THE BUILDER'S WRATH

THE LEGENDARY BUILDER BOOK #4

J. A. CIPRIANO

Copyright © 2017 by J. A. Cipriano

All rights reserved.

No part of this book may be reproduced in any form or by any electronic or mechanical means, including information storage and retrieval systems, without written permission from the author, except for the use of brief quotations in a book review.

WANT TO GET THIS FREE?

Sign up here. If you do, I'll send you my short story, *Alone in the Dark*, for free.

Visit me on Facebook or on the web at JACipriano.com for all the latest updates.

ALSO BY J. A. CIPRIANO

∼

<u>World of Ruul</u>

Soulstone: Awakening

Soulstone: The Skeleton King

∼

<u>Bug Wars</u>

Doomed Infinity Marine

∼

<u>The Legendary Builder</u>

The Builder's Sword

The Builder's Greed

The Builder's Pride

The Builder's Wrath

∼

The FBI Dragon Chronicles

A Ritual of Fire

A Ritual of Death

∼

Starcrossed Dragons

Riding Lightning

Grinding Frost

Swallowing Fire

∼

Elements of Wrath Online

Ring of Promise

The Vale of Three Wolves

∼

Kingdom of Heaven

The Skull Throne

Escape From Hell

∼

The Thrice Cursed Mage

Cursed

Marked

Burned

Seized

Claimed

Hellbound

∼

The Half-Demon Warlock

Pound of Flesh

Flesh and Blood

Blood and Treasure

∼

The Lillim Callina Chronicles

Wardbreaker

Kill it with Magic

The Hatter is Mad

Fairy Tale

Pursuit

Hardboiled

Mind Games

Fatal Ties

∼

Clans of Shadow

Heart of Gold

Feet of Clay

Fists of Iron

∼

The Spellslinger Chronicles

Throne to the Wolves

Prince of Blood and Thunder

∼

Found Magic

May Contain Magic

The Magic Within

Magic for Hire

Witching on a Starship

Maverick

Planet Breaker

1

As Sathanus's axe lashed out at me in an overhead attack that would have split my head like a casaba melon, I darted forward. We were in day six of my training so I could save Gabriella from Dred, and as I moved to counter, I was sure I'd win this time.

My left arm went up, catching the haft as it slammed into me with bone-shuddering force that rang along my entire forearm. Ignoring it, I moved forward anyway, slamming my right hand into her midsection and calling upon my magic.

The earring Sam had given me, The Cold Embrace of Death, blazed in my ear, sending off a stream of black sparks. My hand began to glow, filling with raw Hellfire moments before it slammed into her stomach, blasting her backward in a spray of white-hot heat.

Sathanus grunted, the axe slipping from her grip as she flew backward. Only instead of slamming into the ground, her wings burst from her back, catching her in midair and slowing her like a parachute as she beat them with nearly hurricane-like force.

"I got you—"

"Pathetic!" the Archangel of Wrath roared as she glared at me with so much force, I could literally feel her power trying to tear the flesh from my body against me like a desert sandstorm. "You think that's enough?"

She came at me, her body a blur I could barely see, so I didn't bother. Taking a half step back with my left foot, I readjusted my stance and swung her axe in an upward arc. The silvery blade flashed through the air, glowing with crimson magic as the symbol of wrath on my shoulder blazed to life, illuminating the sigils emblazoned all across the archangel's weapon.

Her arm lashed out, smacking the blade aside and knocking it from my grip. As the axe went flying across the arena, her fist slammed into the underside of my chin.

The next thing I knew, I was on my back a hundred yards away. The metallic taste of blood filled my mouth, and my vision was dark around the edges. I tried to shake my blurry vision back into place as she strode forward like an avenging goddess, but it was no use.

She stood over me, hands on her hips and snorted. "Pathetic." She put one boot on my chest and looked down at me. Then she flexed like she was Hulk Hogan. "One."

I struggled to move, to get up, but my body wouldn't work. Worse, I could tell she'd broken my jaw with that blow, and that was in addition to all the injuries I'd sustained from smashing into the rocky earth at a billion miles an hour. I was pretty sure I'd broken my left collarbone and had a concussion. I was healing, but not quick enough.

"Two," she snarled, glaring down at me. "What's the matter, Arthur? Can't get up?"

"Fuck off," I wheezed, trying to throw her off. Her foot slipped from my chest and landed on the ground.

She smiled. "Oh, think you can get up?" She grabbed me by the hair and jerked me to my feet with one hand. Granted she had to fly a bit to do it since I was taller than her, but still. "Here I'll help." Then she slapped the taste out of my mouth.

I reeled backward a couple steps as my body healed itself. When I'd faced Dred a day ago, I'd used Envy's Armament, the Remorseless Chain of Envy, to steal his ability to heal from nearly anything. Still, the ability wasn't instant, and worse, every time I took damage, the whole of the power reoriented itself on the most devastating injury. So, for instance, if I had a cut, and my leg broke, the skill would stop healing the cut and work on my leg.

It was great when I didn't have too many injuries, but right now, when I had many, it was almost debilitating because it kept healing one until it became less critical to another, at which point it'd switch to that one. Wrath knew that, and she was exploiting it.

"Ready or not, here I come," Sathanus called, springing at me. I ducked her punch, catching her under the arm, and driving her into the rock with the combined strength of me mostly just falling on top of her. As her head slammed into the ground, I took a moment to try to reorient myself.

That was when she head-butted me in the face, shattering my nose. Tears sprang to my eyes, clouding my already blurry vision. As I flopped onto the ground beside her, she sprang to her feet.

"Oh, is that how we're gonna play it?" she asked, jumping backward a couple yards and raising one hand to her ear like she was trying to hear me better. "What's that? I can't hear you."

When I didn't respond because I was too busy trying to crawl to my feet, she launched herself forward, bounding across the earth before leaping into the air. Her leg came down hard on the back of my neck, slamming me face first into the ground.

I'd like to say I was okay, but I wasn't because I was pretty sure she had broken my neck. As I struggled, trying to move my body as the bones in my neck struggled to pull themselves back together, Sathanus grabbed me by the ankle and snapped me outward like a whip.

Vertebrae popped as pain unlike anything I'd ever felt before lit every nerve ablaze. Worse, I could feel my body fighting against her attack, desperate to heal injuries that should have put me down.

As the Archangel of Wrath dropped me limply to the ground, she looked down at me and shook her head.

"Pathetic," she mumbled, climbing on top of me and shaking her head. She leaned in close until her forehead was only a few inches from my face. Then she dangled a loogy from her lips.

"Sathanus, let him up. I think you've proven your point," Gwen said, marching forward, hands on her hips.

The Archangel of Wrath sucked the spittle back into her mouth and smirked at me. "You're lucky," she whispered before hopping off of me and turning to face Gwen. "Have I, Lust?"

"I have a name," Gwen replied, before dismissing the thought. "And yes, you have."

The sad thing was, Gwen was right. Sathanus had proven her point, at least in so far as I still needed a lot more training. That was fine though. I'd train as hard as I could to save Gabriella.

"Good." Sathanus gestured at me and sighed. "Much as I wanted to be wrong, I am right. Arthur is too damned weak." She crossed her arms over her chest. "As much as I hate to admit it, I am weaker than both Lucifer and Michelle." She nodded toward me. "If he wanted to have a chance at stopping Dred, he needs to defeat me in one punch." She spat onto the ground. "Instead, he barely mussed my beard." She drew her fingers down it for emphasis. "Barely."

"As I said, I see your point." Gwen glanced at

me, and I got the impression she wanted to defend me, but couldn't. Actions spoke louder than words, and as it stood, I wasn't capable of fighting Dred.

I'd seen the Darkness's champion beat Lucifer with a single punch after shattering her hammer. A single punch.

And that was after he'd stormed Heaven, having defeated the Archangel of Justice, Michelle. He was an unstoppable juggernaut of power, and I'd gotten my ass kicked by a three-foot dwarf. It pissed me off, but more than that? It made me want to win more than ever.

As the bones in my neck finished stitching themselves back together again, I punched myself into a sitting position. It was hard, and it hurt, but I knew that given two minutes or so, I'd be back at full strength. I could endure a bit of pain.

"How do I save Gabriella then? Because right now, Dred has her locked away in his castle, and I need to figure out a way to rescue her before she gives up her Mark and Armament," I said, and even speaking hurt because my lips and tongue had been shredded into chunks of meat, and while my jaw wasn't broken anymore, it still hurt like a son of a bitch. "How do I beat Dred?"

"You be smarter, dearie." Sathanus glanced at

me like I was the world's dumbest puppy. "How did I beat you?"

"You just kicked my ass." I glared at her as my eyes finally refocused and I felt the confusion of the concussion vanish. "It's annoying."

I touched the earring Sam had given me. It was the armament of Death, but I couldn't get it to work as well as it should. I'd been trying, but I just couldn't master the damned thing. Every time I tried to draw power from it, the thing seemed to fight me, and without my sword, my ability to conjure Hellfire was limited.

"That's a fair point." Gwen gestured at Sathanus. Her armor was scuffed from where I'd blasted her with Hellfire. "Arthur did draw first blood. If that had taken you down, it'd be over."

"And if my grandmam had balls, she'd have been a king." The Archangel of Wrath snorted. "Truth is, you're right as much as you're wrong. He should have killed me or at least taken me down with that hit, but he didn't. That's almost worse." She gestured at the earring. "You need to figure that out because if you don't, all it takes is breaking a couple knees and you're screwed."

"What do you mean?" I asked, getting to my

feet. My body had fully healed, but it was still a bit stiff.

"You can heal an injury, but you fight like you don't want to get hurt, and what's more, your power is dumb." Her boot lashed out, shattering my right knee and causing me to collapse to the ground. As I howled in pain, she kicked me hard in the ribs, breaking them.

"Sathanus!" Gwen cried, rushing forward, but the archangel held out a hand.

"This is a teachable moment." Wrath dropped down beside me right before she punched me in the throat hard enough to break my windpipe. Agony exploded through me, and my good arm instinctively went for my throat while my lungs struggled for breath.

"How is this a teachable moment?" Gwen asked, but she hadn't moved from her spot. She didn't even seem worried, which was bullshit because darkness was encroaching on my vision from my lack of air.

"Notice how your knee and arm have stopped healing." Sathanus gestured at me while meeting my eyes. "It's because your power is focused on keeping you alive." She grabbed my good arm and twisted, shattering my elbow and shoulder. "That isn't healing either."

She was right, of course, my power was focused on healing my throat.

"So what you should do when you fight Dred is give him one big injury, something his body has to heal. Then, while he's healing, incapacitate his arms or legs or whatever." She nodded to me. "Once you overwhelm his ability to heal through your attacks, he'll be easier to fight."

My throat healed, and as my ribs started to pull themselves from my punctured lung, I saw what she meant. When I'd fought Dred, sure he'd tanked my attack, but at the same time, he had stopped, concentrating on healing. I'd seen his organs reform, then his bone, muscle, whatever. In order. If I'd kept attacking, would he have been able to fight back? What if I'd blown off his leg? He might have healed it, but he'd have been hobbled.

"You're a genius," I squeaked even though the words felt like razor blades on my raw throat.

"You get it." Sathanus shrugged. "You need a lot of training." She looked at me. "You're fast and strong. You even have good technique and reflexes, but when it comes to experience, you're a piss poor fighter." She nodded toward me. "I figured that out in one second of fighting you."

"I don't have time for that." I knew she was right, but it didn't matter. Dred had Gabriella, and who knew what the bastard was doing to her. "I need to leave Dagobah and go after her. I don't have time to complete my training."

"Dagobah?" Confusion flashed across the Archangel of Wrath's face. "This is Hell." She glanced around. "The Graveyard of Statues."

"It's a Star Wars reference." I got to my feet once more, though I kept my wary eyes on Sathanus. "In the second movie, Luke left to save his friends before completing his training."

"And how did that work out for Luke?" Sathanus asked, genuinely curious.

"He got his hand cut off, and his friend was frozen in Carbonite." I waved my hand. "Carbonite is a type of stone." I sighed. As much as I didn't want to admit it, Luke had been an idiot. If he'd stayed, he might have won when he faced Darth Vader, but instead? Instead he'd lost his hand, and something told me if I faced Dred unprepared again, I'd lose a lot more than my damned hand.

"Well then, Arthur." Sathanus met my eyes. "I think I've made my point."

2

"We should go again," I said, dusting myself off. "Until I can beat you."

"If you want me to kick your ass again, I'd be happy to do so." Sathanus looked me up and down. "I always enjoy a good fisticuffs." She leaned her axe against one shoulder before holding her other hand out to me and curling her fingers toward herself. "Bring it."

"All right," I said, my hands curling into fists, only before I could strike, her knee lashed out. The blow caught me in the midsection, so hard stars flashed across my vision. Spittle-laced breath exploded from my lips as my feet left the ground and I flew through the air. As I slammed into the dirt a couple hundred yards away before rolling across the rocky ground like a broken mannequin, I finally realized she'd hit me.

Laughter filled my ears, pulsing in my brain as the archangel sauntered toward me. "Sure, I cheated. You weren't ready, blah, blah." She snorted. "But in a real fight, there is no cheating." She looked down at me. "There's just winning and losing. To think otherwise, well, that's scrub talk."

She offered me a hand, which I took. Then she dropped me, letting me hit the dirt. "You were supposed to counterattack instead of letting me help you up." She slapped her thigh. "Pathetic."

"When I heal, we're going to try this one more time," I snarled. Then I pushed myself to my feet. I could still feel my bones healing themselves, but this time it was different. It certainly seemed like once I'd sustained an injury, similar injuries healed quicker the next time I sustained them.

"No." Sathanus shook her head. "We've been at this for hours." She gestured to the horizon where lightning crackled and popped. "I'm going to get myself a mug of ale and then eat a big pile of ribs." She looked at me. "We can resume tomorrow, but I want you to keep something in mind, Arthur."

"What's that?" I asked, and as I spoke, my stomach rumbled audibly. The Archangel of

Wrath's eyes flitted to my gut before landing on my face once more.

"I've been holding back." She shrugged. "You don't have to believe me, but I quickly realized if I went at you full speed, I'd kill you."

"You were holding back?" I asked, unable to fathom it. She'd been so fast I could barely follow her movements, so strong that every blow had broken bones. How could she be holding back?

"Yes." She held up one finger. "I've been using about one percent of my power." I expected her to smirk, but she stared at me stone-faced, making me think she was serious. Only if that was true, I was fucked. "This isn't even my final form."

"Your final form?" I asked, confused. "Is that some kind of joke?"

"You think Envy is the only one with a dragon form?" Sathanus arched an eyebrow.

"I hadn't thought about it." I searched her face, but it didn't seem like she was lying. That made a chill run down my spine. The Archangel of Envy could transform into a massive serpent, and when she did, her power increased by a factor of insanity. That Wrath could do it was simply horrifying, especially since she claimed to be fighting me at one percent strength.

"Think about it." Sathanus met my eyes, and for a second, I felt the enormity of her strength. It was like being thrown into a sun. Heat blasted me, burning my flesh away to atoms before devouring what remained like the endless, crushing void of a black hole. I wasn't sure if Lucifer could bring that kind of power to bear or not, but I had to imagine Wrath was not unique in this way.

"Can Michelle do the same?" I asked, swallowing hard.

"I would assume so. My sister could when I came down here for an extended vacation." Wrath shrugged. "So yes, I'm assuming she went all out and still fucking lost." The Archangel of Wrath shivered then. "That scares me, Arthur, and while I'm happy to keep training you. I don't think it will matter."

The sad thing was, I almost believed her. Still, I had to try, had to get stronger. If I didn't, what was I doing here? How could I save Gabriella?

No. I needed to be able to fight Dred.

"I think it matters." I nodded to Wrath. "As you said before, sometimes experience trumps strength." I took a deep breath. "I assume Michelle and Dred have clashed many times. What we need to find out is why this time was different."

I gestured toward the sky, where I could still see the swirling rift that Dred had torn open when he'd defeated Michelle, driving her from Heaven's hallowed shores into the beached of Hell.

Angelic bodies no longer fell from the sky, but the hole was still there, pulsating like a massive wound in the horizon.

"That's a fair point." Sathanus frowned. "Let us speak more of it over a few drinks." She licked her lips. "I have a massive thirst." She pointed at me with one stubby finger. "And you're buying Mr. I-lost-thirty-six-fights-in-a-row."

"You didn't actually expect me to win, did you?" I asked, following her.

"Not really, but I'd hoped you would." She shrugged. "And you're still buying."

"I'll tell them to put it on my tab," I replied as we stepped through the gates and entered the city. It was a flurry of activity. Those angels that had lived were strewn out across every available space while healers tended to them. The bastards at the healer's guild had tried to argue with us about costs and whatnot, but Lucifer had put a stop to that pretty damned quick when she'd hurled the guild leader into a volcano.

"I hate the smell of healing." Wrath furrowed

her brow as she made her way toward the mess hall. "It's like suffering without the twang of victory from the battlefield." She waved a hand dismissively, and I could tell the sight of so many hurt was bothering her.

"I'm just glad we'll be able to heal most of them." I glanced at the sky. Dred had done this, and I still had no idea what the forces of Darkness were capable of. I mean, I had an army of Archangels at my back, but what if Dred had something similar? After all, that lich I'd faced alongside Sam had seemed tough, but it'd also seemed like a minion. What if they had actual champions similar to the archangels?

"I am as well." Sathanus frowned. "But this should not have been possible from just one man's strength. Even with the Darkness on his side." She shrugged. "It is concerning."

"I've been thinking about that, and I guess we need to wait until Michelle wakes up from when Dred beat her into a coma—"

"If she wakes up." Sathanus sighed before giving me a "go on" look.

"Anyway, I think he's got to have help." I gestured at her. "People like you. It's the only way this all makes sense."

"I would assume there are strong warriors within the Darkness, the likes of which I have not seen. After all, the Empress must be incredibly powerful." Sathanus stroked her lustrous beard as we stepped into the mess hall and moved across the dingy wooden building toward a table in the corner. It was mostly empty, given the time of day. It was really early in the morning, and I figured that was why. That was when I realized I hadn't slept in over a day, and what's more, I wasn't tired. At all.

"I feel like this is going to be one of those bad shounen mangas." I sighed, taking a seat and resting my face in my hands. "The kind where you go through, and there are all these strong people, and then once you get strong enough to win, you find out there's a whole new world of exponentially more powerful people."

"I absolutely hope that isn't the case." Sathanus drummed her fingers on the table. "But it can't be ruled out. Who knows how long this fight will go on?" She looked toward the ceiling. "I know it feels like you've made progress because you have some of the Armaments, but that will not be enough to save Gabriella and stop Dred." She swallowed hard as a waitress came over.

"What will you two have?" she asked, voice

cutesy, and as I smiled at her, taking in her short blue hair, high cheekbones, and supermodel good-looks, I noticed the stain on her right cheek. It was from the chef's guild, and it made me wonder what she'd done to get banished.

"Ale. A lot of it." Sathanus slammed a fist on the table, and the sound echoed through the nearly empty room, causing the few patrons inside to look at us. "And meat. Enough to choke a party of goblins."

"I'll have some water," I added as the girl turned to look at me, her hand whipping out over her pad. "And some breakfast. Whatever is fine as long as it's mostly protein."

"It will be as you wish." She took a look around. "Let me check on the others before I go fix you something special." Her eyes moved to her feet, and her cheeks flushed. "Thank you again for giving me this chance, Builder."

"You're beautiful and special. Why wouldn't I give you a chance?" I asked, trying to remember her name and failing. I was sure I knew it, but then again, so many refugees had come in over the last few weeks, they'd all sort of become a blur, and furthermore, I had never been in the mess hall at this time. It didn't make me feel like less of an ass.

"I, um…" she touched the stain emblazoned on her cheek with one finger. "I just…"

"I don't care about marks or guilds or any of that crap." I got to my feet and reached out to touch her cheek, running my knuckle across the scarred flesh where the guild's banishment stood as a stark reminder to everyone. "I just care about you, and I think you're beautiful." I nodded. "This just shows how afraid of you the guild is."

"Thank you!" she squeaked before turning on her heel and vanishing into a flurry of blue hair.

"Working on a new conquest?" Sathanus raised an eye at me. "Don't have enough already?"

"What? No." I shook my head as I sat down. "I'm just tired of all these people feeling like they're less." I touched my chest. "I know what it's like to feel like you're a piece of shit who won't amount to anything. Then someone finally saw my potential and look." I spread my hands to the room. "I just want others to have the same chance."

"Is that so?" Sathanus murmured as the waitress came back with two frothy mugs of ale. Part of me hadn't even known we had ale, but then again, Buffy, our resident merchant, and the dwarves had hammered out a trade deal, so I guess it wasn't that surprising.

"Here you go," the waitress said, smiling brightly at me, and I could have sworn she looked prettier. Had she done something?

"Thank you," I said, taking my mug from her.

"No." She shook her head, smacking her ruby red lips together. "Thank you, for everything." She moved a bit closer. "If I could, I'd like to *really* thank you sometime."

Sathanus kicked me under the table before turning to the girl. "That would be fine, but I don't want him distracted. Could you come back in a bit?" She winked at the waitress who flushed.

"Right, sorry. You must be busy." She scurried off, and as she hit the threshold for the kitchen, she glanced back over her shoulder. "I'll have your meals soon."

"Why were you so rude?" I asked, narrowing my eyes at Sathanus as the dwarf turned her gaze back to me.

"She wanted to fuck you, and we don't have time for that." Sathanus rolled her eyes.

"You don't know that." I shook my head. "She was probably just being nice."

"Right." Sathanus drew the word out. "Anyway, as you were saying earlier, I think there might be worse things in the Darkness. Strong things." She took a huge gulp of ale, draining half the glass and leaving white froth on her beard. "Be prepared for that."

"Yeah, I suppose you're right. Expect the unexpected." I took a sip of my own ale. It tasted nutty and had a hint of pineapple to it, which was a bit strange.

"Exactly." Sathanus finished her ale and slammed the empty on the table. "That way, when this whole thing jumps the rails, you'll be prepared." She glanced at her empty mug for a second. "Jesus, it's like the Sahara in here." She got to her feet and snatched up her empty glass. "I'll be right back."

3

"You're a goddamned angel," I said, pushing my plate away and leaning back in my chair. I was so full of eggs, bacon, and sausage, I could practically feel it in my throat, and what was more, it had been so delicious, each bite had brought nearly an explosive orgasm of flavor.

"Thanks." The waitress who turned out to be named Takumi said, nodding furiously. "It always makes me happy when people enjoy my cooking." She twisted her hands. "I'd hoped to take over my parents' restaurant in the fishing district, which is why I went to the prestigious cooking academy at Royal Centre." She bit her lip.

"Then what happened?" I asked, glancing from her to the empty seat Sathanus had vacated a half hour ago. She'd grown bored with watching me eat and left to do something else. It was weird because I hadn't expected to eat so much, and to be honest, the sheer volume of food I'd put away was a bit bothersome. Still, a guy has gotta eat, especially when brought a home cooked meal prepared by a delicious woman.

"I, um, well." She swallowed. "One of my professors didn't like that I didn't follow one of his recipes exactly. We had these bad cabbages, so I tried to do a different method to compensate for that, and he didn't like that I veered from his recipe even though it let me finish the challenge. I was expelled on the spot." Tears clouded her vision, and she sniffled. "I never thought I'd be able to cook again." She brightened, wiping her eyes. "But you don't care about that, do you, Arthur?" She nodded. "Come back anytime, and I'll cook my hardest for you."

"Thank you," I said, swallowing hard as I absorbed her story. It made me feel bad that such a thing had happened, and it made me wonder how many other similar things had happened. After all, I'd heard a similar story from countless Stained.

Part of me knew it was to keep the guilds in power, but most of me hated it. Still, now wasn't the time to focus on righting Hell's wrongs. No. It was time to work harder, to train harder. Then I could save Gabriella.

I shut my eyes for a second, thinking about the Archangel of Love. Was she okay? Part of me hoped she was even though I knew that Gabriella was innocent and pure. What was more, she was made to fall in love. If Dred was being nice to her, it was possible she'd fall for him and give him her mark and armament, making him even more powerful.

It was in my best interest for him to be torturing her, and even still, I hated the thought of it. No. At the end of the day, I wanted Gabriella to be okay. Besides, I was coming for her.

"Did my story displease you?" Takumi said, her voice bringing me back to her face. She had her eyes cast down at her twisting hands. "I didn't mean—"

"No. I just have a lot on my mind." I nodded to her and flashed a smile. "Say could you do me a favor?"

"Anything." She flushed. Hard. "What do you require?" She swallowed. "If it is in my power, I will do my best to make it happen, even if it something you think I won't like. I'll definitely try for you."

"Give me the name of the professor who flunked you." I waved a hand at the empty plates. "Because this is the best thing I've ever eaten."

"Oh." Her chest flushed as well this time. "Shino." Takumi swallowed. "She owned the premier restaurant in Royal Centre, so she's probably…"

"Could be." I nodded, getting to my feet. Royal Centre had been destroyed when Lucifer awoke, and while a lot of people had been killed in the blast, many had been in the other cities. If this Shino was alive, well, I wanted to have a word with her. Still, first thing was first. It was time to get a move on.

"Can I make you something for your travels?" Takumi asked as I got to my feet.

"That would be great. I'll come back and get it in a bit, okay?" I nodded to her before picking up my water and downing the glass.

"Sure thing," she squawked before hurrying to clean up my dishes. "Anything you'd like in particular."

"I trust you to make something awesome." I smiled. "After all, you just made me the best breakfast ever."

"You won't be disappointed." She gripped the

plate in her hand tightly and nodded furiously. "I promise."

"I'm sure you're right." I waved. "Now, if you'll excuse me."

"Right, of course. You must be very busy." She took a deep breath, causing her chest to push against the white fabric of her apron, and for a second I wondered if she was wearing anything beneath it. Part of me wanted to look, but that seemed rude, so instead, I waved once more and made my way outside.

It wasn't quite raining, but I could feel the moisture heavy in the air. Ever since I'd used Lucifer's Armament, the Ruthless Crown of Pride, to change the weather to be more conducive to our crops, the air had been humid, reminding me of a Florida summer, or at least what I expected a Florida summer would feel like since I'd never been there.

Rubbing at my arms, I made my way across the town toward Sam's shop. As the Blacksmith came into view, I spied black smoke curling from the chimney. That somewhat irked me because it meant she was still working. If she was still working, that meant she hadn't finished Caliburn. I needed Caliburn finished so I could get on with saving Gabriella.

Intrinsically, I knew Wrath was right and that I couldn't defeat Dred, but at the same time, I needed to go after Gabriella no matter the cost. I couldn't risk leaving her there while I futzed around. Besides, Wrath had made me realize something.

Dred was used to being the strongest dude in the room. After all, if he wasn't, he'd have never fought Lucifer the way he had, never fought me the way he had. He was used to being a hammer to everyone else's nail, but well, not everyone was a nail.

I just had to think of a way to beat him long enough to rescue Gabriella to keep Dred from getting the final Armament. Furthermore, it might let me in on how he'd gotten Belial, The Archangel of Gluttony and Belphegor the Archangel of Sloth to join him.

For all I knew, those armaments were weak just like the one I'd gotten from Sam was too. I needed to find out, and that meant I needed to face off with Dred. To do all those things, I needed my damned sword.

"I'm almost done," Sam said as I stepped through the door. It was weird because the pink-haired blacksmith who was also the Archangel of Death hadn't even looked up.

"Define almost with a timeframe," I said, sidling up beside her. Caliburn was still in the exact same spot on her bench, though there looked to be a lot more rune work inscribed upon the blade. As I glanced over at Clarent, the sword I'd broken when I had saved Mammon's lands from the Darkness, I saw she was right. The runes were done.

"Honestly?" she spun, turning to look at me, and blew a lock of pink hair out of her sweat-streaked face.

"Yes." I nodded to the sword. "The rune work seems almost done."

"It is almost done." She threw an annoyed glance at it before wringing out her arms. "My forearms are cramped because I did a week's work in a day." She took a deep breath and let it out slowly. "I haven't slept, and I've barely eaten." Her stomach rumbled to punctuate the point.

"Should I get you some food? I'm sure Takumi would be happy to bring some by."

"No." Sam shook her head. "I haven't even eaten the last meal she brought me." She pointed across the room to where a sandwich and chips sat barely touched.

"You should eat it. Keep your strength up." I

picked up the plate and held it out to her. "It's probably pretty good."

"You know how it is when I work. I get super focused and forget about eating." She picked up a chip and popped it into her mouth. Only as she did, her entire body shivered, and she let out a soft moan. "Oh man, that's good." She snatched the plate from me and shoved a handful of chips into her mouth.

"Anyway, now that the rune work is done, what's left?" I glanced at Caliburn. "Just moving the power over, right?"

"Yes," she said around a mouthful of sandwich. "But I don't know how long that will take or if I have the strength for it."

"How much strength do you need?" I asked as she shoved the entirety of the sandwich into her mouth and tried to chew around it. "And, you know, tasting usually makes things better."

"You know me, Arthur. I'm a shove it in kind of girl." She batted her eyes at me, which was weird because she was still chewing, her cheeks puffed out like a squirrel.

"All right." I shrugged, picking up Caliburn, and as I did, I felt a surge of strength rush through me that I hadn't before. The runes lit up with sapphire light just how Clarent had. It was a bit crazy.

"Don't touch it!" Sam cried, grabbing it out of my hands and putting it back down. "It's not ready." She shook her head. "You wouldn't walk in on your bride before the wedding, would you?"

"I… um, sorry?" I shrugged. "I didn't realize it was such a big deal."

"You wouldn't." She snorted. "Anyway, I guess now is as good a time to try." She put the empty plate down and moved in front of me, shoving me aside with her hip.

She reached out, running her hand along the broken pieces of Clarent. She'd fitted them back together but hadn't welded them together. We'd talked about doing that or recasting the blade completely, but in the end, Sam hadn't been skilled enough so we'd met with a creepy lady in a lake.

Then I'd punched her and taken the sword. It had been a whole thing.

Either way, I still felt a little bad about Clarent. I'd found it in a pawnshop, and cleaning it had summoned Gwen who had, in turn, brought me here. Part of me knew that without that freak accident, I'd still be the orphan wannabe software engineer in a dreary town.

It was hard to believe how much things had changed, and for a moment, I thought back to Merle. The old man had sold me this sword, and I wondered what he'd say if he saw me now. Part of me wanted to find out, but most of me didn't want to go back to my old life.

After all, what good was being a demigod in the mortal world? I'd be a cubicle monkey just the same. Here though? Here I mattered.

Still, looking at Clarent now, I wondered if maybe we should just weld the blade back together and see if I could regain my Builder powers. Clarent had let me adjust the stats of my friends and allies like I was in a video game, but I had lost that ability when it'd broke. Now Sam was about to put the power into Caliburn, but what if she failed?

Then, not only would Clarent be destroyed, but I'd have lost my primary power as well.

"Are you ready?" Sam asked, glancing up at me. "You know the stakes."

"Yes." I took a deep breath. "If you fail, we'll find another way."

"I like how you worded that." She rolled her eyes. "If *I* fail."

"I didn't mean it that way," I said, putting a hand on her shoulder. That's when I realized how tense she was. Worse, I could feel the fear pulsating through the mark on my abdomen that bound us together. That simple touch let me know how damned scared she was. If she failed, it was over.

"But that doesn't make it less true." She bit her lip and met my eyes. "But I won't fail."

"I know you won't." I gave her my best reassuring smile, and she nodded resolutely.

"Let's get this done." I felt the mark on my abdomen open wide, and felt her strength, her power. It rushed over me in a way I hadn't quite expected. The earring started to flare brightly, and as the specter of death settled over the inside of her shop, her black-feathered wings burst forth.

Black light flowed from her outstretched hand as she shut her eyes and began speaking in the demonic tongue that hurt my brain.

Clarent shattered, exploding into a million scintillating shards every color of the rainbow, and as they did, I felt its power fighting to escape, to disappear into the ether.

Sam wove her hands through the air like a conductor, shaping the very air in a way that reminded me of a sculptor modeling clay. With each stroke, she swept more of the power into Caliburn.

The new sword began to glow, its runes flaring like miniature stars with each pass of the hand.

Sweat began to bead on her forehead as she moved, and I felt the strength inside her begin to weaken. That wasn't good, but fortunately, I had a trick up my sleeve.

"Concentrate on your work, Sam. I've got the power side." I shut my eyes as I reached out through the other marks on my body. "Just think of me as a battery and take what you need."

Pride. Wraith. Lust. Envy. Greed.

As I opened each mark, I felt the archangel on the other side of the tether. I could see through their eyes, feel through their touch, and they could do the same. Then, one by one, they began to lend me their strength.

Gwen was first, and the power of lust flowed into me, heating up my entire body before flowing into Sam like white-hot flame.

The magic around her hands tinged purple as she sucked in a breath, but still, she worked. The cold embrace of Greed hit us next, and as I exhaled a breath of mist, Sam's movements sped up.

Wrath and Envy hit us next, their twin powers so close, that if I hadn't known they were together, I would have wondered if they were. It was a bit weird because while Envy had gone insane, Wrath seemed to take care of her constantly, tending to her in a way that only sisters truly could.

Still, I could tell that even with their boost in power it wouldn't be enough. Sam's form was starting to falter.

"Lucifer," I whispered, focusing on the mark of Pride as I spoke. "Please."

"What if I cannot?" Her response was thready in my ear as she opened her eyes. She still lay in the infirmary, and while I was sure she had been healed, I could still feel her reluctant to share. She'd been less sure of herself ever since she'd been beaten by Dred, but that didn't matter. I needed her help.

Sam's form began to falter, and she gritted her teeth. "I need more." Her words were strained, and as I opened my eyes, I saw she was almost done, but that didn't matter. The glow around her hands was all but gone.

"Lucifer," I said, and this time thunder crackled above me, and the crown she'd given me began to glow. I couldn't force her to help me, but even still we were bound. "Just try."

"Okay."

With that word, her mark opened wide, and the

power of Pride hit me like a lightning strike to the brain. Strength flooded through me and into Sam. Her hands began to glow once more, and this time I knew we'd be able to finish the ritual.

Barely.

4

"It's perfect," I said, holding Caliburn in my hand. The blade pulsed with power in a way Clarent never had. It felt stronger, and well, just more.

"Did it work?" Sam asked, looking at me. Her hair was plastered to her face with sweat, and she was still taking ragged breaths. Oddly, I knew it wasn't just her. I could feel the five other archangels connected me, and they all seemed drained.

To be honest, I'd been tired too until I'd picked the sword. Now I felt like I'd made my coffee with Red Bull. Power thrummed through me as I gave the weapon a tentative swing through the air.

No. That wasn't right. It didn't feel like a weapon. It felt like an extension of myself, of my body itself.

"I think so," I murmured, shutting my eyes for a second and inhaling a breath that tasted of spearmint. As I exhaled, I stared at Sam, bringing up her character sheet.

Name: Samantha (Samael)
Experience: 576,285
Health: 149/149
Mana: 19/190
Primary Power: Smithing
Secondary Power: None selected
Strength: 54/100
Agility: 95/100
Charisma: 20/100
Intelligence: 95/100
Special: 95/100
*Unique Ability: Archangel of Death**
Perk: Rank 3 Blacksmith
Flaw: Badly Marked

"Well, I can see your stats now, so that's good." I pulled Lucifer's crown off my head and set it on the table. Only, Sam's stat boxes remained. Excellent.

I turned my gaze upon Caliburn and nearly shouted for joy when the stat box came up.

Caliburn
Type: Longsword
Durability: 57,000/57,000

Damage: 2D20

Enchantments: Mortal Strike

Ability: Distribution* – Can be used by the Builder to distribute Experience.

"It worked!" I cried, doing a fist bump. "I can see the ability on the sword." I smiled at Sam, and that's when I realized how much experience she had. "Whoa."

"What?" she asked, eyes filling with fear. "Is something wrong with it?" She took a step forward, and I shook my head.

"Give me a second," I said, staring at the flaw listed on her character sheet. I'd not seen it before, but then again, I could see a lot more menus than I could before, and then there was that asterisk on the skill window.

With a flick of my wrist, I opened the ability for Caliburn, and my eyes widened in shock.

Distribution: This Ability can be used to change the Stats of a person, creature, or structure under one's control. It allows the user to distribute unspent Experience points as well as redistribute Experience points that have already been spent. Note: Stats cannot be lowered below their initial levels.

*Note: This ability has been transferred from a lower quality item into a higher quality item. It will be stronger than before. Please exercise caution.

"Okay…" I looked down at the sword. "That's why I see more…" As I spoke, Sam looked like she wanted to ask me something, but evidently, thought better of it. That was good because I wasn't done yet.

Turning my gaze back to her character sheet, I pulled open the Badly Marked Flaw.

Badly Marked – The user was previously been bound to another. While the Mark has been severed, she has not healed from the transition causing a permanent 10% debuff that affects all stats. Additionally, all powers associated with the mark will be lessened.

Would you like to remove this flaw? Cost 68,000 experience. Yes/no?

"Yes," I said, and as I spent her points, Sam cried out in shock. The spot where she and Dred had shared a mark began to glow, and before my eyes, I saw sapphire light leapt from Caliburn and hit her flesh. It writhed along the surface of the scar, and as it did, I felt the mark she shared with me strengthen. I couldn't tell you how, or why exactly, but as the glow faded, it felt like a river had burst through the dam that had been blocking its path.

Power rushed out of her, and as it did, her character sheet changed once more.

Name: Samantha (Samael)
Experience: 508,285
Health: 149/149*
Mana: 22/190*
Primary Power: Smithing
Secondary Power: None selected
Strength: 54/100*
Agility: 95/100*
Charisma: 20/100*
Intelligence: 95/100*
Special: 95/100*
Unique Ability: Archangel of Death
Perk: Rank 3 Blacksmith

"What did you do?" Sam asked, touching the spot, but where before our shared mark had sat atop a scarred chunk of mottled flesh, now the skin below was pristine. I could feel the power radiating off Sam like never before.

Crazier still, I could see asterisks on her character sheet like I had when I'd looked at Lucifer before. I hadn't been able to open them before, but now that I had Caliburn I wanted to try it.

Strength: This Stat represents Physical Power. It determines how strong the user is and how hard she hits.

Current Level: 95/100. Experience Cost to increase

Strength beyond 95 is ten times the current level plus one. (960)

My mouth fell open. I'd never been able to extend stats beyond ninety-five before. It had always been a hard stop, and now I could. It was a bit crazy since those points cost way more experience, but knowing I could was great. Still, that wasn't all. As my eyes read through it a second time, I skipped to the note at the bottom of the menu.

*Note: This user possesses the unique ability **Archangel of Death.** *This unique ability will cause stats to triple when in use.*

"So that's what those asterisks mean!" I nearly shouted as I grabbed Sam and pumped her arms.

"What are you talking about?" Sam asked in a way that suggested that while she knew what I was talking about, it wasn't quite clear.

"Okay, so I spent some of your experience to get rid of a flaw caused by Dred's mark, and when I did, it caused you to get the same asterisks by all your stats like Lucifer had." I gestured at her character sheet even though she couldn't see it. "It makes it so that when you use your archangel abilities, your stats are tripled." I smirked. "You're probably the best blacksmith ever now."

"Wait, I can use my powers again?" She gave me a strange look. Was she unhappy about it?

"You don't seem pleased," I said, suddenly confused. "I thought you'd be happy."

"I am." I didn't believe her because she was frowning. "I'd just, well, I've been without it for so long. I don't want to get my hopes up." She shuffled her feet. "When I stopped being able to use my power, it nearly crushed me. If it still doesn't work…" She took a deep breath.

"Try it," I said, moving across the room and picking up her Scythe. The bone was cold in my hand, like it was trying to suck the heat from my body. Only, it'd never felt like that. As I hefted it, the sigils on it began to glow in the same way that happened when I used any of the archangel's weapons. Only Sam's had never done that before.

"It's glowing," she whispered, and her voice was so quiet, I barely heard her.

"Yeah." I swallowed, offering it to her. "Just try it."

"Okay." She took the scythe from me, and the moment she did, I felt the earring in my ear grow ice cold. Power exploded out from her as a swirling tornado of black ripped from the ground beneath her feet.

The smell of death and decay filled my ears, and when she looked up, I could practically see her skull beneath her nearly translucent flesh. Her dark wings unfurled, spreading out and casting shadow about her like a cloak.

"I'm whole." The words hit me with so much force, I backpedaled. Only, she wasn't paying attention to me. Instead, she inhaled sharply. As her nostrils flared, her eyes widened. "I must hurry."

She darted outside, and as I followed, I saw her moving toward the healers. She grabbed one by the shoulder, causing the demoness to let out a shriek.

They exchanged words before Sam dragged the woman toward an angel who looked to be on death's door. As Sam pointed fervently at the angel, I realized what was going on.

Sam was the Archangel of Death, and she could sense those closest to dying, and as such, she could direct the healers. As I watched Sam shove the healer toward the angel, she spun on her heel, sprinting off toward another healer.

Part of me wanted to help her, but I wasn't sure what I could do. None of my powers moved toward healing, and I'd just be in the way. Besides, now that I had my sword, I felt stronger than ever before.

Strong enough that I was pretty sure I could

save Gabriella. I wasn't sure why, but at that moment I could have sworn I felt her across the horizon. As I turned my gaze toward the Darkness, I knew I had to go get her. I felt the pulse of that need in every inch of my body.

Despite the little voice in my head telling me I was an idiot, I quickly moved back inside Sam's shop and snatched up my crown. I fit it on my head, and a rush of power hit me.

Crazily I saw more stat boxes open around me. While before I could only upgrade the stats of people, I quickly saw I could do more. I stared at the forge before me and opened the menu orb hovered above it.

Black Iron Forge
Type: Forge
Durability: 7,000/7,000*
Grade: B*
Enchantments: None*
Ability: None*

That was all normal, but what was different were the asterisks. This time I opened the Grade menu, just to see what would happen.

Grade – The Grade of this item is currently classified as B. Items up to the level of Grade B can be forged without penalty. Every Grade level beyond Grade B will suffer a penalty of 10%, to stats, abilities, and chance of success.

That was all normal, but what wasn't was the message directly below.

Do you want to upgrade Black Iron Forge to Grade A? Base cost 47 Black Iron ingot (Grade A).

I smiled. I wasn't sure if we had that many ingots or anything, but this meant I could upgrade items as long as we had the materials. I wasn't sure how the costs compared to actually creating or upgrading the forge normally, but it'd definitely be something to check into later.

Still, now wasn't the time for that. No. Now was the time to face the Darkness and save Gabriella. I could see her smiling face in my mind's eye, and as I thought about her, I realized how much I missed her. If something really terrible happened to her, I'd never forgive myself.

I shut my eyes for a second and inhaled, reaching out toward the feeling I'd had before. This time it was more fleeting, but it still pulsed in the horizon, in the area held by the Darkness.

Moving outside, I looked around, even though I didn't know why. I supposed it was because I half expected someone to try to stop me. I wasn't sure what I'd do if someone did, nor did I want to find out.

I was done fighting with my people, and while Wrath's words had scared me, I was sure I could beat her now that I had Caliburn. And if I couldn't, well, that wouldn't help me now. My decision was made.

The walk to the horizon didn't take long, and as lightning flashed overhead, I reached a hand out toward the shimmering wall of absolute black that pulsated before me. It seemed to dare me to enter, and part of me wondered what I'd find inside. Would it transport me to another place, or just be the same place infused with Darkness? I'd encountered both, and I wasn't sure what was better.

"Stop!" Gabriella said from behind me, and as I heard it, I froze. Could it be?

Whirling, I found myself staring at the angel. She looked like she'd been on the wrong end of a brawl, but otherwise, I was sure it was her. Only, how was that possible?

"Gabriella?" I asked, taking a step toward her, one hand reaching out toward her.

"I am not my sister." The archangel scrunched up her nose. "I am Michelle, and you'd do well to heed my warning, Builder. You cannot defeat Dred as you are, and if you enter his domain, you will die screaming and alone."

"You look just like her," I said, only able to focus on how my heart hurt at her words. I'd been so ready for it to be Gabriella that having it not be, nearly broke me.

"We are twins, though I am three minutes older." She waved a hand at me. "And while I appreciate your love for my sister, you are being a fool. Stay, let me help you."

"Help me?" I scoffed. "You lost. How much help could you be? You're practically an invalid."

"And you're weak." She flicked me between the eyes. I didn't even see it coming, not that I could have avoided it if I could have, but I did feel my body hit the ground as unconsciousness overtook me.

5

As my eyes fluttered open, I found myself staring down into the volcano Lucifer had threatened to throw me into. Only, unlike before, I wasn't up on the edge. No, I was just a few feet above the lava. The heat of the magma threatened to overwhelm me, and the smell of sulfur hit me like a punch to the gut, destroying my lungs in a way that let me know if I couldn't heal, I'd have been in trouble.

"What the fuck are you doing?" I cried, looking up at Michelle who held me aloft by one ankle. She was still battered and bruised, but her pearl-white wings were extended as she hovered, effortlessly holding us both aloft.

"Making a point." She looked down her button nose at me. "I spoke to my sister, and Luci told me this would be the best way. She said you were quite dense." She frowned. "I don't normally trust her, but she knows what people want. Can see into their hearts and all that." Michelle stuck her tongue out. "It's disgusting, honestly. All that want and need coming to the surface." She touched her chest with one hand. "That is not the path to victory."

"Is this where you tell me hate and anger is the path to the Dark Side?" I asked.

"Are you making a joke?" Her eyes narrowed, and I realized it may have been a bad idea to joke with her. She clearly didn't get humor.

"Yes but—"

She dropped me, and my face hit the lava before she grabbed me again. Agony unlike anything I'd ever felt ripped through me as my eyeballs exploded and the flesh cooked off my bones in the space of a heartbeat. My bone followed next, and as the magma began to dissolve my brain, she pulled me out. My entire face was nearly gone, and more of my flesh had been cooked by the extreme heat, but even still, I could feel myself heal.

It was excruciating, agonizing, and it made me hate Michelle in a way I'd never hated anyone, even Dred, before. Why? Because I'd known she'd done it simply to make a point. She wasn't fucking around, and if I wasn't serious, I could take a bath in a volcano. Even worse, that wouldn't kill me, at least not instantly, and I'd be stuck in exquisite agony as my power fought to heal me against the might of the volcano. It'd be a losing battle, and it'd hurt so much I'd pray for death.

"What have we learned?" Michelle asked, her blue eyes boring into me. They were devoid of any emotion. She wasn't mad or annoyed. She wasn't pleased or confused. Hell, that was a gaze of someone who simply did not care about me at all. That absence of feeling was scarier than anything I'd seen before.

Dred had at least seemed human. Michelle? She felt like an alien.

"To be serious," I said in my best, most apologetic voice. "I won't fuck around again."

"Good, but that is not what you should have learned." She dunked me in the lava again, and as my body cooked like a roast that had been dropped in the fire, she waited there, holding me by the ankle. Once I'd healed enough to talk, she spoke once more. "What have we learned?"

"I don't know—"

She dunked me again. Over and over again. I

lost count of it because my life became a series of endless agony as the Archangel of Justice bathed me in lava, leaving me in just long enough for me to think I'd die before pulling me out again.

"What have you learned, Builder?" Michelle asked after what had to have been the fiftieth dunking.

"Why do you keep doing this?" I cried, anger flaring in me. "You know I can't stop you."

"Exactly."

I shut my eyes in anticipation of a bath in the lava, but this time none came. As my eyes peeked open, I found her looking at me as stone-faced as always.

"Why didn't you dunk me?" I asked, suddenly very concerned. "I mean, I'm okay with that, but I'm not quite sure you and I are communicating effectively."

"You have learned what I wished you to know. You are weak beyond measure." Her eyes flicked toward the lava beside my head. "You cannot stop me." She touched her chest where it was still bandaged from her battle with Dred. "And I am hurt." She met my eyes. "I am hurt, and you can't even stop me from dropping you in a volcano."

I understood at once. Michelle was badly beaten

from her fight with Dred, a man who had defeated her and the armies of Heaven. He had routed her, presumably despite her best efforts to stop him. He had done all those things, and I couldn't even keep her from killing me if she chose to do it. Hell, I couldn't even pull my ankle free of her grip.

"What would you have me do?" I asked, and oddly, I meant it. Before, I'd been rash. Caliburn had given me a boost in power, a surge of confidence. Only that confidence had been misplaced. I thought back to what Wrath had said. If I'd been smart, I'd have fought with her again, tested myself. I hadn't because deep down, I knew Caliburn hadn't given me that much of a boost.

"You are the Builder." Michelle looked at me, her eyes flashing with something that almost seemed like amusement. "Dred is the destroyer. Your powers are as dissimilar as oil and water. Yet, you seek to meet him on his terms. It is foolish." She swept her hand out. "You have all the resources of Hell, and if you come with me, of Heaven as well. Use that to win." Her lips tightened into a thin line. "Build an army, unlike anything the world has ever seen before. If you do not, you will not win."

"How will an army help when Dred is so

strong?" I asked, meeting her gaze. It was like trying to stare down an iceberg.

"Dred is one man, but with your power, you are many." Michelle cracked her neck as she looked at me. "His Armaments make him strong in a way you can never defeat. Every facet of his power is designed to make him a sword to cut down a single enemy. You are more than that. You are an army of swords." Her wings fluttered as she began moving up the volcano, pulling me away from the heated embrace of the lava.

"I don't follow. Sorry." I cringed as I said the words. "And please don't drop me again."

She almost smiled. "Does not an army of hyenas drive a lion from its meal?"

That was an excellent point. I had an army of archangels, of demons, and angels, and I'd seen enough battles with the Darkness to know they employed a similar tactic. There'd been so many times I'd bemoaned our lack of troops, our lack of resources because I could augment those.

Dred wouldn't have needed that. He could have acted differently, but I wasn't Dred, and if I wanted to save Gabriella, really wanted to save her, I'd be wise to heed Michelle's warning. Otherwise, she may as well throw me in the volcano and get my defeat over with.

The silence between us lingered as she landed on the lip of the volcano and set me down. She stood back, folding her arms across her chest and waited for a beat.

"Your silence makes me think you are smarter than my sisters give you credit for." She nodded once. "Will you use your powers appropriately?"

"Yes." I took a deep breath as I got to my feet. "But only if you can help me save Gabriella."

"I would do that, anyway." She shoved me hard, knocking me back down the volcano. I tumbled, breaking bones and getting my flesh ripped to shreds before I slammed into a rocky outcropping at the bottom. As I lay there dazed and confused, Michelle landed lightly next to me.

"What was that for?" I snapped, feeling anger rise in me as she settled down beside me.

"I need you to know this is not a negotiation. You will not have terms. You will do as I say because I command of Heaven. I know what we lack, and I know Dred. I have fought him many times, and I can help you beat him, but if you stray from me even once, I will end you." She watched me for a long time. "This is where you point out my shortcomings, and I beat you to death again and again until you concede. I would rather skip it, for as you know, time is of the essence."

The truth of her words hit me hard. I knew she would do it. Hell, not just that. Doing so would be her duty because she wanted to win. She would be just and fair, but she would be equally blind to my suffering along the way. I could respect that, and if I was being really honest, I sort of liked the idea of people listening. My time in Hell had been littered with endless infighting and strife. If they'd banded together, we might have pushed the Darkness back further.

Hell, maybe things would be different now.

I wasn't sure, but either way, what Michelle offered, I wanted.

"Okay." I held up my hand. "I will help you."

She seemed slightly surprised, and though it flashed across her countenance for only an instant, I'd seen it. "Oh?"

"Yes." I got to my feet and held out my hand. "Help me to defeat Dred and rescue Gabriella, and I will do all you ask."

She took my hand, and as she shook it, I felt her strength, but more than that, I felt her resolve. It was as unshakable as an oak tree, and for once in my life, that was what I wanted. I was tired of trying to get people to help me, even when it was for their own good.

No. I just wanted to build my army and save Gabriella, and if I was being really truthful with myself, that was why I'd wanted to go into the Darkness. I knew that if I stayed here with things as they were, I'd never win.

And more than anything, I wanted to win.

6

"So, that's what is going to happen." Michelle's tone left no room for argument, but even still, I half expected someone to say something. After all, Michelle had just told everyone I was leaving them to go to Heaven and do whatever the fuck she said.

For a moment, I thought Gwen was going to say something, but she didn't. Instead, she met my eyes and nodded.

"I'll be back soon," I said, meeting her eyes.

"You will not," Michelle said, glancing at me. "This place is a cesspool." Her gaze flitted to Lucifer, who stood in the back looking pissed off. "You have done a poor job, Sister." She spread her hands. "I expected more from the *most high*." She spat the words like a curse.

"Hell is not as it should be." Lucifer strode forward. "That is my fault, and I *will* fix it. This, however, is not the time to point fingers because if one was so inclined to do so, they might think that a man has grown strong enough to rival the entire divine company on your watch." She looked toward the sky. "It is no excuse, but I have been imprisoned for eons. You have roamed free and spectacularly failed, but no matter." Lucifer put a hand on Gwen's shoulder. "I spoke with Lust earlier, and we have come to an agreement. Arthur's talents are wasted with Hell as it is. Hell must be united into a blade that can strike out at our enemies."

"Gwen?" I asked even though Lucifer's words were aimed at Michelle. It was a touch strange because the Archangel of Justice hardly seemed perturbed. No. It more seemed like she took in Lucifer's words, weighed and measured them, and then ignored that which she felt irrelevant.

"Lucifer is right." Gwen met my eyes. "I always knew this day would come, that you'd be forced to leave." She swallowed. "We're the minor leagues, at least now. We should have had Royal Centre and the others to back you, but ever since Queen Nadine left, it's all been a giant mess. It's gotten worse, and that needs to be fixed. You can't spend your time getting jerked around by those too stupid to get behind the war effort." She nodded once. "Go, Arthur. Use Heaven to rescue Gabriella. When you are done, come back and see what we have made Hell."

"It is settled then." Michelle's eyes flashed as she surveyed the crowd. "We will leave immediately. For now, I will leave the soldiers currently here to help bolster your defenses, but I may have use of them."

"Wait, you're leaving the angels here?" I asked, confused. "Won't we need them?"

"She can't heal them," Mammon said, speaking for the first time. "She's trying to play it like she's doing us a favor, but the truth is, Heaven doesn't have enough healers. They really subscribe to that whole 'return with your shield or on your shield' thing." Mammon waved a hand. "Trust me, as soon as these angels are able, she will want them back."

"Is that true?" I asked, turning my eyes to Michelle. "You don't have enough healers?"

"We have some warrior healers, but not many." Michelle looked at me, and in her eyes, I saw only resolve. She paused for a split second before continuing. "It is best that you come and see what we have to offer. You will find all this to be meaningless." She waved a hand at the surroundings. "You do not need sculptures and ice cream. You need to be strong, to overwhelm your enemy with force."

While that was true, I also saw it as a way to lose a war of attrition. It had always seemed like the Darkness had infinite warriors to throw at us in ever increasing waves, to think they were not investing in healing their warriors because it was a sign of weakness? That was insanity.

"Suddenly rethinking your plan on abandoning us, eh Arthur?" Mammon asked, and before I could even respond, Michelle's wings burst from her back. Golden sparks flitted from the individual feathers as she gripped my wrist.

"Enough. It is time to leave." Michelle took a deep breath and leapt Heavenward, bursting through the air like a rocket, and dragging me effortlessly along behind her. Above, the swirling hole in the horizon Dred had punched through the sky lay open and raw.

"Wait, you mean to fly through that?" I screeched, barely able to speak from the air whipping by me.

"How else would you expect us to get back to Heaven? You have no stairway?" Michelle glanced at me, and I swallowed hard. She was right. We'd never even completed the stairway, and as I watched the rift above get closer, I realized we had a problem. I had no idea how long this rift between Heaven and Hell would remain open, and once it closed, I might not be able to return.

"What if it closes?" I asked as we burst through the rift. The change in temperature was immediate. The sweltering heat of Hell dissipated, and I suddenly felt comfortable in a way I'd not expected. It was strange but not as strange as Heaven.

Truth be told, I'd expected clouds and pearly gates, but what I saw was hardly that.

Row upon row of squat, featureless gray buildings filled the white sand for as far as I could see. The sky above was a blank, opaque blue color, and as I looked for wisps of clouds, I couldn't find any. No, the whole place was a monochromatic Hellscape. Where Hell had shades and degrees, Heaven had been painted with a matte palette. Like they only had time for one wash of paint.

"Come. There are many soldiers for you to make stronger. Many defenses for you to upgrade." Michelle strode forward, practically dragging me along. As we moved across the sand, I turned back toward the rift. It had been punched straight through a golden gate, and I could see twisted shards of metal on each side.

"Was that how Dred got in? Did he open a rift on top of your gate?" I asked, pulling my hand free from her wrist and staring at it while rubbing my chin.

"Yes." Michelle stopped and looked at the spot for a moment. "I never expected it. Once he'd done that, his forces came inside by the millions. It was overwhelming, and while we managed to push them back, it wore out my best troops. By the time Dred showed up, we were all but exhausted. Still, we fought, but it did not matter." She frowned. "You will make up for this. Increase my people's strength so we cannot be rushed again."

"There's more to fighting than that," I said, staring at the hole. "We need to fix the gate for one."

"We cannot fix the gate. We have no resources." She scrunched up her nose. "Though it should be better guarded. I only see one contingent there."

I looked but didn't see anything at all. Was there really a contingent of angels there? Only, as I thought about it, I saw twelve menu orbs appear spread all around, and beneath them, the shadowy outlines of more women appeared. Interesting.

"That's amazingly good stealth," I said with a whistle. "That's quite impressive." My hand when to Caliburn, so I could look at the ability, but Michelle gripped my shoulder, stopping me.

"Your job is not to gawk, builder. It is to build." She moved me around. "I will tell you what to do, and you will do it." She met my eyes. "Or do I need to teach you a new lesson?" The way she said it chilled me.

"No. It's fine." I sighed, turning off my curiosity as well as I could. Then again, it wasn't that hard. Heaven was so ticky tacky that it wasn't that interesting. Every building and structure looked like it'd been pushed out of a mold. Worse, it wasn't even a pretty mold. It was all utilitarian and ugly.

"So, what is the plan, exactly?" I asked Michelle, looking at her. "And are there other archangels here?"

"There are. Why do you ask?" Michelle seemed confused, which was a first. Up until now, she'd had all the answers or at least the appearance of having them.

"Um..." I touched my chest. "I am the Builder. I want the Heavenly Armaments and the marks. Speaking of which, I'd like yours too."

"What are you talking about?" Michelle shook her head. "You cannot use our marks nor our armaments. You are the Builder, not the Destroyer. They are not built to function for you."

"That's not true," I said, reaching up and pulling off the armament I'd gotten from Sam. "Do you recognize this?"

"Yes." Michelle nodded. "That is Samael's Armament. The Cold Embrace of Death." Her eyes widened. "Wait, did you take it from Dred?"

"No." I shook my head. "I broke the link between Dred's Mark and Samael." I waved a hand. "It was a thing. Then she crafted this for me." I pulled up my shirt, revealing the mark of Death on my abdomen. "Once Sam gave me the mark, I could use the armament, but it doesn't work that well."

"Of course not." Michelle sighed. "Still, it is interesting." She chewed on her lip for a moment. "We must speak with Raphael." She nodded once, veering sharply to the right. "She will know."

"Raphael?" I asked, trying to keep up with her as she pulled me along.

"Raphael is the Archangel of Providence. She is also the keeper of the archives." Michelle frowned. "As much as I hate to use such a valuable resource in this way, knowledge is power and power is strength. We cannot forget that."

I wasn't sure what to make of that, but as we approached a massive building, I felt my heart hammer in my chest. The place could have fit half the western United States. Could it really all be filled with knowledge? I found it hard to believe, but then again, this was Heaven. Nothing here made sense.

"Come." Michelle moved toward the door, which was when I realized she had released me. So far she had dragged me around, but now, as she approached the archives, she seemed hesitant. Interesting.

I watched her for a heartbeat before following her across the sand to the door. When I reached it, I felt something buffet against me moments before I was flung backward across the ground.

"Be gone!" The word echoed across the horizon, and as I felt it pulse inside my brain like a gong blast, the door opened to reveal a short woman with skin like coal and hair like spun copper. She was dressed in a long white lab coat over a white button up, red tie, and pleated navy skirt. She pushed her glasses up her nose and glared at Michelle. "How dare you?"

"How dare I?" Michelle asked, raising an eyebrow. "Watch your tone, Raphael."

"Excuse me?" Raphael asked, one hand jerking out to point at me. "Am I the one who has brought a human onto the hallowed grounds of Heaven? Do you not remember what happened last time?"

"I remember quite well, but this is different."

"It is not." Raphael looked at me. "I might have believed you if he wasn't cute."

"That isn't it at all, Raphael." Michelle sighed. "We require information."

"Of course you do." Raphael took a step back into the building, and for a moment I thought she might close the door on Michelle's face. "He cannot come in."

"Fine," Michelle growled, and it was crazy because I'd seen Michelle show more emotion in the last few seconds than I had in all the time until now.

"Very well." Raphael stepped outside, shutting the door behind herself. "I would ask why this time is different, but I know you do not know because you are dumb." Her gaze moved to me. "Justice may be blind, but that blindness is often dumb. There's a difference between the letter of the law and the soul of the law. She'd know that if she studied for a single second."

"Raphael, I do not wish to have this argument

with you now. I have many things to attend to." Michelle paused. "I do have a question, or I would not be here."

"Ask your question," Raphael huffed, crossing her arms over her chest.

"Why has he been able to use Samael's armament?" Michelle gestured to me. "He has her mark as well."

"Oh, that's easy." She looked at me. "Tell me, what is your legitimacy with the item?"

"Legitimacy?" I asked, raising an eyebrow.

"Oh, another dumb one. Awesome." Raphael rolled her eyes. "When you look at the item, it should have a legitimacy stat. Tell me what it is."

"Um…" I swallowed because I'd never seen a legitimacy stat on any of my items, but then again, I'd not looked at this particular item since I'd gotten Caliburn. Reaching down, I gripped the hilt of my sword and opened the menu for the armament.

The Cold Embrace of Death
Type: Earring
Durability: 1,300
Defense: 1D5
Legitimacy: 25%
Enchantments: Armament of Death
Ability: Ethereal Armor– Allows the user to coat his

body in Ethereal Armor that absorbs three times the user's health in battle before being destroyed.

"Twenty-five percent," I said, trying to hide my surprise as I opened the new stat.

Legitimacy – The user's ability to harness power from a faction other than his own. By building up reputation with opposing factions, the user can increase his legitimacy, allowing him to harness a greater percentage of an item's power.

"Right, okay." Raphael gestured at me as her eyes moved to Michelle. "So he can use about twenty-five percent of Samael's power. If he raised his legitimacy, he could do more, but as it stands, he can only get that. Still, it's better than nothing."

"So this means that we can increase his strength by giving him our marks?" Michelle asked, staring at me. "This is excellent news, even if your legitimacy is low."

"Um… in theory." Raphael looked at me. "I'm guessing something happened to Samael's bond with the Destroyer, yes?"

"Yes." I nodded.

"It is as I thought." Raphael sighed. "I do not know how easy it will be to break those marks here. Down there, she will experience a debuff based upon being in Hell where the Builder's power is strongest. Here he will be unlikely to break those bonds, at least without increasing his affinity."

"Oh." Michelle nodded, dismissing the idea. "Well, let us move on then."

She turned and began to walk away, and as I glanced at Raphael, wondering whether or not I could get the archangel to tell me more, she smiled at me.

"It's okay. You can come back later, Arthur. You intrigue me." Raphael glanced at the Armament of Death. "Samael was a good friend."

"He will not have time for your poking and prodding. He is busy." Michelle stopped and waited for me. "Come. Not all of Heaven is as nice as this."

7

Michelle was right. The rest of Heaven was a fucking pit. I wasn't sure how I hadn't noticed it before, but it became immediately clear as we left the Archives and headed back toward the zillions of barracks. From a distance they had seemed okay, but as we approached, the full extent of the damage became clear.

Most of the buildings were dilapidated, and while I wasn't sure how much of that was from neglect and how much was from the Darkness's forces running roughshod inside the town. The wounded were another matter.

They were fucking everywhere. It was like the stained problem back in Hell, but almost worse because they were hurt.

"You need healers," I said as we passed yet another broken down building. This one looked like it had been lit on fire for a while. Inside ten angels lay on the charred floorboards inside, blood staining their bandages crimson. "A lot of healers."

"That is not what we need." Michelle tossed a sidelong glance at me. "We need to be so strong we cannot be hurt."

"Sure, right." I sighed. "You keep saying that, but you can't get stronger if you're dead."

"Battle weeds out the weak." Michelle looked at me for another moment, and while she wasn't annoyed with me yet, I could tell that was going to change if I kept it up. Images of being doused in a volcano over and over again filled my mind, and for a moment, I kept my mouth shut.

Only as we passed more injured and more burnt out, halfway condemned buildings, I started getting pissed. This wasn't right, wasn't fair.

"We need to help these people." I stopped and put my hands on my hips. "Now."

"No. We must make those who are strong, stronger. We have no time to waste on this chaff." She gestured at an angel who had one bloody arm wrapped against her chest.

"You're wrong." I glared at Michelle. "It isn't a

crime to get hurt in battle. Hell, if we hadn't healed you, we wouldn't even be talking because you'd be dead."

"Be that as it may—"

"No." I shook my head. "I will not 'be that as it may.'" I pointed to the woman. "She could be you. Hell, she could be the most powerful angel here. We should heal them." I gestured around. "This whole town is a slum. Why aren't you fixing this?"

"I already told you that we cannot." Michelle crossed her arms over her chest. "Must we have this conversation again?"

"Yes." I glared at her. "This is almost worse than Hell. It's like you took a well-oiled machine and ran it into the ground." I threw my hands into the air. "I'm not doing a damned thing until we get some healers here."

"And how would we do that?" Michelle raised an eyebrow at me, and for a moment, I thought she might be placating me, but when she waited for my response, I realized she really wanted an answer.

"Um… we get some from Hell?" I shrugged. "If you don't have any, that is."

"We cannot allow demons and the fallen to set foot on our hallowed shoes. It is unacceptable." She snorted. "As if."

"Are you being serious right now?" I asked, barely resisting the urge to throttle her. I might have done it, but I didn't want to fight here and now. I wanted to help these angels.

"Yes." She waved a hand. "This conversation is over. Think of another way, and I shall entertain it. Until then, we will carry on with my plan."

I wanted to argue, to come up with a way to make everything work, but I couldn't. Hell, as I pulled up the stats for the woman, I felt my gut sink. For one, she had no healing trees of any kind, but for two, I couldn't even heal her injuries with experience because they weren't considered flaws.

"Arthur, come along." Michelle slapped her thigh in a way that pissed me off. "We have much to do."

"What other archangels are here? Can one of them heal?" I asked, looking at Michelle.

"Theoretically." She paused for a moment. "But it is unlikely."

"Tell me, or I'm not moving. I'll just go back to Hell and take my chances." I crossed my arms over my chest.

"Mammon misspoke when she said we had no healers." Michelle sighed. "But she was not wrong when she said we could not heal our own." She gestured at the injured angels everywhere. "Our battle medics can do simple things, but nothing to this extent. The best thing for our people it to take care of them until they heal on their own." She gritted her teeth. "It is not normally this bad. We were just attacked by the Darkness a few days ago."

"You're dumb." I shook my head before hitting my chest with the flat of my hand. "I am the Builder. I can modify the healer's stats. Take me to them, and let me see what I can do."

Michelle stared at me for a long moment. "I have been trying to do that this entire time."

"Why didn't you say that?" I snarled, moving toward her. "Let's go."

"I do not wish to tell you my every thought. It is enough for you to know that I consider all options." She held her hand out to me. "Do not think me unkind or uncaring. Neither of those are true."

"Fair enough," I said, taking her hand and her skin felt cool to the touch. Only as she squeezed my fingers, I felt something from her I never had before.

Pain.

An endless rush of pain and misery. This was her fault, and she knew it. She hadn't been strong enough, and now she was worried those she'd sought to protect would turn on her. It was why I was here. To back her play, to keep them strong to fight the Darkness, and right now, I wasn't helping. I hadn't noticed it before, but all around us, I could see the injured tittering about my defiance.

Heaven needed to be strong, and I was fucking it up.

"I'm sorry," I said, louder than I needed to. "I should not have presumed to know everything about Heaven or your leadership." I nodded. "Take me to your healers."

"I'm glad you're starting to understand." She released my hand, and as she moved, I could see thanks in her eyes. I wasn't sure how she'd conveyed so much with only a brief touch, but she had nonetheless.

"I still think you're a bit wrong though." I moved beside her, careful to keep my voice low enough so no one else would hear me. "You should take the help from Hell if they offer it."

"You are wrong." Michelle looked at me. "Trust me on this above all other things."

"I will for now, but I think it's wrong. The Darkness is the enemy. Hell is not." I sighed. "But it's your show. I don't even work here."

"That is where you're wrong, Builder." Michelle stopped in front of a large building. "We are here."

"Here?" I asked, looking over the structure. It was about three times the size of the other buildings but was as equally unadorned.

"Yes." She marched up to the doors and pulled them open.

The first thing I noticed was the stench. Like blood, shit, and vomit. I staggered backward, and as I did, Michelle furrowed her brows.

"What is this?" she asked, and as she spoke, I saw a figure in the middle of the room rise. She took a step forward, and I realized she only had one wing. The other had been shorn off, and she dragged it toward us.

"All are dead, Michelle." The voice that spoke was low and melodious, like a female James Earl Jones. "We pushed them back, but it was obvious this was their goal from the start." The woman stopped in front of us. Her entire body was covered in dried blood, and as she looked at me with her one good eye, she laughed. "Welcome to Heaven."

8

"Uriel!" Michelle exclaimed, showing more emotion in that single word than she had in all the time until now. "What has happened to you, to our battle-clerics?"

"Jophiel," the bloodied woman replied right before she shoved the shorn wing into Michelle's chest. "She has happened."

"That... that isn't possible." Michelle swallowed hard, hands instinctively reaching to grab the angel wing against her chest. As her fingers closed around the bloody feathers, Uriel pushed past her.

"You must be the Builder." Uriel looked me up and down, her good eye taking me in. She wasn't that tall, standing only about my height, but she looked built. Her body was all lean muscle, and what was more, she had that intrinsic feel of danger I'd seen many times walking by thugs after dark. "It is good to meet you before I die." Her green eye flashed. "That seems melodramatic. I am far from dead." She smirked. "That isn't even my wing." She threw her head back and laughed, howling like a crazy person. Then her hands went back to the nub where her one wing had been torn from her body. "I can't seem to find mine though." She frowned.

"Whose wing is that?" I asked, suddenly confused. "And why do you have it?"

"Why?" Uriel tapped her chin with one stubby finger. "That is the question, now isn't it. Wish I knew the answer." She smirked again. "Not true. I know the answer, but it is far from a good one. Truth be told I wanted it, so I took it."

"You wanted a busted angel wing?" I asked, suddenly confused.

"Uriel, who owns this wing?" Michelle said, turning to look at the one-eyed woman.

"I own the wing." She smacked her thighs and laughed again, her green eye flashing with delight. "I took it with my own hands." She held them up and clapped them together. "I ripped it from that stupid bitch's body when I found her within." Uriel snorted. "Thought she could take me, just 'cause I was down a wing. Well, I showed her. Took her damned wing." Uriel smiled. "Fair trade, I think."

"Okay." I clapped my hands together and looked Uriel over. Only, as I did so, I realized I couldn't see her menu. That was a bit odd. "Say, what's wrong."

"Wrong?" Uriel asked, raising an eyebrow. "Nothing is wrong. Now if you'll excuse me, I have some falling to do." She smirked again. "All the cool kids do it."

"You can't fall," Michelle stated the words so sharply, Uriel actually stopped moving. Then the archangel whirled around.

"And why should I not?" Uriel poked Michelle in the chest. Hard. "You're not the boss of me. I quit. Resign. Throw in the towel."

"You can't do that either." Michelle dropped the broken angel wing to the ground.

"I can do whatever I damned well please, Michelle." Uriel snorted. "I'm the biggest, strongest, baddest mama jama in Heaven, and right now, I'm about to pull a Lucifer and do whatever the fuck I want." Uriel's wing extended, and as she did, emerald fire sprang from her feet.

"Lucifer is not to be envied, nor followed,"

Michelle said, shaking her head. "She abandoned the cause."

"Well, I'm about to abandon the cause. Y'all can suck it sideways." Uriel made a wiping motion with her hands. "Because I'm done."

"Can you just hold on a teensy second?" I asked, looking over Uriel. She seemed like a twisted ball of energy, like a coiled spring just ready to explode or a jungle cat ready to pounce.

"For you?" She nodded toward Michelle. "Or for her?"

"For me." I smiled. "Because I'm totally lost."

"Ain't it the truth?" Uriel threw an arm around my neck. "We're all lost, kitten." She shrugged. "But what do you want to know?"

"Who is Jophiel?" I asked.

"The Archangel of Wisdom." Uriel shrugged. "Got any other brain busters?"

"And why did she kill everyone?" I said, turning over that in my mind. "Because I thought angels were the good guys."

"Angels are dicks." Uriel snorted. "Including me and especially including her." Uriel jerked a thumb at the Archangel of Justice. "There's no good. No evil. No right or wrong or just. There are just a buncha slobs." Her eyes twinkled. "Hell, for all we know, God is a slob just like one of us."

"I guess I'm not following." I took a deep breath.

"Here's the thing. Miss High and Mighty likes to put on a pleasant picture, but angels have been defecting for years." As Uriel started to say more, Michelle huffed, loudly, drawing my eyes to her.

"That isn't true. Only Jophiel has defected." Michelle snorted. "She's barely an archangel. She has the title, but no power."

"She is the Archangel of Wisdom, and rather than follow you, she chose to join the Darkness." Uriel didn't look at Michelle as she spoke. Instead, she met my eyes as she touched her temple. "Think about that."

"So, the wisest angel abandoned us?" I asked, dread filling my gut. "That seems really bad."

"It is bad." Uriel laughed, delirium filling her voice. "It's so fucking bad I could scream." She screamed. "And I'm dumb enough to still think we could win without her."

"Is that why you guys have been losing, why Dred pushed so far into Heaven?" I asked, suddenly confused.

"I doubt it." Michelle crossed her arms over her chest. "Jophiel defected only a few days ago."

"She just defected, and in that time you guys got owned?" I took a deep breath and hoped that the loss of the archangel hadn't royally screwed us. "How long had you stood before that?"

"Millennia." Uriel sighed. "Michelle doesn't get it, but without Jophiel we're pretty much fucked. She made all the plans, all the defenses. She knows how to beat us." Uriel gestured toward where we'd come. "That gate rift bomb? That has Jophiel all over it."

"Why would Jophiel defect?" I asked, not quite understanding. "Something had to have happened."

"Cause she's a tool." Uriel jerked a thumb at Michelle. "No, not a tool. An entire toolbox full of tools. She's a big old box of tools."

"That isn't as helpful as you'd think." I sighed.

"How did she get you to come here?" Uriel got really serious as she spoke. "Was it torture?"

"Well—"

"Jophiel said we needed you to win, needed your help." Uriel glanced at Michelle. "She wouldn't hear of having your stain on our hallowed shores, blah, blah, blah no one cares."

"So Jophiel defected, just like that?" I asked, suddenly understanding.

"Yup, she wanted you to come. What's more, she wanted us to help you." Uriel looked at Michelle. "Tell him I'm lying."

"You are not." Michelle sighed. "Yes, it is true, I did not want you. Now though, with Dred able to break in and the Archangel of Wisdom helping him, we need you."

"Right, okay." I took a deep breath and rubbed my temples. This had just gotten a lot harder than I'd thought. "Then we need to do some things my way."

"Arthur, that is not—"

"Michelle." Uriel turned toward the Archangel of Justice. "I want to hear his plan. If it sounds good, I'll stay. If not. So long and thanks for all the fish. Are we clear?"

"Yes." That single word seemed to hurt Michelle, but if it bothered Uriel, it didn't show.

"Good." Uriel gestured at me. "Tell me your plan, Builder."

"I think we get some of the people from hell to help us." I waved my hand at the surroundings. "It's obvious some very basic stuff could move things in the right direction. You don't have stat boosting sculptures or rune work for one. You also need healers, smiths, craftsmen. Unless I've not seen them, you don't have any of those, do you?"

"We don't," Uriel said with a nod. "Not anymore anyway. All dead. That's who the forces were after. Not that we had much of a force to begin with."

"Right, so we need some, and Hell has some. We bring them here."

"And after you've sullied Heaven with Hell's rejects, what then?" Michelle asked, anger filling her voice.

"Then we figure out how the hell to raise my affinity with you guys' armaments so we can give them to me and I can crush Dred." I shrugged. "How does that sound for starters?"

"I like him. He has pizzazz." As Uriel spoke, her menu orb appeared over her head. "Guess I'll stay." Her eye flashed with mirth. "If only to see how much he annoys you, Michelle."

9

"You're sure you're okay with this, Michelle?" I asked, looking over at the Archangel of Justice. "You can still say no."

"No." She shook her head. "I cannot."

"Yeah, you can." We stood just in front of the rift connecting Heaven and Hell, and while I couldn't see all the way down into the depths of Hell, I could feel the rush of sweltering heat from below. It was weird. I'd only been in Heaven a few hours, and already I found myself accustomed to the more moderate climate.

"If I do, Uriel will leave. We cannot lose the Archangel of Forgiveness. She is the strongest among us." Michelle looked over at me. "I have not won in millennia, and Jophiel said to trust you, to bring you aboard. Not heeding her has cost me so much already." She put her hands on her hips. "And we need their skills, much as I hate the idea of demons coming into Hell."

"Good." It was weird though, as I let her words roll around in my head, I was brought back to something my aunt said after they'd taken me in. She'd told me that people often did things they didn't like because it made those around them happy, and to suck it up when people asked me to do things I didn't like.

Now those words rang truer than ever, and I realized that as much as Michelle didn't want to let demons into Heaven, she needed them. What's more, she was trusting me. Both of those felt like heavy burdens, and for a moment, I wondered if I could shoulder it.

Then I decided I didn't care. If I couldn't Gabriella would remain with Dred, and I couldn't let that happen.

"Good." Michelle offered me her hand. "Let us go get your crafters."

I took her hand, and as I did, she stepped off the edge. We plummeted down through the air, and for a second I worried we'd slam into the ground. Only as it rushed up toward us, Michelle unfurled her awesome wings, catching us in midair and slowing our descent.

A second later, we were back in the sweltering heat of Hell. The sky crackled overhead, swirling around the hole in the sky overhead.

"Let us be quick," Michelle said, looking me over. "And as I said before, only three may come. I will not be able to carry more." She met my eyes then. "And not Samael."

"Why not?" I was suddenly confused. "She's a great blacksmith, and we will need her."

"She is fallen." Michelle crossed her arms over her chest. "I cannot have her back. It will send a very powerful message to the angels who have stayed. That cannot be allowed to happen. Not if Heaven is to remain a well-oiled machine."

"Fine." I thought about fighting, but it hardly seemed worth it. We could only bring three back, and of them, one had to be Sally, and the other had to be Annabeth. It'd always been a tossup between Maribelle and Sam, and I'd leaned more toward Maribelle, anyway. After all, the angels had their own magical weapons.

"I expected more of an argument," Michelle sighed. "You seem to love arguing with me. It's infuriating."

"Look, I'm just trying to do my best with what I've got." I shrugged as we made our way to the Graveyard, and when I knocked on the door, I heard a squeal of commotion inside.

As the door opened, I saw Buffy the goblin merchant standing there with a shit-eating grin on her face. "Well, look what the cat dragged in." Her grin got wider. "Let me guess, you need supplies."

"Actually, we do." I nodded to her. "How'd you guess?"

"Everyone needs supplies, and they just got ransacked." Buffy walked over to us and put her hand out and looked at Michelle. "I'll be happy to help you with supplies." She smiled. "Just tell Buffy what you need."

"Well, this is unexpected." Michelle looked from the goblin to me, and when I shrugged, she turned her eyes back to the goblin. "Why would you help us?"

"For the money of course. So much money." Buffy put her arm through Michelle's and while the archangel looked like she didn't want to be touched, allowed it. "But enough of that. Let's talk about what ol' Buffy can do to help you."

Michelle shot me a "help" look, but I ignored it as I waved to her. "I'll be back in a bit, okay?" With that, I left them to chat. I'd just make sure I looked over any contracts before Michelle signed them so I could keep Buffy from skinning her alive. Then again, maybe not. Heaven was kind of lame.

As I walked into the town, I was immediately surprised by how little it changed. I know I shouldn't have been because, realistically, I had only been gone a few hours, but I don't know, it had felt longer.

Still, as I made my way through the bustling streets, I could tell things were going to change. There were more workers for one, and a lot of the angels were already up and on their feet. Many of them were working under the tutelage of demons. Was this because of Lucifer?

I wasn't sure, but whoever had gotten the angels and demons to work side by side was a damned genius and definitely needed to talk to Michelle.

"Hey, Sally!" I called, waving at the healer as I approached. "How goes the healing?"

Sally turned to me, her deep blue eyes flashing as her long golden hair whipped around her body.

One hand went to her heart as though she was trying to keep it from racing out of her chest.

"Arthur, you scared the bejeezus out of me!" she exclaimed, eyes sweeping over me. "I thought you were in Heaven?" She gave me a wry smile. "Did they kick you out already?"

"Nearly so," I joked, moving toward her. "You've done great work. When I was walking around, I saw most of the angels were better. It's insane."

"There were only a couple hundred." Sally shrugged, her cheeks flushing. "And we had a lot of help. Ever since Lucifer threw their leader into a volcano, they pretty much do as she says." Sally covered her mouth conspiratorially. "She commands them with an iron fist."

"Yeah, getting tossed into a volcano has a way of making you listen." I shuddered at the memory. "Anyway, that's sort of why I'm back."

"To throw someone in a volcano?" She arched an eyebrow as confusion spread across her face.

"No." I shook my head as I reached out and took one of her hands in mine. "I came back for you."

Sally's cheeks flushed as she met my eyes. Then

she swallowed, once, twice, three times. "You left Heaven for me?"

"Yeah." I nodded, my free hand sweeping out toward the few injured angels that remained. "You thought this was bad? You haven't seen anything. Heaven is a goddamned murder pit, and they have *no* healers."

"Oh." Sally looked away from me, eyes distant as she took in the scene. "Right, of course." She nodded slightly. "I'd be happy to help." The thing was, she didn't sound happy, only I didn't know why.

"That's great!" I hugged her. "You're the best."

"Yeah." She nodded. "Let me just gather some things and tell Crystal—"

"About that." I kicked absently at the ground. "She can't come."

"Oh?" Sally stared at me for a long moment, and when I didn't respond, continued, "Why not?"

"I can only bring three people, and the other two spots are for Annabeth and Maribelle." As her eyes bore into me, she nodded.

"Crystal will not be pleased." She said it like she was also not pleased.

"I'm sorry." I sighed. "It was like pulling teeth

to get you three up there." I shook my head. "You'll understand when we get there."

With that, I made my way toward the center of town. I'd expected to find Annabeth there, but she was noticeably absent. Usually, her sculpting setup was by the fountain, but it wasn't there either. That was odd. I wondered where she went.

10

Fifteen minutes later, I still hadn't found Annabeth, but I had found Maribelle. She was admonishing a group of angels who didn't seem to know how hammers and nails worked.

"No, you idiots!" Maribelle hollered, gripping a hammer in a white-knuckled grip. "You hit the nail in one smooth motion so you can drive it into the wood and not bend the fuck out of it." She put a nail against a board and smashed it with her hammer, driving it into the wood with one stroke. "Like that." She threw her hands into the air. "Honestly, it's like you've never seen a hammer before."

"Well, they've likely not seen a hammer before," I said, approaching.

"Well, that's just pathetic…" Maribelle stopped as she turned and saw me. "Arthur! I thought you were in Heaven?"

"I came back to get you," I said, smiling at her.

"You did?" Maribelle asked, suspicion filling her features. "Why?"

"Because I need a carpenter," I said, nodding toward her. "And you're an awesome carpenter."

"Okay, good." She let out a breath of relief. "For a moment, I thought you just came back for another foursome." She rolled her eyes. "That was a onetime thing."

"Yeah, I figured," I mumbled as the memory of her and her two apprentices flashed through my mind. At the time, we'd been overtaken by the power of Lust, and it had driven all sensibility from our brains. It was especially strange because of all the women I'd been with, Maribelle had been the most, um, boy crazy. She'd also seemed the most disgusted by seeing other women naked. Not that I'd tried to recreate the moment or anything…

"Anyway, I'll need some help." The blue-skinned Maribelle gestured at the angels who were practicing driving nails into wood. It was almost comically bad. "These gals suck. I'm assuming Heaven isn't much better."

"It's worse." I shrugged. "And you can't bring anyone else. I just need you and that pretty brain of yours."

"Of course you do." She rolled her yellow eyes. "And you can lay off the compliments." She gave me a sly grin. "They're unnecessary." As she licked her lips, I felt my body react as all the blood in me rushed south.

"Right, okay." I shook off the sudden need to see just how unnecessary they were and sighed. "Anyway, I need to find the last of our party. Do you know where Annabeth is?"

"Oh, um…" Maribelle looked heavenward as she started to think. She tapped her chin a couple times with one stubby finger. "Isn't she still with the dwarves?"

"That's right," I said, suddenly feeling bad. Annabeth had been with the dwarves. I'd meant to pick her up, but I never had. Worse, now that I'd traded Wrath's teleport ability for Dred's healing power, I couldn't click my heels together and go get her.

"Well, that seems like it'll be the trip." She smirked at me and ran a hand through her long red hair. "Let me know when you're ready. Until then… I'll be trying to teach these nitwits."

"Right, okay. Sally is coming too, so if she comes looking for me, let her know." As Maribelle nodded, I turned and made my way back toward where I thought Buffy and Michelle would be. Last time I'd been here, Buffy had the only Nexus Gateway Conduit, and with it, she could transport me to the dwarven stronghold.

It took me a few minutes longer to find them than I'd have liked, and when I finally did, I was surprised it was in the mess hall.

"So, then she comes over and smacks me in the chest with a wing and is all 'it's not even my wing,'" Michelle mocked in a perfect rendition of Uriel as she tossed back another gulp of ale. "What did you say this stuff is again?"

"Ale." Buffy eyed the angel carefully. "And maybe you should stop. You've only had one, and you're all…" the green-skinned goblin waved a hand at Michelle. "This."

"What do you mean? I feel great," Michelle said, finishing the drink in another long gulp that caused dribbles of fluid to spill out from the corners of her mouth. She reached up and wiped the froth away with her forearm as she set the mug down. "What other flavors are good?" She hiccupped.

"Is she drunk?" I asked, coming over, and

before Buffy could say anything, Michelle jumped off her barstool and wrapped her arms around me, crushing my face into her chest in a way I'd have really enjoyed under different circumstances. Worse, the angel was a damned sight stronger than she looked.

"Arthur! You've returned." She pulled me off her chest and looked at me with glassy eyes. "Your short friend has shown me this thing called ale. We simply must bring it back to Heaven." She hiccupped again and smiled at me as her eyes raked over me. "My, I've not noticed it before, but you're quite cute." She broke into a wide grin as her gaze settled on my crotch. "Say, do you have a big one?"

"A big one?" I asked, looking at Buffy for help. Only the goblin wasn't even looking in our direction. In fact, she was very pointedly looking away from us and pretending to sip her own drink.

"A big peeeeenis," she said, drawing out the word. "I've never even seen one before." Her gaze flicked up to my face. "Would you show me?" She smiled again.

"I don't think that's a good idea," I said, and she frowned for a second before brightening.

"Oh, I get it." She nodded three times in rapid succession. "You don't want to show me because it's not a fair trade." With that, she unhooked the straps of her armor with her thumbs and flicked them off her shoulders. The Greek style plate mail slid off her lithe form and hit the ground with a clang, leaving her standing there completely naked.

I'll be honest. I looked. I'm not proud of it, but at the same time, she was really damned hot.

Worse, as the chilly air of the mess hall hit her exposed flesh, her pink nipples jutted out like they were standing at attention, and as I stared, she put her hands on her hips, drawing my eyes down to her golden crotch.

"Well." She gestured at me with one hand. "Your turn."

I again looked to Buffy for help, but as I caught sight of the goblin, her eyes went wide, and she looked away. Great. Just great.

"Michelle, you're drunk," was what I should have said, but I didn't. Instead, I just sighed.

"Fine, but that's all," I did say, and then before I could really think about what I was doing, I dropped my own pants to the ground.

"Hmm…" Michelle said, eyes settling on little me. "It um… I thought they were." She held her hands apart. "Bigger."

Buffy cackled.

"It's cold in here." I swallowed. "He's not quite ready to go."

"Not ready to go?" She looked at me in confusion. "Oh, does it get bigger?"

"Yeah, it's um, not in its final form." I couldn't believe I was having this conversation.

"How do we get it in its final form?" Michelle asked, coming closer to me, and I realized I could feel the heat wafting off her body.

"You, um—"

"Oh, it's starting to get bigger," she said, clapping her hands and bouncing excitedly. And let me just say, that when she bounced, she did bounce. "Oh, that did something!" Her eyes widened as she dropped to her knees in front of me, mouth slightly agape.

"Michelle, um, I think—"

"Can I touch it?" she asked, holding her index finger out toward me. "Please?"

"I think maybe I need to go." Buffy slid off her stool. "Don't do anything I wouldn't do." She winked at me, and sidled out, leaving us all alone in the mess hall.

"Hmm… why did she leave? She was nice. I think I'll miss her." Michelle said, looking up at me from her position in front of me. "She's going to help with the trade in Heaven. I'm not sure what that will mean exactly, but I have high hopes."

"That's awfully nice of her," I said, and she nodded.

"So then, back to the matter at hand." Michelle looked right at my cock. "We were having another negotiation." She hesitated. "I suppose you can touch me in return. Would that be an okay trade?"

"Michelle, I don't think that's a good idea." I sighed, wanting more than anything in the entire world to not be me right now. If I was someone else, well, I'd be getting a blowjob from the archangel about ten seconds from now.

"Why not?" She furrowed her brow. "I've never been with a man before. Is that why?"

"No, it's because you're drunk." I shook my head. "And I'd never forgive myself if we did something like this while you were." Then as the angel looked at me like I'd grown a second penis, I sighed. "I think we better get dressed."

"I think I get it." She stood, not bothering to cover herself. "It's because I drank those drinks." She swallowed. "I'm acting different, I suppose." She sighed, reaching out a hand and touching my arm. "Thing is though, I'm always so careful, and for once I feel free." She met my eyes. "Do you understand what that's like? To have to show a different face to the world." She bit her lip. "Maybe I just don't want to do that. Maybe I want to stop thinking and have some fun for once."

"That's fine, and if you want me to fuck your brains out when you're sober, I'll totally do it." I looked her up and down. "Totally." I sighed, taking her hand.

"Arthur." She reached out and grabbed little me. The warmth in her grip rippled through me, and before I could stop myself, I moaned. "I think you might be right. I probably did drink too much." She dropped down in front of me again and began to slowly stroke me. "But it'd be okay if we just played a little, right?" She stared intently at me, mouth open slightly. "You seem nice enough, and I'm so lonely. *So* lonely." She looked up at me and smiled. "We don't have to do anything you don't want to do, but I'm a big girl." She nodded once. "I can make my own decisions."

11

"No!" Lucifer snarled, kicking in the door and marching toward us.

Michelle looked over at her sister, one hand still stroking me and smiled dumbly. "Oh, hi Luci!" She beamed. "Do you want to try?" She frowned then. "Why do you seem upset?"

"I'm not upset." She came to a stop beside us and looked right into my soul. "I'm disappointed."

"I can explain," I said, even though I had no fucking clue what to say. I mean, I was standing here naked with a drunk angel who was giving me a hand job. It pretty much was what it was.

"Don't." Lucifer shook her head right before she grabbed Michelle by the arm and pulled her away from me. "And you need to stop."

"Luci!" Michelle glared up at her older sister. "Let me go."

"No." Lucifer knelt down in front of Michelle. "Listen to your older sister. You don't want to do this." She shot me a look. "Not with him, and not like this."

"But Arthur seems like a nice boy," she pouted, crossing her arms over her chest. "Why does everyone else get to do what they want? Why not me?" She thumped her chest. "What about Michelle?"

"You're drunk." Lucifer let the words hang in the air, but the only one of us it had an effect on was me. Actually, that wasn't quite true. It had an effect on little me, who quickly went into hiding.

"I know that. Arthur explained it already." Michelle huffed. "We weren't going to mate." She looked over at me, and her face fell. Her gaze swung back toward Lucifer. "You made its final form go away."

"Its final form?" Lucifer glanced at me, and her cheeks colored. "Do you mean his erection?"

"You made his penis small again." Michelle held up her hand. "I can't rub it when it's small." She sighed. "Now I have to make it big again."

I'll be one hundred percent honest here. I never

thought I'd be privy to a conversation like this. And especially not between Lucifer and Michelle. Worse, I never expected Lucifer to be the voice of fucking reason. My life was weird. Good, but definitely weird.

"Right." Lucifer met my eyes. "Arthur, pull up your pants and wait outside please."

"Yeah, okay." I nodded because the look she gave me made me think my little bath in the volcano would be a day at the park in comparison to what she'd do to me if I stayed.

"No. Don't go," Michelle whined, and as she tried to get back to her feet, she stumbled against her older sister. "Oh, you're warm."

As I exited the mess hall, I felt like an ass, and that feeling was only amplified when I saw Buffy standing there looking distraught.

"You're welcome," Buffy said, looking up at me.

"I'm welcome? You left me in there and now Lucifer—"

"Who do you think got Lucifer?" Buffy asked, not meeting my eyes. "I wasn't even going to try to stop Michelle from doing whatever the fuck, but Lucifer could." She sighed. "And I know you, Arthur. You're not a bad guy, but you are a guy, and she's like a perfect twenty. You were totally going to fuck her if she kept pressing the issue." She waved a hand. "Sure, you'd feel bad about it afterward. The thing is, you can't unfuck someone."

"Thanks." I nodded to her. "Truth be told. I'm glad it sort of worked out this way." I glanced back at the mess hall. "Really glad." I took a deep breath, trying to reorient myself to reality, and as that reality settled around me, I could still tell myself I was a decent person. It might not be true, but then again, it might be, and that was important.

"So, why were you looking for us?" Buffy asked, pointedly changing the subject. "I doubt it was because you like my sparkling personality, and Michelle is about as fun as a bag of stumps under normal circumstances, so…"

"You know you both started and ended that with the word 'so' right?" I asked, and when Buffy glowered at me, I smiled. "I need to go get Annabeth from the dwarves. Part of me thought she'd returned, but I might be misremembering."

"Oh?" the goblin snorted. "Well, either way, she is with the dwarves." She reached into her satchel and pulled out the Nexus Gateway Conduit. "Let's go get her."

"You seem pretty pleased," I replied, following her toward the Nexus Gateway. "Why?"

"I'm going to skin the angels alive." Buffy rubbed her greedy paws together. "I will have so much money I will literally build a giant fortress of money to hold my money in."

"You know, there's more to life than money, right?" I asked, and the goblin glared at me.

"You shut your whore mouth." She crossed her arms over her chest and hugged herself like she was trying to ward off a chill. "I can't believe you'd talk about money that way!"

"Uh huh," I said, shaking my head. "And as a point of fact, Lucifer seems quite protective of her sister. You sure you want to, what was it you said? 'Skin them alive?'"

"I'm not trying to fuck her." Buffy didn't look at me.

"You got her drunk during negotiations." I sighed. "You're a bad person."

"At least I know what I'm about." She looked over at me.

"Money?"

"Money," she affirmed.

"Right, I hope that makes you feel better when you're swimming in a volcano." I stared out at the horizon, remembering my bath in lava. Fun it had not been.

"My money always makes me feel better. When I'm sad, it makes me happy. When I'm cold, I fill a big sack with it and crawl inside for warmth." She smiled. "When I'm in danger of a lava bath, it buys me SPF one billion."

I wanted to respond, but it seemed a silly thing to do. To be honest, I literally did not care either. Buffy was, more or less, on my side, and if she made us richer, that could only help. Besides, as stuck up Heaven seemed to be, they could do with some good old-fashioned capitalism. Then maybe they wouldn't be a bunch of mindless automatons who got owned by a single angel.

"All right, let's get this show on the road," Buffy said, switching open the portal, and as it burst to life like a glowing blue pustule of energy I shivered. I always hated gateway travel. Teleportation had been way better, but so was not dying. It almost seemed unfair I had to choose, but I wasn't sure who I was supposed to bitch at about it.

"Yeah, time is money, and all that." I jumped through the Nexus Gateway, and the familiar sensation of being torn down to my composite atoms before behind reassembled filled every inch of my being with pain. That pain was always a little strange because, during the near instantaneous transit, I had no body.

"I love that you're learning," Buffy said as she appeared beside me on the stone platform the dwarves had erected.

"That time is money?" I asked, quirking an eyebrow at them as we made our way to the gateway.

"Yes. It's like watching a baby bird fly for the first time." The goblin beamed at me as we approached the stalwart dwarf at the gate. Unlike Mina, the guard I'd first met, this one reminded me of Nurse Ratched only bearded. Her long black beard fell to her knees, and as she squinted at me with her dark eyes, I got the feeling she didn't much like me.

"I don't like you." Well, that answered that question.

"I don't like you back." I stuck out my tongue. "Now open the doors, or I'll tell Sathanus you're being mean to me."

"One day you will not have the Archangel of Wrath backing your play. On that day I will find you, and I will cut off your balls." She glared at me before turning and hitting the button to open the massive stone doors. As they swung open on gears that shrieked like a banshee, I tried to ignore her piercing stare.

I wasn't sure what I'd done to piss off the dwarf, but it was enough that Buffy stepped pointedly away from me so she wouldn't be contaminated by my presence.

"I'll wait out here," she said, looking at me as I moved toward the door. "Just in case they decide to kill you, anyway."

"Smart goblin," the dwarf intoned, and I sighed.

"Okay." Not sure what else to do, I made my way inside. Every single dwarf who saw me gave me the stink eye, and as I moved forward, I got the impression I'd wronged them in some way. Still, I didn't much care. I was going to save their whole race. If they disliked me because of it, who was I to complain?

Still, after a few minutes, I realized I had a problem. I'd never really walked through much of the town the dwarves had carved into this mountain, and what little I had explored had been with a guide. I mulled that thought over for a second before moving toward the closest dwarf.

"Excuse me, can you help me?"

She spat on me. Literally hocked a huge loogy

and spat it onto my chest. As I looked down at the gob of spittle sticking to my shirt, I was too shocked to even say anything.

"Why don't ye go on home, Builder? We don't want yer kind here," The dwarf snapped before shouldering me aside and walking away. As I turned to watch her go, I couldn't help but be more shocked than annoyed.

"I'd love to leave, but I'm trying to find Annabeth." My words caused the angry dwarf to stop in her tracks and glance at me over her shoulder.

"Is that so?" she asked, and her tone had softened. "Have ye really come for the Sculptor Queen?"

"The Sculptor Queen?" I asked, confused. "Um… I guess. I'm looking for Annabeth. I'm supposed to pick her up." I rubbed the back of my neck and looked at her sheepishly. "I'm a bit late, but in my defense, I got my chest caved in by Dred."

"But ye came." She nodded. "I'll reserve my resentment for the time being." She stuck a finger out at me. "But ye better watch yerself. One wrong move and it's curtains." She drew her hand across her throat which seemed too dramatic and a bit unnecessary. Still, if she'd bring me to Annabeth, I could put up with her for now.

"Right, let's just go." I glanced down at my shirt and wiped away the spittle. It was gross, and while part of me wanted to throttle the rude little dwarf, I didn't. Throttling could wait.

I have no idea how long we moved, or where we went because after the sixth left, I was totally lost. As the minutes dragged by, I found myself wondering when we'd ever find Annabeth.

"So, uh, why is everyone pissed off at me?" I asked, and my voice seemed unnaturally loud in the silence of the cavern.

"Yer the daft boy who left the Sculptor Queen to rot here. Mina told us how you said you'd come pick up Annabeth, but then you never did." The dwarf glared at me. "Just because Annabeth is a good person and makes excuses for your actions, we hate ye on her behalf."

"Oh." As her words settled in me, I couldn't help but feel like a total jackass. I know out of sight out of mind, and that I'd been busy, but it would have only taken me a few seconds to come get Annabeth. That I'd left her here for the last few days was pretty douchey of me. "Guess I deserve that."

"And more. Why if my beard had it her way, ye'd be strung up by yer balls." The dwarf snorted as she came to a stop beside a massive metal door with such a spectacularly designed dragon etched into it, my breath caught in my throat. It looked real.

"Did Annabeth make that?" I asked, gesturing at the door as the dwarf pushed it open.

"Yes, she did. She's done many sculptures while here. Each better than the last. Her talent is truly transcendent." The dwarf glowered at me. "What she sees in the likes of you is beyond my ken." She looked skyward. "Hell, tis beyond the ken of mortal demons."

"I'm a nice guy."

"A nice guy wouldn't leave someone stranded on a mountaintop." The dwarf sneered before gesturing toward the door. "Either way, she's in there. I suggest ye apologize for being, well, you."

As I looked at her, I couldn't help but agree. A nice guy wouldn't do that, but then again, a nice guy wouldn't bang a drunken angel. So maybe I wasn't a nice guy.

12

"Arthur!" Annabeth exclaimed, looking over at me and blowing a lock of dark hair out of her face. She was in the middle of carving something from a massive piece of rock, but since it was covered with sheets, I couldn't make it out. "Are you back already?"

"Um… yes?" I looked at her confused. "Is everything okay?"

"Yeah," she got to her feet and wiped her hands on her trousers. "I've been keeping myself busy." She gestured around the room where a dozen half-finished sculptures sat. "Trying out new techniques." She smiled. "It's been kind of nice. The dwarves mostly leave me alone to work."

"Wait, you're happy?" I asked, suddenly confused.

"Why wouldn't I be?" She waved off my comment. "Oh, because you left me here for a few days?" When I nodded, she continued. "It's sweet of you to think of me, but I know you're busy. Truth be told, I was kind of peopled out." She frowned. "I've always been a wandering sculptor. The whole staying in a town for so long had made me reach my limit. I was getting up in the morning and strengthening myself to deal with all the people. It was exhausting."

"I didn't realize." I suddenly felt bad for coming to get her which was crazy because only a few moments earlier I'd felt terrible for feeling the exact opposite.

"I never told you, so how could you?" She winked at me. "You're cute, but perceptive, you're not." She sauntered over to me, picking up a satchel of tools along the way. "Besides, it takes two for a conversation." She smiled at me. "Ready when you are."

"I'll be honest, this isn't going like I expected. I mean, I'm glad you're not mad, but still." I sighed. "Anyway, yeah, I did come to get you. Buffy is waiting."

"You can't teleport anymore?" Annabeth raised

an eyebrow. "I can't believe you gave up that ability."

"Dred caved in my chest and stealing his healing ability was the only way I could survive." I shrugged.

"Dred came?" Annabeth's eyes went wide. "Is everyone okay?"

"No." I shook my head. "That's why I came to get you. Dred shattered Heaven, and we need to go fix it." I thought about telling her about Gabriella's capture, but I didn't want to make her more upset.

"Oh." She frowned. "I'm not really good at the whole town building thing. I'm just a sculptor."

"You're not 'just' anything." I patted her shoulder. "You're the Sculptor Queen!"

"That's what the dwarves say too, and it seems so pompous." She blushed. "I'm not even that good."

"Are we really having this conversation? You won the sculpting tournament." I shook my head. "Take some damned praise."

"Fine," she grumbled, but I didn't get the impression she actually agreed. "So why do you want me in Heaven? To make sculptures?"

"Yes." I nodded. "Your sculptures give stats and

buffs and all that goodness. We'll need that to help repel the Darkness. You up for the challenge?"

"I suppose, but I'll need good material for that." She looked around. "The better the material, the better the sculpture."

"Buffy is working on that." I shrugged.

"So you turned Buffy loose on the angels?" Annabeth said as we made our way out. "I almost feel sorry for them."

"Me too," I replied as the dwarf who had shown me the way looked over at us.

"Did he apologize?" the dwarf asked, looking over at Annabeth. "Because if he didn't, well…"

"He did. It was very sweet." Annabeth nodded. "Thank you for asking." She frowned slightly. "I didn't quite finish the sculpture, but I will when I finish up in Heaven okay?" She paused for a second. "And don't go peeking."

"I wouldn't dare." The dwarf totally lied.

"Mmm hmm," Annabeth said, sighing. "You'll be disappointed if you do. It's barely halfway finished." She shrugged. "And if you do peek, I'll know, and I won't come back. How would you like to be responsible for that?"

The dwarf looked like someone had stolen her lunch money. "I would not like that at all."

"Well then, seems we have a decision, don't we?" She gestured down the hallways as she smiled. "Can you show us the way out?"

"I'd be honored, Sculptor Queen." The dwarf threw another glare at me, but it was different this time. She was mad I was taking the sculptor home, which was a bit odd because she'd originally been mad because I hadn't done that. Dwarves.

It didn't feel like it took nearly as long to make our way out, and as we stepped through the doorway and Annabeth made her goodbyes to all the dwarves who had followed us out, I spied buffy. The goblin as waiting by the courtyard exit, either staring at one of her many watches or tapping her foot.

"Finally!" Buffy said, nodding at us. "It's been a dog's age. Do you know how much money I've lost waiting? No, of course, you don't. Just know it's a lot."

"Sorry." I shrugged. "But if you think about it differently—"

"I still lost money." Buffy paused a blink. "Man, I sound like a cardboard cutout villain." She scratched her head. "I do care about things other than money."

"Of course you do, Buff," I said, as Annabeth

came over and the two of us followed the goblin toward the Nexus Gateway.

"I do!" Buffy stamped her foot.

"You do what?" Annabeth asked as Buffy switched on the portal. I was surprised it worked because normally they needed to recharge for an hour, but then again, the trip had taken a while. It'd probably been an hour or more. No wonder Buffy was peeved.

"Care about more than money."

Annabeth laughed, and not just laughed, but thigh slapping, tears rolling down her cheeks, laughed.

"I do!" Buffy growled.

"Oh, you're serious?" Annabeth said, between gulps of air. "Sorry."

"It's not funny," Buffy snapped. "If you cut me, do I not bleed?"

"I dunno, what's it called when gold coins flow out of your veins?" Annabeth looked over at me. "Is that bleeding?"

"I do not find this humorous in the least." The goblin's gaze swiveled to me. "In the least."

"I don't know what to tell you," I said, shrugging, and then before she could argue with me about it, I leapt through the portal. It was just as painful as before, but when I emerged on the other side, I was glad. I didn't really like the dwarves and having miles and miles between myself and them was pleasing.

As my compatriots emerged behind me, I stared up at the rift merging Heaven and Hell. In just a little bit I'd be back in Heaven, and while the weather was nice, I wasn't quite sure I was up to the task. I was also, sort of dreading seeing Michelle after our whole, um, thing.

"Well, my work is done now." Buffy met my eyes. "I'll have the order ready tomorrow. Assuming she remembers, Michelle is supposed to send some angels to get it." Buffy pointed to the loading bay a few meters away. "It'll be there. Don't forget to get it or there will be a late fee."

"That's paid in money?" Annabeth joked, and as Buffy turned to look at the sculptor, a wry grin split her lips.

"Usually, but I accept many things." Her eyes flicked to me. "Ass, grass, or cash."

"Well, that's just swell," I muttered, shaking my head.

"Hey, I'm equal opportunity." Buffy shrugged.

"I'm not even slightly surprised to hear that," I said, already trying to put the idea out of my mind.

Even still, it was hard to not picture Buffy as Jabba the Hutt, covered in slaves while smoking from a pipe and wearing gold chains.

"Anyway, I'll be taking my leave. Money to make and all that." She paused a touch. "Not that money is all I'm about." Then before anyone could say anything, she scampered off toward the loading dock where a group of angels were arranging boxes.

"I feel like we hit a nerve with her," Annabeth said, looking over at me. "I didn't mean to upset her."

"It's fine." I waved a hand dismissively at her. "Some people are hyper-competitive, and money is a way of keeping score."

"I suppose," Annabeth said as she followed me toward the town. "So who else is coming to Heaven?"

"You, Maribelle, and Sally." I glanced at her. "Why?"

"I just wondered if Sam was coming. You know, because of that whole fallen angel thing."

"Yeah, Michelle wouldn't allow that." When Annabeth gave me a blank look, I explained further. "Michelle is the leader of Heaven. It's really different from here. You'll see."

"I suppose I will," Annabeth mused before lapsing into silence for the rest of our trip. That was fine though because I had to round up Maribelle and Sally before heading off to find Michelle.

It was a bit weird because I could tell Sally was still annoyed at me, but she was doing a good job of not letting it show.

Even still, I would have almost rather talked to her about her feelings than face Michelle. Only as I found the archangel, she was fast asleep. She was curled up into a tiny ball, head on Lucifer's lap. The older archangel was staring down at her, absently brushing her hair.

"Is it time for you to go?" Lucifer asked, and she seemed strangely saddened by the idea. "I suppose so." She gently shook Michelle. "Wake up, sweetie. It's time to go home."

"Just a few more minutes," Michelle murmured, batting her hand at Lucifer.

"Sorry. This is all the time we have." Lucifer swallowed and looked at the sky. "Sorry."

"You said it twice," Michelle mumbled, stretching before rubbing her eyes. Then she looked around, and I could tell she was still drunk. It was a bit weird because I'd expected her to be sober, but then again, it'd only been an hour or two tops. Maybe she'd drank more than I'd thought?

"I meant it twice," Lucifer said, brushing Michelle's hair out of her face. "I am sorry."

"Okay." Michelle nodded before wrapping her arms around Lucifer and hugging her tightly, causing Lucifer to stiffen, obviously uncomfortable. "I believe you're sorry." Michelle turned to look at me. "Are these the crafters?" Her gaze swept over my trio.

"Yes." I turned toward them like I was Vanna White on Wheel of Fortune. "This is Annabeth, she's a sculptor. Sally who is a healer, and Maribelle. She's the carpenter."

"We do love carpenters in Heaven." Michelle gave me a small smile. "And we can definitely use the healer, but why the sculptor?"

"See, I told you this was a bad idea—"

"Annabeth," I said, cutting her off. "Can make sculptures that enhance the abilities of those around them. Putting a few of those inside heaven will vastly strengthen the entire place." I looked over at Michelle. "Isn't that what you want?"

"You know what I want." She met my eyes.

"Did I miss something?" Annabeth asked,

glancing from Michelle to the other girls who just shrugged.

"I think we all missed it," Sally replied.

"What's there to miss? I think it's pretty obvious the angel wants a trip to pound town." Maribelle sighed. "And I somehow doubt she'll be the only one."

13

As we landed in Heaven, and the sight of broken buildings and injured filled our vision, the girls I'd brought let out a collective gasp.

"Oh my god," Sally said right before clamping her hands over her mouth and looking sheepish. "Wait, is He here?"

"No." Michelle shook her head. "God is not here. Not any longer anyway." She sighed. "Your reaction makes me feel as though I have been a poor steward for Heaven."

"It's pretty bad," Annabeth said, glancing at her.

"Pretty bad?" Maribelle cried, moving forward and pointing at a half-burned building. "Do you see this joint? It's terrible! I could build something better with my ass."

"I don't think that's what she meant—"

Maribelle cut me off as she pulled a board off the frame. "And this shoddy nail work?" She shook her head. "This is an absolute nightmare." She dropped the board and put her fists on her hips. "Who the hell built this? I need to tear them a new asshole."

"You won't be able to do that," Michelle said, gaze moving to the horizon as her hand swept out toward the injured, dead, and dying. "Unless you find them in there somewhere."

"Right." Maribelle almost looked repentant for a second. Then she rolled up her flannel sleeves. "Guess I've got my work cut out for me." She pulled the hammer from its sling on her belt. "Send me your huddled fuckin' masses. Cause shit is about to get built."

"Did you expect that?" Sally asked, glancing at Annabeth. "Because I for one, didn't."

"Not really, but I guess I don't know her that well," Annabeth replied, shrugging. "Anyway, do you need my help or can I get to sculpting?" She rubbed her chin. "I think some healing sculptures would be helpful."

"Yeah, you do your thing, I'll do mine." Sally's face fell as she looked around. "Are there any injured healers I could start with?"

"Or carpenters?" Maribelle called right before she kicked in a stud that caused the entire structure to collapse in upon itself. "Fuckin' pathetic."

"Or carpenters?" Sally asked, glancing at Michelle who already seemed bored.

When the archangel caught sight of Sally looking at her, she gave a tiny shrug. "I have no way of knowing. You'd have to ask Uriel. She deals with non-combat staff." Michelle looked to me then to the three I'd brought. "I'll go get her."

As the archangel hurried off, I heard Maribelle yowl. "Why isn't this working?"

"Eh?" I asked, moving over as Sally hurried over to the closest injured angel.

"Something is wrong, Arthur." Maribelle pointed to a beam she'd been pulling nails out of. Only the holes in the wood were torn instead of seamless like normal. "That shouldn't happen. At first, I thought it was an accident, maybe altitude sickness or something. Then I tried a couple more times. Something is wrong."

"Arthur!" Sally called, and as I turned back to her, I saw she was already sweating, and the angel in front of her looked no better. "Something is interfering with the magic."

"Fuck," I mumbled, trying to think quickly. "Maybe you need electrolytes? That helps with altitude sickness, or you know, go down a thousand feet?"

"We're in heaven," Annabeth said, meeting my eyes. She had a small chunk of wood in her hand, and I could see even from the cursory marks it wasn't as good as normal. "Not on a mountain. We're like a billion miles above sea level."

I shut my eyes for a second thinking, and as I did, a horrible thought struck me. When I was in Heaven, despite the perfect weather, it always felt draining, like the place was actively fighting my power. I'd assumed it'd go away, but what if it was an intrinsic part of the place?

After all, both Gabriella and Sam had complained that hell sapped their powers. Maybe it was the same here, only in reverse?

I opened my eyes and quickly looked over my three girls, and as I did, my heart sank.

Debuff – Unwelcome: The user is currently in an enemy faction. All skills, abilities, and stats will temporarily be reduced by 25%. This debuff will be removed when the user leaves enemy territory, or the user's faction reputation increases.

"Well, that blows," I muttered, glaring at the message like I could somehow change it. "We're afflicted by a debuff that reduces everything by twenty-five percent. No wonder we all suck."

"Speak for yourself," Maribelle said with a snort. "Me at seventy-five percent is still world's better than whoever built this garbage." She glared at the boards in front of her.

"I guess I know what I'm doing," Annabeth said, nodding to me.

"Creating sculptures to combat the debuff?" I asked.

"Creating sculptures to combat the debuff," she affirmed. "I have no idea how to do that exactly, but I'll try." She thought for a second. "Can you read me the exact wording of the message?"

I nodded and did as she said, only as I finished an explosion filled my ears. I spun on my heel, turning toward it in time to see black smoke rising from just beyond the western gate only a few hundred meters away. Worse, I could see what looked like an enormous dragon made of pure Darkness flying toward us. Only, I'd never seen anything like it.

As I stood there in shock, a claxon sounded, and while I was sure that was to spur the heavenly host into action, with all the wounded, I had no way of knowing what kind of force they could bring to bear. Worse, I was pretty sure they wouldn't make it here before the dragon attacked.

"Holy fuck," I mumbled, and before I realized what I was doing, I was racing toward the gate. I could see lizard men, beholders, and even ravagers moving from the Darkness strewn horizon in numbers I'd never seen, and as I hopped over the gilded gates, I remembered what the lich had said.

When we'd fought, he said the Darkness could only bring forth a force approximate in strength to that of Hell. Maybe it was the same for Heaven, and if that was true, maybe Heaven was stronger than I realized?

Only, I didn't have time to think about it. As my feet hit the ground and I drew Caliburn from its scabbard, I found myself confronted by an entire legion of lizard men. Only there were more kinds than before. Axe men, sickle users, archers. Hell, there was even a bunch with halberds. It was a bit crazy, but I didn't care because I was too busy attacking.

As nunchucks whipped out at me, I sidestepped,

slashing outward at the lizard man and cutting it in half. As it fell to the ground in bloody chunks, I whirled on the ball of my foot and drove my elbow into the face of another, shattering its skull into a fine gray mist. My sword whipped out again, hobbling another right before its friend threw a spear at me.

I caught the weapon and smashed it into another lizard man, shattering it like a homerun swing. My sword blazed as I called upon my power and unleashed a sapphire blast that blew a two-man wide hole in the lizards.

As crumpled bodies hit the ground in front of me, a dragon swooped down at me. I'll be honest, fear filled me because the thing was supermassive. Like a goddamned flying building filled with fangs, claws, and flaming breath.

Smoke poured from its huge nostrils as I raised my hand, calling upon the power of Caliburn and letting Hellfire fill my palm. The smell of sulfur hit my nose as I flung the fireball at the dragon. The blast slammed into it, causing it to shriek in pain as it swerved, trying to fly back into the air.

Only before it could escape, I sprang into the air, driving Caliburn into its side. As my blade sank into its flesh, another screech tore from its maw.

Then it bucked, trying to throw me off. Resisting, I reached out with the power of Mammon's gauntlet, the Relentless Grips of Greed. As soon as I did, I felt everything inside the creature, including the gob of Dark Blood that powered the creature.

I yanked on it with everything I had, and as sweat beaded on my brow, I felt something within the creature give. The Dark Blood within it ripped free, slamming into my palm an instant before the creature evaporated.

That was a problem because I was a couple hundred feet in the air. Yes. I tried to flap my damned arms like I could fly. It didn't help, and oddly, knowing I'd heal was a small comfort as I hit the ground at a billion miles an hour.

As my outstretched arm shattered beneath my weight, followed by pretty much every other bone in my body, Darkness and agony ripped up inside me. Even as I felt my powers struggle to heal me, my only solace came from the fact that the Darkness warriors were too busy trying to tear down Heaven's gates to pay me much mind.

That's when I saw the angels descend on the battlefield. Michelle stood front and center, a glowing sword of fire in one hand, and as she touched down with a multitude behind her, she whipped the blade outward. The edge snapped outward like a whip of flaming steel, and as it hit the creatures closest to her, they disintegrated into ash.

She strode forward, her weapon whirling around her in a blur of flame, and crazier still, every time she swung, entire legions fell. No wonder she was the leader.

As I watched her cut down a ravager like it was made of tissue paper, I had a horrible thought. Dred had utterly destroyed her in battle. How was that even possible?

No. I couldn't think about that right now. I had to focus. Shutting my eyes, I reached down and let my marks open. This time, as power flowed into me, I felt my healing quicken, spurred on by the six marks I now held. Wrath, Pride, Envy, Greed, Lust, and Death.

Strength filled me, and when I opened my eyes a second later, I had been reformed. Part of me was shocked, but most of me was just glad to be whole again. Pocketing the Dark Blood I'd taken from the dragon, I leapt to my feet and rejoined the fight.

I can't tell you how long I cut, and punched, and kicked, nor how many Darkness warriors I fought, but it felt like it had to be hundreds. Yet, even as they fell before my blade, more came charging from the Darkness.

I'd worried about that for a moment, but a quick glance behind me, made the worry dissipate. The angels had formed a line, standing shoulder to shield in a way that reminded me of the Spartans from 300. Mounds upon mounds of Darkness warriors rushed them only to fall to decisive spear thrusts. For everything else, the angels knew how to fight.

In fact, almost all the angels were fighting in that solid, unbreakable line, and even when one fell, another moved to take her place.

There was only a scarce few, like Michelle and Uriel who found beyond the line, and even then, they more seemed to be in a supportive role, moving quickly to where the legion seemed thickest and thinning it out, or focusing on the specials like ravagers.

It was a bit crazy, and I quickly realized that had I not taken down the dragon, Michelle or Uriel would have. Well, maybe not Uriel since she had only a single wing, but still.

"You need to get behind the line," Michelle said, moving next to me and destroying the pair of beholders I'd been fighting with a casual swing of her flaming whip-sword. "The boss will show up soon."

"Boss?" I asked, confused. "What do you mean, boss?"

"During these attacks, they throw minions at us, and when we've killed enough, a really powerful monster comes. I don't want you out here until I know what it does." Michelle, Archangel of Justice looked at me. "At the end of the day, I'm more expendable than you."

"I'm not leaving," I said right before the horizon shattered into iridescent shards, and a lich rode through on another dragon. Only if I thought the other one was big, this one made it look like a baby.

"Get to Uriel," Michelle cried as the lich sighted on us and raised its staff.

As she shoved me backward behind her, a fiery blast of silver light slammed into her, blowing a hole clean through her armor before exploding outward with so much force I was thrown from my feet by the shockwave.

Michelle collapsed forward on her knees, her abdomen a bloody ruin, and as she looked at me, the lich charged her on its dragon, staff raised high as it summoned more energy.

14

"Get away from her!" I cried, leaping to my feet. Caliburn blazed in my hand as I flung a sapphire blast at the creature.

The lich batted it away with ease, and as my attack shattered into ethereal shards, it began to laugh.

"I wondered if we would meet, Builder," the lich cackled in its half-dead Morgan Freeman voice. "Now, prepare to die, so that I may raise you as a zombie. Then you can serve me grapes for all eternity."

"Or you can just go back to being a corpse!" I snarled, and as I glared at it, I felt the earring in my ear pulse with cold remembrance. What I'd seen Sam do when she completely obliterated the creature with her power over death filled my brain, and I realized I could see a thousand blue dots all over the lich's body, reminding me of stop-motion capture.

"Such big talk for one who will be a feast for my dragon!" The lich charged, its steed tearing up the distance between us.

"Get out of here, Arthur," Michelle wheezed, pushing to her feet with the hand that gripped her sword. Blood dripped from her mouth while her other hand clutched her wound. More blood flowed from between her fingers.

"No. You go, Michelle. Have Sally heal you." I held out my hand, and once again focused on Mammon's power. As I did, I felt the dark blood within the dragon. I yanked once more, ripping it free with a surge of demonic energy. As the glowing green crystal hit my outstretched hand like a basketball, the dragon erupted into flames.

The lich screamed as its mount was reduced to ash, and as it crashed to the earth, I squeezed the dark blood, drawing upon its power. The crown on my head began to flare as I focused on the weather.

With a shriek, the piece of dark blood shattered into dust, and as it fell from my hand in a billion pieces, a tornado exploded into the middle of the battlefield. It whipped outward, tearing through the armies of Darkness and ripping them to pieces.

Even still, I knew the display wouldn't last long because even though I'd powered it with the energy contained in the lich's mount, this was a tornado. I had ten seconds at best, but that would be all I needed.

As the lich climbed to its feet, I stepped in front of Michelle, who still stood there bleeding. Her eyes were wide in shock as I clutched Caliburn tight.

"You won't be able to do that to me," The lich snarled, its bony hand gripping its staff as it conjured a swirling ball of power and sent it flying at me. "My magic protects me."

"That's fine. I plan to rip out your heart the old-fashioned way," I said, realizing I couldn't feel the dark blood within it like I had with the dragon.

As its spell flew toward me, I slashed at it with Caliburn, cutting the explosive blast in half, and sending it spiraling off behind me. It exploded on either side of me, and the shock wave of the blast turned my stomach, but I was just glad none of it had struck our fellow fighters.

"Then come, Builder." The lich planted its staff in the ground as the tornado cleared a path between us. "Face me."

"With pleasure." Only instead of charging the creature, I stared at all the pinpoints of light holding it together. I wasn't sure if they were each there, but from what it seemed like, it sort of resembled a puppet on strings.

As I focused on the power of Death, I reached into my pocket with my free hand and grabbed the dark blood from the other dragon. Power coursed up in me as I pulled it free and pointed it at the lich.

With a flick of my wrist, I once again broke open the Dark Blood. Energy surged forth in me as I concentrated on ripping those strings out of the creature. To be fair, I wasn't sure if it was from Death's power or Greed's, but either way as my power grabbed hold of those strings and jerked them free, the lich screamed. I didn't get enough of them to completely hobble the monster, but I got enough for its legs to give out beneath it.

"What have you done?" the lich cried, and for the first time, I heard the fear in its voice.

"Defeated you," I said, sprinting forward and slashing out at it with Caliburn. My blade cut through its magical barrier with an earsplitting shriek that ripped across my brain, like nails on a chalkboard.

Then my sword smashed into its skull, shattering its unlife into a spray of bone and brain matter. An explosion of light and sound filled my ears moments before I was flung backward across the landscape by the lich's death spell.

As I landed hard on the ground, the tornado burned itself out, leaving only scattered remnants of the army. Only without the lich to guide them, they were mostly running away from us rather than toward us.

I picked myself up and moved toward Michelle who was on her knees, blood still flowing from her wound, but even still, she looked better than she had only a second before.

"Need a hand?" I asked, offering her my free hand.

"How did you do that?" Michelle asked, not taking my hand because she was too busy staring at the crater left behind by the lich. "I've not seen someone do that since Samael." She swallowed. "Normally we need to beat on them until we shatter their shield with force. It's difficult and takes a lot out of me and the others."

"I have Samael's mark." I touched my abdomen, and the movement drew her eyes to me. "It let me see the power animating the lich and negate it. I could have done more, but you know, I'm only at twenty-five percent."

"This is you at twenty-five percent strength?" She took a moment, trying to absorb that.

"Yeah." I nodded as she licked her lips. "It is."

"If this is you at twenty-five percent, then we must get you to one-hundred percent." She forced herself to her feet and extended her hand to me. "Come, Arthur, there must be a way. Let's go see Raphael."

15

"You just storm over here and demand I help you?" Raphael asked, glaring at Michelle from the doorway to her archives where she kept all the information Heaven had gathered throughout the years. "I'm busy doing important work."

"Is this where you make a big deal about having to help, so that when you succeed, I praise you?" Michelle asked, raising an eyebrow. It was a little crazy because she was still bleeding, but she hadn't wanted Sally to bother because she would "heal it like an angel should" and that "scars are good reminders to be better."

"Don't be a bitch," Raphael snarled, blowing out an exasperated breath and shaking her head so her copper curls fluttered around her head.

"Excellent," Michelle smiled before turning to me, and I must have looked as lost as I felt because Michelle's smile slipped a touch. "What?"

"I have no idea what's going on." I pointed at the pair of them. "This is way over my head."

"Oh." Michelle nodded to me. "Raphael is mad because she figured it out and wanted to make a big deal about it, but I stole her thunder."

"You figured it out?" I asked, sort of surprised. "Already?"

"Yes." Raphael gave me a hesitant look, like she was waiting for the other shoe to drop. "Is that a problem?"

"It's fucking awesome, and you're awesome." I moved forward and clasped her hands. "Thank you so much."

"Well, I, er, it was nothing." She pulled her hands away and pushed her glasses up her nose.

"It's not nothing. You figured out how to overcome my inability to effectively use Heaven's armaments. That is game-changing." I smiled.

"I suppose it is, isn't it?" Raphael's eyes moved to Michelle before settling on me. "Come, I'll show you." She stepped back, gesturing for me to enter. I was a bit surprised because the interior was all plush red carpet and gold filigree. Artwork I was pretty sure had been lost for centuries filled the walls, and as I stared at what I was pretty sure was an original Da Vinci, my eyes nearly popped out of my head.

"You're letting him in?" Michelle asked incredulously. "You don't even let me in."

"You're a bitch, and he's nice." Raphael grimaced. "And you'll bleed on the carpet. I just had it cleaned."

"You had it cleaned?" Michelle said, clearly confused as she looked down at the carpet. "But it's red. Blood won't even show."

"Some of us don't like to live in hovels." Raphael snorted. "Now come along, Arthur. It is okay that I call you Arthur, right?"

"Yeah, it's fine." I smiled at her and cast one last look at Michelle. "I'll be back in a bit okay?"

"Okay…" Michelle said, clearly at a loss for what to do. I sort of felt bad about it, but at the same time she'd had eons to be nice to Raphael, and being nice never hurt anyone. Still, I knew that deep down Michelle really did want friends. Or at least she did when she was drunk, anyway.

As the door closed, blocking off Michelle from view, I turned to find myself staring at the world's largest museum. Artifacts, books, and everything in between filled shelves, cases, and displays. There was so much that even a cursory glance at this very tiny room let me know it'd take a lifetime to look through, and this was just the entryway of a building that seemed to rival the whole of Earth.

"What do you think of my collection?" Raphael asked, clearly enjoying my awe. "It used to be bigger, but sieges destroyed some artifacts before I could move them here." Her face soured. "Damned heathens always destroy things."

"I think it's amazing." I took a step forward and stared at a map of what looked like America. Only it was hand drawn. "Is that what I think it is?"

"The Amerigo Vespucci? Yeah." Raphael nodded. "But I doubt you came to see old maps." With that, she spun on her heel and moved toward the far door, her hips swishing with each step in a way that made me wonder if it was natural. Either way, I liked it.

"So how did you figure it out?" I asked, following behind her into the hallway. It was filled with so many life-sized suits of armor, that it could have outfitted an entire battalion.

"Figure what out? The armaments thing?" Raphael cast a glance over her shoulder at me.

"Yes." I nodded. "Seems like you did it in just a couple hours."

"Well, I knew where to look. Knowing where to look is eighty percent of the battle." She gestured at me. "It's like the book I asked Gabriella to give you. It talks about your powers."

"Sort of. It more displays information after I encounter something." I shrugged, wondering what the book would say now. Would it have entries on Heaven, on the angels? I wasn't sure, but the moment I got a little time, I was going to look.

"That's true, but not the point." She turned the corner and stopped before a silver archway. Beyond it was a football field sized room all filled with tomes, artifacts, and paintings. "I bring you to what I call the wing of the Builder and Destroyer."

"You found it in here?" I asked as she gestured for me to enter.

"Yes. I have all the collected works on you and your rival." She shrugged. "Does it seem like something I wouldn't have?"

"I honestly, never thought about it really." I felt a little dumb. I'd never even considered where Gabriella had gotten the magic book from nor if there were others. From the look of things, there were *many* others.

"You should think more. Not all women like the muscles and brawn thing." She frowned. "Anyway, I found it in a book that talked about achievements." She pointed at a book that lay open on a desk near the center of the room. It was piled high with other books beside a notepad with an honest to god quill pen in an inkwell next to it.

"What are achievements?" I asked, moving closer, only as I glanced at the page in the book, I realized I couldn't read it, and while a menu appeared above it, opened it revealed only strange, nonsensical characters.

"Achievements are special, um, hmm…" Raphael thought for a moment. "Let me start over. When you accomplish certain tasks, it will cause you to gain an achievement." She waved her hand. "I recognize that doesn't explain much but just go with me for a second here, and it will sort of make sense." When I nodded, she continued, "If you accomplish a bunch of tasks, you will gain reputation with our faction in Heaven. That faction boost will basically eliminate the debuff affecting you and the armaments."

"Okay, I guess that makes sense." I took a moment, thinking it over. While I didn't quite understand, it sort of made sense. Often in video games, by building reputation with various factions, you could gain access to rewards from that particular faction. Evidently, Heaven worked similarly to that. I must have started off with a higher reputation with Hell because I was the Legendary Builder, but conversely, that ruined my reputation with Heaven. Now I had to quest to raise my reputation.

"It does?" Raphael seemed surprised. "I feel like my explanation was terrible."

"I need to do quests to grind out faction reputation. It makes perfect sense. At least to me, anyway." I shrugged. "So, what are the quests I need to complete?"

"They aren't quests. They are achievements." She gave me an annoyed look. "It's different."

"Right, okay." I sighed. "What are the achievements?"

"There are five, and each one will increase your reputation by ten percent. Once all are completed, you will get an additional twenty-five percent bonus, effectively giving you seventy-five percent." She smiled at me. "Since you already have twenty-five percent, that additional seventy-five percent ought to give you one-hundred percent legitimacy with Heaven, allowing you to wield all of our Armaments."

"I think I get it. So I should know out the easy ones first." I bit my lip, thinking. If I did that, I could progress toward full affinity and even more power with my Armament of Death. Then I'd have the strength to break these angels free of their mark to Dred *and* use that power to save Gabriella.

"None of them are easy," Raphael said, tapping the page, and as she did, the characters in the tooltip finally resolved from gibberish into something I could read.

Rebuild Heaven – Heaven has been decimated by recent attacks. Rebuild it to its full glory. Current Progress: 12%

Outfit the Troops – Heaven's forces are badly in need of upgraded equipment. Bring their current weapons and armor out of the dark ages. Current Progress: 0%

Those who were Lost are Found – The ancient warriors who once protected Heaven have been lost. Return them to Heaven so that they may once again guard against the forces of Darkness.

Restore the Hallowed Host – The Holy Grail has been lost. Return it to Heaven! Current Progress: 0%

Heal the Rift* – A wedge has been driven between Heaven and Hell. Reunite the two factions and forge them into a unified blade. Current Progress: 60%

*Note – This achievement is a dual faction achievement.

Progress must be made by both sides, or this achievement cannot be completed.

"Arthur, are you listening to me?" Raphael asked, bringing me back to reality. I shook my gaze from the tooltips and looked at her.

"No, sorry. I was reading the tooltip for the achievements." She gave me a confused look, and I sighed. "It's a Builder thing. Either way, I totally get it now. I need to accomplish the five achievements to get stronger."

"It will not be easy to find the Holy Grail or the warriors. I don't even know where to begin looking for those." Raphael sighed, turning to look at the stack of books. "Guess I know what I need to do."

"I'd really appreciate it," I smiled at her. "And I think you'll figure it out." I glanced at the floor. "Until then, I guess I'll try to talk Michelle into letting me bring more people. We have to pick up supplies anyway, so I guess that even if she says no, we can hide them in boxes."

"Or make a Trojan Horse." Raphael smirked. "I do so love that story." She looked at the ceiling. "Can you imagine being so loved that entire civilizations went to war for you?"

16

With the achievements fresh in mind, I made my way back outside. I'd hoped to find Michelle there, but I guess she'd left during the time I had spent with Raphael. Part of me was annoyed because it'd probably only been a half hour or so, but then again, she'd had a horrible wound. Maybe she'd gone to take care of that?

I wasn't quite sure that'd be true, but since I had to find Sally anyway, that seemed like a good place to start. Unfortunately, while it didn't take long to find Sally, Michelle was nowhere to be found. One thing at a time I guess.

"I see you've found some helpers," I said gesturing at the three angels nearby. They were busily tending to people, and all worse silver chain mail with crimson crosses etched between their breasts, on their shoulders, and on their backs.

"These were the only three who survived out of an entire battalion." Sally gave me a tired smile. "Took a lot of energy but I managed to get it done." She took a deep breath. "I need to rest though. I'm pushing myself, but it's just so much harder here."

Name: Sally
Experience: 87,700
Health: 105/105
Mana: 42/190
Primary Power: Healing
Secondary Power: Alchemy
Strength: 10/100
Agility: 95/100
Charisma: 25/100
Intelligence: 95/100
Special: 95/100
Perk: Rank 4 Alchemist
Perk: Rank 4 Healer

"You've got a lot of experience though," I said, surprised. While I'd seen that the others had a lot, I'd expected Sally to be lower, since I'd drained her to next to nothing many times before.

"What do you think you'll spend it on?" she

asked, acting like it was my decision. I mean, ultimately, I suppose it was, but at the same time, it was her skills, stats, and experience. Besides, I'd long since sort of given up on knowing what they needed. Usually, I found it better to ask them.

"How are the clerics working out?" I gestured to them, popping open their stat windows. I was unimpressed, to say the least, but they all at least had a lot of experience.

"They're fine, but a bit slow." She bit her lip. "I could probably teach them a bit better, too. That might help. They're all pretty good at battle magic, but deeper stuff, well, they just have never seen it before. It's mostly triage medicine."

Looking over their skill trees, I quickly agreed. They had the battle-medicine down pat, but only cursory skill in the main healing trees. It was nearly the opposite of Sally's tree, except, well, she was also better at battle healing.

"I'm going to increase your teaching Proficiency," I said, pulling up the skill.

Teaching Proficiency
Skill: 3/10.

The user can teach Skills up to a maximum level of 3. Increasing this Skill increases the speed with which knowledge is imparted as well as the maximum level of Skill that can be learned.

Like before there was an upgrade tab. This time the message was a bit different.

Do you want to upgrade Teaching Proficiency to Skill level 4? Base cost 800 Experience. This price can be reduced by attaining an overall Rank of 3 in Healing.

I quickly spent the eight hundred experience, followed by twenty-two hundred more to increase the skill all the way to six. That felt like it'd be enough, at least for the moment. After searching the rest of her skills, I made an executive decision.

"I'm going give you some more mana regeneration abilities." I looked at her sheet and dropped another ten thousand experience. "Anything else you feel you need?"

"Not particularly." She glanced back at the clerics. "I can take care of most everything if I had the strength. I'd rather save the rest in case something new comes up."

"Sounds like a plan." I turned my gaze to the clerics. "What do they need besides base stats? They all have a lot of experience to work with so, just let me know, and we'll work it out if you decide they need too much."

"Probably mana regeneration." She sighed. "It

sounds weird to say because I don't even really know what mana is." She waved off the comment. "And some more basic healing skill. Broken bones, minor cuts, lacerations. That sort of thing. Maybe concussions if there's room. I can take the stuff beyond that, I think, but I keep wasting time on that stuff when I should be triaging the ones with real damage."

"Okay." I glanced through the skill trees. "I can up their skills in Broken Bones, minor wounds, and major wounds…" I looked to Sally again. "You're at pretty high rank at those things. You have eight in broken bones and major wounds. Nine in minor wounds. That's out of ten." I gestured at the clerics. "These guys all have one or two in the first two, and only one even has a point in major."

"Yeah, they said they were apprentices, so that doesn't surprise me. It's probably why they were left alive." Sally shrugged. "I'd say five at least."

"Right, okay." I bit my lip, thinking. "That combined with the stat requirements is gonna cost in the neighborhood of twenty thousand experience. They all have around thirty thousand give or take. Anything else you'd like, instead of or in addition too?"

"Is that with the mana regeneration?" she asked, looking at me.

"Yeah, getting it to eight or nine in a couple different skills. They actually have it pretty good already, so it didn't cost a lot." That made sense to me. Most of their skills were battle oriented and had big costs to them. They'd need major mana regeneration to keep up with battle.

"Then let's save it for a while." Sally nodded. "Who knows what will happen." She bit her lip. "You need to go back down though."

"Why in particular?" I asked, looking at her.

"Some of the angels down there are healers. We'll need them here." She sighed. "I'd say to get the demon ones because they are better, but with the debuff…" She wrung her hands.

"I get it." I nodded. "Next time I go down, I'll try to retrieve them."

"Good." She yawned and took a drink from her canteen. "Now if you'll excuse me, I have work to do." She gave me a quick peck on the cheek before hurrying off.

I watched her move, and as I did, I realized the angels were being separated into groups based on the severity of their wounds.

"You're doing well," Uriel said, her deep voice startling me.

"Thanks," I said, turning to look at her, and that was when I realized her wind had been regrown. "Did Sally do that?"

"Yes." Uriel reached back and touched the shimmering feathers. "We've never had such magic before, so I'm still in shock." She smiled. "Seems we have a lot to learn from those down below."

"So, it'd seem." I gestured around. "Though I saw you guys fight. Hell could learn a lot from you too."

"And no doubt they will." Uriel nodded. "I have spoken to Michelle. She won't let more up here now, but I think, given time, she will. Already, she is pleased with how powerful you are." Uriel smirked. "Way to her heart, that is."

"Is that so?" I asked, raising an eyebrow. "Cause I was sure I just needed to get her a few drinks."

"That likely works too." Uriel nodded. "With how hard she works, I bet she parties hard."

"Anyway, I doubt you came to talk to me about Michelle's love life." I looked the angel up and down, noting how she was still in full battle dress. It showed off the muscles in her bare legs, and while before I'd wondered why they used armor that covered only their torso, I had realized during the battle it was a range of motion issue. Sure their thighs and arms were somewhat exposed, but they were also proficient in using their bracers and greaves to block blows.

"I am told you can increase our strength." Uriel touched her chest. "I wish you to do that for me."

"I've never been able to increase the strength of an archangel before." I gestured at her. "And you're a Heaven angel. That's probably even harder.

"Have you tried recently?" Uriel asked, and after watching for a moment, she smiled. "I'm taking it from the look on your face that you have not."

"I haven't," I conceded.

"Then try. What will it hurt?" She crossed her arms over her chest.

"Okay." I nodded, wondering if it would work. After all, Caliburn seemed more powerful than Clarent had been, and I also had Lucifer's crown. Maybe I could do it. After all, I had been able to mess with Sam's stats. I'd assumed it was because of the flaw, but maybe it was because I was stronger?

"Okay? Just like that." Uriel frowned.

"Is that a problem?" I asked, confused. "Isn't that what you want?"

"Yes. I'm just surprised." Uriel shrugged. "I am one of the strongest archangels, and you would make me stronger just because I asked?"

"We're on the same side, Uriel. I know that seems crazy cause I'm Hell's champion, but honestly, I just want to stop the Darkness."

"Your words are wise, but still I find myself surprised by you, Arthur." She nodded. "Please try."

Name: Uriel
Experience: 3,765,484
Health: 194/194*
Mana: 184/184*
Primary Power: None selected
Secondary Power: None selected
Strength: 98/100*
Agility: 96/100*
Charisma: 80/100*
Intelligence: 87/100*
Special: 92/100*
Unique Ability: Archangel of Forgiveness

"Um, what do you want me to upgrade, assuming I can?" When Uriel gave me a blank look, I continued. "I can try your primary stats, your abilities. I mean, you don't even have a primary skill tree…"

"I don't know what any of that means, Arthur." Uriel shrugged. "Just use your best judgment." She shrugged again. "I trust you."

"Great, just modify the age-old angels stats using my best judgment. What could go wrong?" I rolled my eyes as I selected her intelligence stat since it was lowest and would affect her mana pool.

Intelligence: This Stat represents Magical Power. It determines how smart the user is and how hard her spells hit.

Current Level: 87/100. Experience Cost to increase Intelligence is current level plus one. (88) Would you like to upgrade? Yes/No.

I confirmed my choice, moving her Intelligence to eighty-eight, and as I did, I nearly whooped. It had worked

"Well, you're in luck," I said, grinning like an idiot. "I *can* upgrade your stats, and you have a shit ton of experience."

"Good." Uriel nodded. "Finish me, and I'll take you to Michelle. This will please her."

"What do you want me to do…?" I shook my head. "You know what, let me just look around a bit."

I wound up spending a bunch of her experience to increase her regeneration abilities, to move her stats to all one hundred, and to upgrade some combat skills, but even after all that, I'd barely spent a half million experience. It was sort of crazy because, at the same time, I was willing to bet she was maybe ten percent better. While part of it was she was so strong to begin with, I also knew that we'd need all the help we could get.

17

I'll be honest, the last two days of my life had sucked. My life had become a nonstop blur of stat and skill upgrades. It'd started innocently enough with Uriel explaining to Michelle what I'd done, whereupon I'd done the same to her.

That's when the Archangel of Justice decided to take advantage of me, and not in a good way. She sat my happy ass down and made the entire Heavenly host form a straight up line in front of me.

Somewhere after the first thousand or so, my brain went totally numb. It was like at some point my brain just gave up trying exhausted and gave me a second wind. Then a third, fourth, and fifth.

The good news? I'd actually gained an achievement that reduced the cost of skills for me, as well as a few others that didn't seem to have bonuses attached to them. The bad news? I was tired. More tired than I'd ever been. Everything hurt, even my hair.

"What's that sound?" I asked, blinking a couple times as a vicious claxon sounded. It was hard to think, hard to concentrate, and as I tried for the life of me to figure out what it meant, the angels in front of me broke their line and sprinted off into the distance. "Wait, where are you going?"

"That's the alarm," Uriel said, turning back to look at me in confusion.

"What alarm? Is there a fire?" I looked around, but not seeing any flames, I sniffed the air. I didn't smell smoke either. Odd.

"There's no fire you idiot." Uriel gave me a concerned look. "Well, probably not." She pointed out toward the gates. "There's an attack by the Darkness."

"Oh." I nodded. That made a lot more sense. "Sorry, it's been a few days."

"Maybe you sit this one out?" Uriel said as I got to my feet and stumbled slightly because walking was hard.

"Or I could go stabby stabby on the Darkness." I pulled our Caliburn. "Would you deny me that?"

"Yes." She pointed at my chair. "Just relax.

We've done this a billion times. Besides, I'm way stronger now."

"You're like two or three points stronger. That won't do jack." I glanced out at the horizon. "I'm coming."

"I could stop you." Uriel held out her hand and her weapon, a gilded trident appeared in her hand.

"You could fucking try!" I snarled, suddenly angry. "I've been a good little Builder. I've upgraded lots of stats. My people are rebuilding your entire city in addition to training carpenters, sculptors, and healers." I pushed past Uriel. "Get out of my way. I wanna punch something."

"Can't really argue with that," Uriel said, her wings unfurling. "But stay with me just in case."

"Fine." With that, she grabbed me up under my armpits and sprang into the air. As she carried us forward like a goddamned bullet train, I almost regretted giving her that flying speed upgrade. Almost.

We hit the ground outside a second later, and the angels were already in their line. While Michelle was busy taking out ravagers with her glowing whip sword of fiery doom, I spied an angel I'd never seen before. She stood next to Sally and her group of healers just behind the lines.

She was tall and had skin like white snow. Like the battle clerics, she was dressed in crimson-stained chainmail, and she held what almost looked like a healer's staff in one hand.

"Who is that?" I pointed at the angel.

Uriel glanced over. "Phanuel?"

"Yeah, I guess. Is she the one with the chainmail?" I asked.

"She's the Archangel of Peace. She almost never comes out to fight. Goddamned hippie is what she is." Uriel shook her head. "I mean, I'm the Archangel of Forgiveness, and I still bust heads."

"Can you introduce me?" I asked, not sure how to proceed.

"Are you dense? We're in a battle right now." Uriel swept out with her trident, skewering an unfortunate lizard man who had gotten too close. As it writhed on the end of the tri-prongs, its body began to glow with silvery light before it exploded.

"After the battle then." I took a step to my left and decapitated another lizard man. It was almost too easy. They were so slow, and even as tired as I was, they were no match for me.

"Fine." Uriel lashed out once more, smashing in

the skull of another lizard as it approached. "Can we fight now?"

"Yeah." With that, we charged into the thick of it. Uriel's fighting style was nothing like Michelle. Where the Archangel of Justice took out large swathes of the enemy with her whip-sword, Uriel cut down each enemy with precision before moving to the next.

It made me think that in single combat she'd be nearly unstoppable.

"You're the one who normally fights the boss, huh?" I asked as I sidestepped a lizard man and drove my hand into its buddy's face and unleashed some hellfire.

"Yes," Uriel replied as the headless corpse fell to my feet.

"Thought so," I said as the horizon rumbled. I turned toward it to see another lich come forward. Only unlike the others, this one was cloaked in red.

"Builder!" the lich called, immediately fixating on me. "I've got a bone to pick with you!"

Its hands extended, and as I readied myself to parry whatever it did, red light collected on the bodies around me.

"Corpse explosion!" Uriel cried, grabbing me by the collar and leaping into the air, right before all the decimated bodies erupted in geysers of blood and bone.

"That's new," I mumbled as Uriel made a beeline for the lich. Only, before we reached it, the rest of the bodies began to rumble and shake. Then they slammed into one another as huge flesh golems rose in their place.

"Damn, I hate flesh golems," Uriel snarled as she dropped us back down on the battlefield. "I'll get left and you right?"

"On it," I said, taking off after the right one. I sprang into the air, and slammed into the creature, planting my sword into what it thought was its face.

"GrargH!" it shrieked, grabbing me with one fleshy hand and tossing me across the field like I was a sack of smelly laundry. After all, no one would handle clean laundry that way.

I smashed into the ground and rolled a few times before coming to my feet. Only, my attack had cost more than me. Rather than keep attacking, the flesh golem had turned on Uriel, causing her to have to backpedal to avoid their attacks.

"Sorry," I muttered as Michelle leapt into the fray, smashing into the one I'd been fighting and body checking it across the field. Only before she could capitalize on the blow, the lich launched a torrent of flame at her.

She caught it on her whip-sword, but even still the attack was enough to let the golem regain its footing.

That was its plan. To let the golems pound on the two archangels, while keeping them off balance. It was a standard mechanic, but the thing was, this was real life, not a game.

I raised my sword and pointed it at the lich, calling upon my power. As sapphire energy cascaded off the blade, I let loose in a torrential blast.

The lich never saw it coming. I don't know if that was because it was focused on the archangels new threat generation skills, or what but either way, my attack slammed right into the side of the lich's skull, sending it cartwheeling across the battlefield.

I launched myself forward, and as the lich struggled to its feet, it still didn't seem to notice me. Moreover, both golems were now solely occupied with dealing with Uriel while Michelle continued to wail on them, taking off chunks of flesh with each fiery attack.

As I swung at the lich, it didn't even glance at me. My blade caught it right on the back of the neck, severing its head from its shoulders in a single blow. As the skull hit the ground and bounced a couple times, the flesh golems just stopped moving. All at once, they dissolved.

I glanced down at the lich and saw it too was dissolving. Only, this time it'd left something behind. I knelt down and scooped up the amulet it'd been wearing, and as soon as I touched it, a tooltip showed up.

Mark of Death

Type: Enhancement

Ability: Permanently increases the effects of Death magic by ten percent when used. Can only be used in Heaven.

"That was amazing," Michelle said, coming toward me, glee in her voice. There were still lizards and whatnot on the field, but like last time, after we'd killed the lich, they were fleeing.

"What was?" I asked, glancing at her.

"The skills you gave Uriel. They just kept attacking her while we hit them hard." Michelle made a fist. "It's a game changer."

"Yeah, it's mechanics. We used a similar trick back in Hell." I shrugged. "Threat generation and a big tank."

"I like it," Uriel said, coming toward me.

"Makes it so I don't have to chase them around. I hate chasing monsters around."

"I think we all hate that," Michelle said, surprisingly happy.

"Not more than me. I am the queen of hating it." Uriel smacked her chest. "Queen."

"Have you guys seen this before?" I held the Mark of Death out to them. "The lich dropped it."

"No." they said in unison before looking at one another.

"What's it do?" Uriel asked, peering closely at it. "Smells like death magic."

"It says it can raise the user's death magic skills by ten percent, which seems insane to me." I had half a mind to use it on myself, but I didn't really have death magic. Fortunately, as I looked down at my abdomen, I realized I knew someone who did.

"Seems like it is meant for Samael," Michelle said slowly. "You should bring it to her."

"That won't work," I said, leveling a glare at her. "It can only be used in Heaven."

"Arthur…" Michelle said, but before she could let the silence sink in, Uriel threw her arm around Michelle.

"Aww, come on Shelly. Why don't you turn the

other cheek? Forgive and forget, etc, etc." Uriel smiled as Michelle rolled her eyes. "Do it!"

"Fine. You can bring Samael back here, but just her." With that, Michelle stomped off like a sullen child.

"It's okay," Uriel said, elbowing me in the ribs. "I won't tell her you're totally staring at her ass."

"Hey, what can I say," I said, trying to ignore how hot my cheeks felt. "As much as I hate seeing her go, I love watching her leave."

18

"I still can't believe you didn't tap that ass," Uriel said as we made our way toward the rift that separated Heaven and Hell. "Are you gay?"

"I'm not gay," I replied, glaring at the Archangel of Forgiveness. "She was drunk, and Lucifer interrupted." I waved my hands helplessly. "It was a whole thing."

"That sounds like the beginning of an awesome threesome." Uriel elbowed me in the ribs. "I dunno how you fucked that one up."

"I didn't fuck it up." I sighed, remembering the look of disappointment on Lucifer's face. "I'm sort of glad about it."

"Whatever." Uriel rolled her eyes at me. "I'd have been like, hey, Lucifer, wanna join in?" She mimed pushing the Devil's head against her crotch. "I mean two of you were already naked. You were like eighty percent of the way there."

"I find it hard to believe you'd have a threesome with the Devil and the archangel who threw her out of Heaven." I glanced at Uriel who was thrusting her hips with each step.

"Oh, it'd be great." She licked her lips. "They have a lot of issues to work out." She met my eyes. "In bed."

"Is that so?" I asked. Part of me couldn't believe I was even having this conversation. My life was majorly fucked up. To think, I was standing in Heaven talking to an archangel about having a threesome with her two hottest sisters was just... I dunno, but my ability to even was almost more strained than my pants.

"Oh yeah. It'd probably be some kind of hate sex that turned into like forgiveness sex." Uriel nodded, eyes distant. "That's like the two best kinds of sex at once."

"You have issues." I sighed, turning away from the archangel.

"I know what I'm about." Uriel shrugged. "Seems, you don't." She thrust her hips again. "You should figure that out because as far as heroes go, you're lame." She looked me up and down. "I can get behind the scrawny weakling thing you've got going on, but you need to start getting laid."

"I get laid plenty." I sighed. "Can we just focus?"

"You get laid plenty?" She cocked her head and looked at me. "You're the only fucking guy in all of Heaven and Hell. The fact that you're not having sex at this very moment means you suck."

"I like doing things that aren't sex." I gestured toward the crackling horizon that marked the Darkness's territory. "I wanna beat back the Darkness for one."

"And I get that. Really, I do." Uriel sighed. "I'm just trying to help you out. Get my boy some mad pussy." She threw her arm over my shoulder. "Let Uriel help you with that, and thereby live vicariously through you."

"Even if I was okay with that, I don't need your help." I shrugged off her arm. "Besides, I don't want to think about—"

"You know what your problem is?" Uriel asked, ignoring my attempts to escape by putting her arm back around me and pulling me against her. "You haven't even tried to sleep with me. I mean, here I am talking all about threesomes, and you keep making excuses when you should be whipping it out and being like 'suck it, bitch.'" She paused. "But don't do that. The moment is ruined."

"I thought you were gay," I said, suddenly very confused. "I was literally one hundred percent sure of it."

"I am most certainly not gay." Uriel gave me a sour look. "I'm just equal opportunity." She looked me up and down. "Except for you. I prefer men with meat on their bones." She rubbed her hands together. "When you get some big muscles and can bench press a tractor, we'll talk. Until then, don't go whipping out your dick."

I'll be honest, the way she looked at me made me want to do just that. I wasn't sure what would happen, but I had a "you know what, fuck it" moment.

"I don't believe you," I said, and with that, I whipped out my cock.

Uriel stared at me like I was a crazy person for half a second. "I just told you not to do that." She glanced down at little me. "Like literally three sentences ago."

"All I hear is you not sucking it." I gave her a wry smile. "You know you want to."

"This is a decidedly strange turn of events," Uriel said, reaching down to grab me. As she closed her hands around me, a surge of heat rushed through me, making me moan. "I think if we proceed this way, you'll find out the only thing that stops me from having sex is clothing." She bit her lip, glancing down at me. "I mean, that's mostly true, but still." She began stroking me. "I want you to think I have standards."

"Oh, trust me," I said through quick breaths. "I absolutely respect you."

"Really now?" She raised an eyebrow at me. "Well, that has got to change."

With that, the Archangel of Forgiveness was on her knees.

"Nothing quite like a mouthful of come and a sore jaw for my troubles," Uriel said, getting to her feet an appropriate amount of time later.

"I still think you should let me return the favor," I said as I pulled up my pants. "I feel sort of selfish."

"I'm good. I don't really like getting oral sex." Uriel frowned. "I'm more of a giver I guess." She clapped me on the back. "Just think of me like one of your bros."

"My bros don't give me blowjobs," I said,

unsure of how to proceed with this conversation. "Nor do I want them to."

"You know what I mean," Uriel replied. "You need another later, just come ask."

"We could do more than that," I said, and as I reached out toward her, she smacked my hand away.

"No. I'm saving the rest for marriage." She glanced away from me. "Maybe that sounds silly, but that's my thought on the matter."

"I'll be honest, a lot of me wants to engage you in this conversation further, but wouldn't you know it, we're at the rift." I pointed at the gateway that led to Hell before sighing. "Aww shucks."

"Wow, you give a guy one blowjob, and he gets all weird." Uriel rolled her eyes at me. "Trust me, if I wanted more from you, I'd have made you put a ring on it."

"Fair enough." I paused as she reached her hand out to me so we could begin our journey to hell. "You're not like any other angel I've ever met."

"I know. I'm a unique snowflake, you fuck." With that Uriel leapt off of Heaven, pulling me along with her.

19

"Hell is kind of a dump," Uriel said as we made our way through the Graveyard of Statues. "I mean, Heaven sucks too, but I sort of expected more." She waved her hands at the people bustling about to and fro. "This is like the Chinese sweatshop version of Hell. And not even a bad one." She flailed a bit. "Where's the torture, the suffered, the goddamned fire?"

"Did you just say goddamned?" I asked, glancing at her.

"I did, didn't I?" She smiled at me. "You think you know me?" She began to walk off before stopping. "I also have no idea where we're going."

"Right, follow me." I shook my head at her. I still had no idea what to make of Uriel, but oddly, she was sort of starting to grow on me. Not in a good way or a bad way either. At times she just reminded me of the strange growth my Uncle Larry had on the back of his head. I'd once asked him why he never had it removed and he had told me that he'd grown used to it, and besides, it helped keep his hat straight. That bastard had loved his hats.

In a land of stuck up angels, hot as hell demons, and everything in between, Uriel was my weird lump of flesh. It was sort of nice in a fucked up way.

"I like what you've done with the place," Uriel said as we made our way through town. "I mean, it's not the Hell I'd envision, but it's sort of, I dunno, peaceful. You'd never know the Darkness was seething just over there." She gestured at the horizon. "They also must not try very hard."

"Not really compared to Heaven." I shrugged.

"I wonder why that is," Uriel replied, rubbing her chin. "You'd think they'd just crush us." She pointed at me. "For one thing, why aren't you just dead?"

"What do you mean?" I asked, suddenly confused.

"Well, you say you've fought Dred, right?"

When I nodded, she continued. "Well, I've fought Dred too, and the motherfucker is all man in a way you just aren't. Don't take that the wrong way."

"I'll do my best." To be fair, I sort of agreed with her. Dred was a big strong warrior with millennia of experience, and I wasn't. I was a scrawny software engineer with a magic sword. If I was going to beat him, it had to be on my terms, not his.

"Anyway. I just think that if he wanted you dead, you'd be dead. Only he should want you dead." Uriel gestured around. "This little town of yours should be a smoking pile of ash."

"I've had a similar thought myself…" I mumbled. It was true. Sure, Gwen had pushed Dred through the portal before he could have killed us all, but that was the thing, he could have killed us all. Hell, Nadine could have killed me ten times over, and she hadn't. I'd always gotten the impression Nadine hadn't wanted to really kill me, had given me every opportunity to not die, but Dred didn't strike me that way.

"Exactly. See, I knew you weren't dumb. Well, at least about things that aren't fucking Michelle." She took a deep breath. "I'm not going to bother telling you're an idiot again."

"Thanks for that." I waved off the image of Michelle's naked body as it filled my mind. "But yeah, Dred should have killed me. Hell, what the fuck is he even doing right now?"

"Probably trying to beat Gabriella into submission." Uriel sighed as my heart threatened to break and rage exploded through me, so hot and furious I couldn't even breathe. "That's a downer if there ever was. She's so sweet."

I took a deep breath and let it out slowly. Getting pissed off right now wouldn't help. No. Only outthinking Dred would help.

"Okay, but this is Dred. He's strong enough to come down here right now and kill us all. So why isn't he here?" I gestured at the town. "Why?"

"That's a question I'm not sure I want answered because, honestly, when we find out it's gonna suck." She shuddered. "You're not even close to being able to fight him, either."

"I've got that." I made a fist. "Even with everything I've done, he stands on a plateau far beyond me." I sighed. "I feel like I'll never get there."

"Arthur." Uriel met my eyes, and for once she seemed totally serious. "What were you doing before you came to Hell?"

"Um… making Slurpees at a Seven Eleven." I

could almost see myself standing behind the register as whiny toddlers complained that the red one wasn't working. Then I'd have to go fuck with it while the stoners stole Doritos and cigarettes.

"Right, and now?" She gestured around us. "You're basically the only thing standing between Heaven *and* Hell getting crushed by overwhelming Darkness."

"I get that, but—"

"It hasn't even been that long and Dred? That guy has been fighting us for millennia." She patted my head. "Imagine what you could do given the same amount of time."

"That's a fair point, but I'm unlikely to get the same amount of time. Ever since I've gotten here, it seems like things have shifted into high gear." I sighed. "I just worry that Dred will kill us all before I get strong enough to stop him."

"It's totally possible, and when your battered, bloody corpse is getting the flesh picked off it by crows, I'll be pissed, but until then, just work harder." She poked me in the chest. "I believe in you, Arthur."

"Thanks." I meant it, but somehow, I couldn't help but think it wouldn't be enough.

"You're welcome." She looked around. "Now,

where is Samael? I haven't seen that pink-haired vixen in a dog's age."

I laughed. I couldn't help it. Uriel sort of reminded me of a frat boy with tits. Admittedly, that brought some very strange thoughts to my mind, but I ignored them as I stopped in front of Sam's shop. Smoke was pouring from the chimney, and I could hear clanging inside.

"Just inside, I think." I pointed to the Blacksmith's shop. "This is her place."

"What's she doing?" Uriel asked, inhaling sharply. "It smells like smoke and metal. The Sam I knew wouldn't be caught dead doing manual labor."

"Oh?" I asked, raising an eyebrow at Uriel. "She's totally into the manual labor thing."

"I don't believe you for a second. Sammie was always a little princess complete with ribbons and bows." Uriel smacked her leg once. "It always made me want to see her get down and dirty if you know what I mean. Why this one time I saw her in the shower…" Uriel whistled.

"Right," I said, knocking on the door, and when there was no immediate response, I pushed the door open.

Sam stood with her back to the doorway, her

two apprentices busily working on something I couldn't discern.

"I'm busy," Sam said, not bothering to look up. "Leave your order with Gwen, and I'll get to it," she paused, glancing at a kitten calendar on the far wall, "fucking never."

"Sam, it's me," I said, and at the sound of my voice, she whirled around.

"Arthur?" Confusion flashed across her face as she stared at me. "Why are you here?"

"Sammie? Is that you?" Uriel cried, pushing past me, only when she saw Sam, she stopped in her tracks. "You've changed."

"I had to change," Sam said, taking in the big angel with one quick, dismissive look. "I fell, remember?"

"It isn't for the better. Not really, anyway." Uriel moved closer, surveying Sam like she was a sideshow attraction. "Where's the makeup? The frilly dresses? The bows?" She squinted at Sam. "Where's the Archangel of Death?"

"She died when she fell out of Heaven you big lug." Sam crossed her arms over her chest and blew a lock of pink hair out of her face. "I've had to improve, adapt, and overcome."

"So you became a blacksmith?" Uriel asked,

right before she reached out and poked Sam in the shoulder. "Not a dressmaker or a home decorator?"

"Wait a second," I said, glancing from one to the other. "You mean to tell me the Archangel of Death used to dress in ball gowns and wear make-up?" I tried to picture it and couldn't.

"With frills!" Uriel added.

"It wasn't my finest moment," Sam said, glaring at Uriel. "I haven't been that person for a long, long time."

"Well, it's time to look around for your inner vagina and find her," Uriel said, nodding. "Because you're coming back upstairs."

"What the hell are you talking about?" Sam asked, confusion and anger filling her face.

"I talked to Michelle. She's agreed to let you come back to Heaven," As I said the words, Sam glared at me so hard, I thought I might melt. I'll be honest, I looked around for somewhere to hide.

"And why the fuck would I want to do that?" Sam took a step forward. "They threw me out, Arthur. Made me have to change who I was, change everything just to survive." She gestured around. "They didn't help me at all."

"Aww, sis, Come one. Forgive and forget," Uriel

said, and while her words were full of cheer, doubt had clouded her eyes. "I'm sure once—"

"No." Sam crossed her arms over her chest. "I'll not do it."

"If you don't, Dred will win," I said, hating that I was about to make her feel like shit. "And don't you want to try to stop him, after, you know…"

"I do not like the tone or implication of your words, Arthur," Sam said, and I felt the mark on my abdomen go colder than ice. "Tread carefully."

"Look, all I'm saying is that we need you, Sam. We need a smith who knows the angels and can outfit them to stop the Darkness. You're the best person for that job." I smiled at her. "Help us, Sam. You're our only hope."

20

"I see Heaven hasn't changed much," Sam said when we arrived on its hallowed steps. She probably said more, but I was suddenly too distracted because I was busy checking the progress of the achievements.

Just like I'd thought *Healing the Rift* had increased. Just by having stepped foot in Heaven, my progress had gone from sixty percent to seventy percent. Even better, the *Outfit the Troops* achievement had increased to five percent. It wasn't a lot of progress, but it since I'd been at zero before we went down, I was pleased to know we were on the right track.

"Arthur, I'll need a place to work," Sam said, and her tone was angrier than I expected. "Is there somewhere?"

"Um… You know, I'm not sure. Let's find out." I nodded to her. "I'm sure Maribelle is around here somewhere."

"Right, that sounds super boring." Uriel yawned. "I'm gonna go do anything else." With that the big angel walked off, leaving me alone with Sam.

"I cannot believe I let you talk me into coming back here," Sam said once Uriel was out of earshot.

"I get it—"

"You don't get it, Arthur." Sam shook her head. "Michelle banished me, and now I'm supposed to help her?"

"It's the right thing to do."

"The right thing to do wasn't to throw my ass out of Heaven. We all made mistakes." She crossed her arms over her chest, clearly still angry. Then again, she'd had a long time to stew.

"Fair enough, but you pretty much have two options. You can let it go, or you can stew." I smiled at her. "I know letting go isn't easy, but you'll be better for it."

"I recognize that, but it doesn't make me less angry." Sam stamped her foot. "Fine, let's just find Maribelle. Once we get this show on the road, I'll have work to distract me."

"Works for me," I said, looking around for Maribelle. While some of the buildings nearest the rift had been rebuilt, most had just been demoed for parts. Worse, while we had received some supplies from Hell, it hadn't been nearly enough. That was compounded by there being no resources to harvest here. Heaven was basically a desert made of clouds. There was no stone, no wood, no nothing.

Not that we'd have been able to harvest things anyway given the standard profession of nearly every angel was a generic soldier.

"What happened to the gate and why haven't you guys fixed the gate yet?" Sam jerked her thumb toward the twisted wreckage behind the rift.

"Jophiel used some kind of rift bomb to blow it open, and we don't have the expertise to fix it. At least, Maribelle didn't." I stared at it for a moment. "So far, the guards have done a good job of keeping the Darkness warriors from getting through. That combined with the threat generation techniques I taught them seems to be keeping us from a full-scale invasion."

"Perhaps," Sam rubbed her chin. "But without that gate, the wards keeping the Darkness at bay are greatly weakened. It has to be fixed." She sighed. "Find me somewhere to work, and I can do it." She glanced at me. "We'll probably need more Heavenly Gold though."

"Do you know where to get that?" I asked as we began making our way through the buildings. I wasn't quite sure where Maribelle was, but I was hoping if I followed the sound of work, I'd find her, or at least someone who knew where she was.

"I've been in Heaven all of ten seconds. How would I know where to find it?" Sam glared at me. "I wasn't a blacksmith when I was here before."

"Fair enough." I sighed, wishing once again I could use my builder powers to just repair stuff. Alas, it didn't seem like I had that ability. While I could upgrade things if I had the materials, they had to already be in pretty good condition for me to do so. I couldn't just spend materials to repair it no matter how much I wished I could.

Then again, if I could do that, I'd just build myself a giant mechanical suit of armor and every time it got damaged, I'd spend resources to fix it and be unstoppable.

"Hey, I think that's Maribelle." I pointed to a blue speck in the distance.

Sam put one hand over her eyes like she was shielding her face from the light and squinted. "She seems annoyed." Sam glanced at me. "It looks like she just threw a hammer at Phanuel."

It did look like that, which was sort of funny because Phanuel was the Archangel of Peace. Only, as I watched Phanuel shake her head in dismay before moving to pick up the hammer, an idea struck me.

"I'm an idiot," I mumbled, glancing at Sam.

"I know that, but why specifically?" Sam asked, looking at me.

"After we broke your link with Dred, I talked to Raphael about it, and she said a buncha stuff that basically you being in Hell made it possible." I gestured at Phanuel. "What if they came down to Hell, and I broke the marks down there?"

"Won't work." Sam shook her head. "I know it seems like it will, but I can just tell it won't. When I was down there, I sort of became part of the local fauna. Even up here again, I can feel myself acclimating to Heaven. They would have to spend a lot of time down there to do what you want, and if they did that, they'd grow weaker like I did."

That made a certain amount of sense, and while I wanted to try anyway, I wasn't sure we could risk it. If something happened to one of the

Archangels, it'd make it that much harder to stop Dred.

"I think what you need to do is figure out how to complete the achievements you told me about. Then when you have earned the power of Heaven, kick Dred in the balls and rescue Gabriella." Sam frowned. "I hope she's doing okay."

"Me too." I shut my eyes, taking a breath as I tried to dismiss the feeling that I wasn't doing enough, wasn't working hard enough. I knew that wasn't true per se. I'd been moving toward completing the achievements to gain the strength to face Dred, but at the same time, I worried it wouldn't be enough, and if it wasn't, who would save Gabriella?

No. I couldn't think like that. I had to succeed, to push forward. Gabriella was counting on me, and every moment I spent doubting myself was a moment spent not saving her.

"Hello, Phanuel," Sam said, and her reverent tone shocked me from my thoughts. I looked up to see that while I'd been thinking we'd somehow crossed the distance to where Maribelle was working with the archangel.

"Samuel. I am glad to see you again. I hope you are staying for a while." Phanuel bowed her green-haired head before straightening so her lithe, eight foot tall body strained against the too small armor she always wore. It wasn't her fault exactly, more that all the other angels were shorter than her, and since she never actually engaged in combat, well… Guess she hadn't been deemed worthy.

"We'll see," Sam said, sighing. "It still feels a little weird to be here. The air even tastes different than I remember."

"Heaven is just a place." Phanuel smiled. "Home is where you make it. This is no longer your home, though I hope it will not always be that way, sister."

"Thank you, Phanuel." Sam nodded as Maribelle came storming over with a bucket of nails.

"Are you taking a break?" Maribelle sighed, glaring at Phanuel. "The infirmary isn't going to build itself." She gestured at the frame of the building. "You wanted to help and while I appreciate that, helping should mean I need to work less hard, not more hard."

"Maribelle," I said sternly. "That's not nice."

"Oh, I'm sorry, was I supposed to be nice. Very well then." The carpenter cleared her throat. "Thank you, Phanuel. Why don't you take a break, maybe go see if Sally needs anything? I hear you're a good healer."

"Sally asked me to come help you though." Phanuel looked confused. "It's only been an hour. I doubt she wants me to return already."

"Nope, I talked to her. She *totally* needs your help." Maribelle smiled brightly. "Totally."

"Oh, okay then." Phanuel nodded to Maribelle before looking at Sam and me. "I will be seeing you sister." Her eyes flicked to me. "Builder." With that, the Archangel of Peace trudged off to find Sally.

"Does Sally really want her help?" I asked, watching Phanuel go.

"God no." Maribelle sighed. "She's nice enough, and she tries hard, but I swear she's all thumbs. With her help, it's taking me longer to do the job."

"Phanuel was always strange like that." Samuel smirked. "I don't know what it is about her, but everything just sort of goes slowly when she's around."

"Which is why Sally sent her to you, eh?" I asked.

"Turnabout is fair play," Maribelle said, looking from me to Sam. "I suppose you'll be wanting a shop?"

"Yes." Sam nodded. "Then I can fix the gate and work on weapons and armor."

"Figured." Maribelle chewed on her lip. "There is an old armory we scavenged. It doesn't have a lot of equipment, but the basics are there. I can probably get it done in a day or two. I'd have to stop working on the infirmary though."

As she spoke, I glanced at the building in question.

Infirmary

Progress: 18%

Use: Allows for the creation and training of healer classes

Bonus: 10% to all healing related activities carried out within its walls.

"I can see why Sally wants this built," I mumbled. "How long do you have left on it?"

"Two, maybe three days?" Maribelle shrugged. "Unless you want to get people who know what they're doing from Hell."

"And how long to do the retrofits on the armory?" I asked, ignoring her gripe because if I could have done that, I damned well would have done that. Getting Michelle to let anyone up here was almost harder than convincing the Guilds down below to do what they should.

"Same amount probably," Maribelle looked at the sky, clearly mulling it over. "But we don't have the equipment for the inside, anyway. Not that we have equipment for the infirmary." She sighed. "I never realized how much easier it was down below. Here, I go, okay, I need a toaster, but I can't just go buy a toaster, I have to make a toaster, so I go okay, I need some wire, only they don't have wire, so I have to figure out how to make wire. It's like that for every damned component, and it's infuriating." She gestured at the torn down buildings all around. "Right now we've been salvaging things, but soon enough that won't work anymore."

"We need industry," I agreed. Both Sally and Annabeth had similar concerns, and I knew Sam would as well. Hell, she'd been here ten seconds, and I already needed to go mine Heavenly Gold.

"No." Sam shook her head. "That's not what we need." She turned and looked right at me. Then she poked me in the chest. "You need to make Michelle really open up trade down below. Get contractors and materials here. This piece-mealing bullshit won't work."

"Getting Michelle to do anything is impossible." I crossed my arms over my chest. "I've tried."

"Try harder," Sam snapped. "Look, I get it. I

know Michelle. Just figure it out, or this is going to take so long Gabriella will give Dred the argument. Once that happens we're toast."

"You know, that's an excellent point," I said. I mean I'd known that before, but Sam was right. Michelle had promised me a well-oiled machine, and thus far, she'd given me a machine with no gears, sprockets, or whatever else a machine needed to run. It was almost the exact opposite problem I'd had in Hell. There we'd had no labor force but had resources. Here we had labor and no skills or resources.

"Of course it is," Sam said, blowing a lock of hair out of her face before sighing. "Come on Maribelle, let me help you. Then maybe we can do the armory afterward. There's no point in abandoning the infirmary when I still need to get my forge and other equipment from below, and that won't happen until at least tomorrow."

"Do you know anything about carpentry?" Maribelle asked warily.

"I know how to hit stuff with a hammer. How hard can it be?" Sam asked, and that was my cue to leave.

I spun on my heel and made my way toward the training grounds. More often than not, Michelle would be there drilling the troops endlessly. I'd always wanted to join in, but so far, I'd been too busy. Besides, the run-of-the-mill angels were a bit too weak to spar with, and the archangels were too strong. I really needed a different grade of opponent to face off with if I wanted to learn anything.

21

"You call that a thrust?" Michelle cried, smacking the spear from one of the angels, sending it spinning across the sandy grounds of the training arena. The place sort of reminded me out of a cross between a high school football field and a roman coliseum because it had cheap bleachers, but the grounds were just bloody sand.

"You do it like this!" Michelle demonstrated, striking out with the spear in a perfect blur of precision.

"Sorry," the angel squeaked before snatching her fallen spear and trying again.

"Better, but as punishment, all of you do a run around the arena. Then fifty pushups." The rest of the battalion scowled at the girl standing before Michelle before taking off to run the six-mile loop.

"Do you need something?" Michelle asked, turning to me and looking me up and down. "I'm busy trying to get these soldiers back into shape." She snorted. "A few days in Hell and they became soft."

"About that," I said, taking a deep breath and exhaling slowly. "Things need to change."

"I agree." Michelle nodded to me. "You shouldn't let Uriel blow you in the middle of town." She glared at me. "I don't want to hear excuses or anything, just keep that shit behind closed doors." She shook her head. "I don't know what's wrong with the two of you where you'd think that was appropriate."

"Right, sorry about that." I felt my cheeks flush as Michelle stared at me with her piercing blue eyes.

"Is that not what you wanted to speak about?" She looked at me for a moment longer. "I have no claim over you, Arthur. It really is okay with me."

"That is one hundred percent not what I wanted to talk about," I said, waving my hand dismissively.

"You didn't come here to apologize?" Hurt flashed through her eyes.

"Um…" I said because I was a master of oratory function.

"You didn't." She sighed. "I'd thought…" She shook her head. "What did you come for?" She did a very good job of hiding how upset she was.

I stood there for a moment and realized I had two roads I could travel down. One would be to address the elephant in the room, and the other would be to ignore it and go on.

"This isn't working for me," I said, going with option B because feelings were hard.

"What isn't working for you?" Michelle asked, and she seemed genuinely concerned. "Is it the lack of sex? Is that why you were with Uriel in such an obvious way." She looked at her feet. "I know I haven't taken care of your needs, but I've never done that sort of thing before…"

"That isn't what I'm talking about at all." I made a time-out gesture. "I one hundred percent do not want to talk about sex or relationships or any of that stuff with you right now. Maybe later, but not right now."

Michelle looked at me for a moment. "Okay." There was a lot of pain in her eyes, and it hit me like a punch to the gut. I was hurting her despite trying very hard not to hurt her. "What do you wish to speak to me about?"

"We need to vastly open up trade with Hell." I gestured to the soldiers. "Your soldiers are a billion times better than those in Hell, but after that you have nothing. We need crafters, supplies, tools."

"I have allowed you to bring four people here." She looked at me quizzically. "Do you need more?"

"Fuck yes." I rubbed my face with my hands. "Do you need more than four soldiers?"

"Depends on the situation," she mused, watching her angels run. "But I see your point." She frowned. "I dislike it though."

"How do you feel about Gabriella?" I asked, turning and pointing toward the Darkness. "Because Dred has her and is doing god knows what to her. Don't you want to save her?"

"I do." Michelle sighed. "But what does that have to do with letting demons and the like up here?"

"I need to complete the achievements to get enough power to stop Dred. Once that happens, you, Phanuel, Uriel, and the others can mark me, and I'll be strong enough to save her." Michelle stopped me with a wave of her hand.

"We spoke about that. An army, not a lone

warrior is what we need." Michelle gestured to the girls. "I am building you the army."

"And they need better armor and weapons." I moved forward and poked her hard on the right hip. "And don't you want to be free of that mark? Of that link to Dred."

She looked down at my finger and took a long, slow breath. "Yes."

"Then trust me, Michelle. We need to get the achievements done." I smiled at her. "I'm not saying to stop what you're doing. I'm saying we need to do more, work harder in addition to smarter. If we can do both, we'll win."

"Okay." Michelle nodded. "There is a problem though. Even if I allowed the demonic crafters to come here and work, we cannot afford to pay for the work." She pulled out a piece of parchment and showed it to me, and I was surprised out how reasonable it seemed at first glance given it looked like Buffy's handwriting.

"That's easy." I glanced over at her girls. "Hell needs warriors. Trade them. The rest is details, and I bet Buffy can figure it out."

"You want me to send my angels down to Hell to work as guards?" Michelle didn't seem to like that idea. I could tell in the way her body stiffened and her voice became clipped.

"And have Hell's guards come here for training. You're clearly a lot better at it than them." I took a deep breath. "It's like Athens and Sparta."

"Athens and Sparta?" Michelle repeated, obviously confused.

"Back in ancient Greece, Sparta was a military powerhouse while Athens produced trade, and inventions, and all those other things a society needs. Individually they were lacking, sure, but together they were much stronger." I pointed at her. "You're Sparta. You need to ally with Athens."

"Fine," Michelle said, and she actually seemed less upset than I expected. "I will send my warriors down there to teach them, and in return, I will agree to allow their people to come here to rebuild." She looked over at me. "That just leaves one more problem."

"What's that?" I asked, wondering what she was talking about and really hoping we weren't about to have another sex talk.

"Only an archangel can ferry people between Heaven and Hell. How will you fix that problem because I've barely managed to do the trips I do now with what little time I have? I cannot afford to spend more time as a ferrywoman." Michelle was right, but as I stared at her, I had a horrible, awful idea.

"Oh, I think I know how to fix that," I said, grinning at her, and when she made a motion for me to go on, I continued, "Do you know where Phanuel is?"

22

"Good luck," I said, leaving Buffy and Phanuel to figure out the details of the whole Heaven and Hell trade merger thing. Honestly, I wasn't sure how it would work out in the end, but either way, I was feeling pretty good about myself. With Phanuel to constantly ferry goods and people between Heaven and Hell, that would fix two problems. The first, of course, was that we'd have someone to do the job. The second was that no one seemed to want the Archangel of Peace around.

Still, Buffy seemed to like the archangel well enough, and as I left them to do whatever it was they were going to do, I hoped their friendship would last until we got Heaven up and running.

It was actually kind of nice because as I walked

back through town on my way to visit Raphael, a runner had come and told me she wanted to meet with me, I could see what Heaven would look like.

Once all the rubble was moved away, there'd be a trading post right there, along with a few other shops like a cobbler and a haberdashery. Truth be told, I had no idea what they did exactly, but I did know from the plans I'd seen that one they gave bonuses to shoes and hats.

That said, we were a long way from that point. Even with the demon salvage team Buffy had already brought up, it'd take a few days to clear the broken buildings and tear down the damages structures that couldn't be easily repaired. Then there was sorting and refining.

I almost didn't want to think about all the work left to be done, especially since I needed to find some Heavenly Gold for the gate, but that could wait until after I spoke to Raphael.

The door opened before I even knocked on it and I found Raphael standing there looking like she'd been about to leave.

"Finally," she heaved, grabbing me by the arm and dragging me inside. "I was about to go get you myself." She shook her head. "Didn't my assistant tell you it was urgent?"

"She did, but everything is urgent," I said with a shrug. "That makes nothing urgent."

"I found a clue about an achievement." Raphael stopped and looked at me. "I figured you'd want to know, but if you don't…"

"I do, sorry." I wiped my brow with my free hand. "Sorry. It's been a long few days. I can barely remember the last time I slept. Between planning, and upgrading skills, I've gotten pretty rundown." I tried to smile. "Still, none of that is your fault."

"Indeed." She pushed her glasses up her nose. "Anyway, I think I know where you have to go to complete the *Those who were Lost are Found* achievement."

"That's the one about the hidden army of warriors, right?" I asked, trying to remember. It was hard because I only saw updates for the achievements when the percentage complete increased, otherwise, unless I was looking at the page in the book, I had no way of knowing how far I'd progressed.

"Yes." Raphael nodded. "There's just one minor problem."

"Oh?" I asked, looking at her. "What's that?"

"You need to go to the Plains of Desolation to

find them." She looked at her feet. "That's not an ironic name either like Iceland."

"Why would it be," I said with a sigh. "What's there that's so bad?"

"I have no idea," Raphael swallowed. "It was overtaken by Darkness centuries ago."

"This gets better and better," I said, rubbing my chin. "What do you know about it?"

"Not a lot. It was a place for warriors to go to test their mettle. I've never gone, but Michelle has. She'd be the person to ask." Raphael gave me a small smile. "I can give you a map though. To the Plains of Desolation, that is."

"That would be great," I said, and before I could thank her further, she handed me a piece of rolled up parchment.

"I've enchanted it, so it should show where you are in relation to the plains in real-time." Raphael turned like she was ready to leave. "I'll try to find out more about the other achievements in the meanwhile." With that, she disappeared into her study, leaving me standing there in the hallway. I thought about following her, but honestly, what was the point? I had what I needed.

No, it would be better to find Michelle, get a

small contingent of soldiers and go kick the Darkness's ass.

Finding my own way out, I quickly made my way to the battleground. Michelle was there, as per usual, only she now had several demons mixed in among her angels, and from the look of things, the demons were struggling to keep up. Worse, I knew Michelle wouldn't cut them any slack.

"If any of you thinks it's too hard, feel free to go back to Hell," Michelle said, boredom filling her voice. "Otherwise pick up your pansy asses and run." She whipped her flaming whip-sword through the air eliciting a sharp crack. "Now move it." She glanced at another angel, a girl with blue-green hair that fell about her shoulders like seafoam. "Keep pace."

The angel nodded before taking off after the running demons, blowing her whistle like it was her job.

"If you've come to see the prospects, I'm afraid you'll be disappointed." Michelle turned to me, addressing me in that uncanny way she always did when I approached. "I'll be surprised if there's any potential between the lot of them." She shook her head. "I find it disgusting that the denizens of Hell are so soft."

"In their defense, they make really good doughnuts." I shrugged.

"Great. When their entrails are spread across the battlefield, I'm sure that will come as a quiet comfort." Michelle sighed. "What do you need now? Do you wish to turn my glorious city into a latrine in exchange for additional funding?"

"Is that a joke?" I asked, confused.

"No." She shook her head. "Your goblin proposed that."

I almost laughed but caught myself. Michelle was barely okay with this, so I found it hard to believe Buffy would propose such a thing.

"Why?" I asked, genuinely curious.

"Something about creating viable farmland by covering it in shit." Michelle held her nose. "Unthinkable."

"Oh." I thought about explaining further but figured whatever farming representative Buffy brought from down below could handle that. So far as I knew, the angels didn't really have any form of agriculture. Instead, they mostly subsisted on foraging for wild berries and roots and off the flesh of slain Darkness warriors. Yes, it was as disgusting as it sounds. Roots and berries were gross.

"If you're not here to talk me into the cesspool,

why are you here, Arthur?" She glanced at the sprinting demons. "I really doubt you care to see their progress."

"I came to ask you about the Plains of Desolation." As I said the words, Michelle's face hardened.

"Why?" That single word was so angry, it actually took me a moment to process.

"Um… Raphael said I needed to go there to complete an achievement—"

"Then you should consider it lost." She squared herself like she was getting ready for a fight. "Even if it wasn't overrun by Darkness, you would not be able to complete the trials within." She looked at her shoes. "Neither Uriel nor I could do it." She blew out a long breath. "Dred got close, but still he failed too."

"Wait, Dred has been there?" I asked, confused.

"Yes." Michelle nodded. "Before he was a champion of the Darkness, he sought to overcome the ritual despite my best efforts to tell him otherwise. He joined the Darkness shortly after."

"Are you worried I will fall to the Darkness too?" I asked, raising an eyebrow at her. "Because that's never going to happen." I made a fist. "I want to beat the Darkness."

"As did Dred, once upon a time." Michelle met

my eyes, and there was real pain there. "You do not know what the trial is like, Arthur. Once you are within the Plains of Desolation, you will be all alone with only your strength and wits to save you."

"Then tell me what to expect. Help me win."

"I cannot." She shook her head. "It is different for all who step within."

"Oh." I took a deep breath. On the one hand, that worried me, and not just because of what Michelle had told me. I was worried because I *needed* to complete this achievement or I wouldn't be able to save Gabriella. That meant I had to go in there and try. No. I had to go in there and win. Trying wouldn't be enough.

Worse, I had no way to prepare for it. That seemed like a recipe for disaster.

"I can see you're scared." Michelle put a hand on my shoulder. "That is good. You should be fearful." She swallowed and shut her eyes. "You should figure out another way to save Gabriella."

"There's a reason it's an achievement no one has gotten before." I crossed my arms over my chest. "If it were easy, you would have succeeded. Uriel would have succeeded, and Dred would have succeeded."

"Do you think you can do what we could not?

That you are so much better?" The eyes of the Archangel of Justice narrowed.

"No." I shook my head. "I do think I'm different though, and you said the trial changes based upon who faces it. Maybe mine will be one I can defeat."

"It is a nice thought, but you are wrong." Michelle shook her head. "I want to admonish you, to tell you no." She sighed. "But I also want you to win, Arthur. Maybe you will win. I do not think so, but lately, I have done many things I thought I never would." Her cheeks reddened. "If you decide to go, you must promise me one thing."

"What's that?" I asked as she looked me up and down before settling her gaze on Caliburn.

"You will win."

23

It didn't take long to arrive at the Plains of Desolation, in part, because Michelle carried me. She'd barely spoke during the entire hour-long trek and, after dropping me off, made her way to a small tree and sat down beneath it.

Still, I'd learned something during the trip. Heaven was bigger than I expected. It had seemed small because everything was centralized within the gates, but Heaven was a vast place, easily as large as Hell, and there were tons of resources once you got a few miles outside the gates. It seemed that what I'd called Heaven was just a tiny bulwark right at the edge of the Darkness, and behind it was miles and miles of uninhabited territory.

Sure, there had been splotches of Darkness peppering the lands, but it hadn't been like Hell where the Darkness seemed to come from everywhere.

Or at least it hadn't been until I'd reached the Plains of Desolation. Now I stood at the threshold of a border with the Darkness, and while I couldn't see through it, I could feel the cold, insatiable hunger within.

"This is your last chance to turn back," Michelle said before taking a bite of the apple she'd plucked from the tree. "I will not think ill of you if you do." She shook her head. "It is not cowardice to run from a fight you cannot win. It is wisdom."

"Yeah, well, the last angel who claimed to be wise joined the Darkness." I shrugged, turning away from her and stared at the border. It was now or never. "Wish me luck."

"Good luck, Arthur. May you succeed where all others have failed." As Michelle's words filled my ears, I stepped across the threshold.

Nothing happened. Well, nothing like the normal scenario happened. Usually, when I entered the Darkness's lands, it was like being teleported to some other place. This wasn't like that at all. Instead, it just felt like a colder version of where I'd been. Trees and whatnot still littered the countryside, and as I glanced over my shoulder, I realized I could see through the veil.

Michelle sat there, staring at me with concern etched onto her face as though she could see me. I wasn't sure if she could actually see me or not but was leaning toward not, since when I had waved to her, nothing had happened.

Well, either way, it was time to do this. Gripping Caliburn, I pulled the blade free and ventured forth.

The Plains of Desolation reminded me of the Graveyard of Statues in that it had twelve statues of what looked like medieval knights all around, but that was the only similarity. Worse, as I crept around, while the feeling of unease and dread filled my belly, I didn't see a single enemy.

I also couldn't see any tooltips or menu icons next to the closest statue, nor any of the others. Making my way to the statue, I knelt down in front of it and tried to read the inscription on the base. Unfortunately, it was all in that same angelic gibberish I'd seen all throughout Heaven.

"I wonder what it says," I mumbled, standing up and looking at the eight-foot tall statue once more. It was of an armored man with long hair. He held a giant shield in one hand, and his other gripped a large claymore that rested over his shoulder. His eyes stared off into the distance like he was scanning the horizon for threats.

"Who are you?" A voice boomed from everywhere and nowhere. It was the crashing wave, the grinding rock, the crackling fire.

"Arthur Curie," I replied without thinking. "The Builder."

"I have never met a Builder before," the voice answered, and it was both closer and farther, both angry and pleased. "Tell me, Arthur Curie, the Builder, why have you come to my small slice of Heaven?"

"Are you making a joke?" I asked, confused. "With the slice of Heaven crack? Because if you are, it didn't work."

"Would that please you?" it asked both bored and curious.

"I don't know, to be honest," I said with a shrug.

"Why are you here?" it repeated a little angrier this time. "Arthur Curie, the Builder?"

"I am here to complete the trial." I nodded to the statue because it was the closest thing. "To complete the achievement."

"Oh?" the voice responded, and this time the ground beneath my feet shook. The sky overhead opened, and a crimson sun shone amid a cotton candy pink sky. "Do you truly think you have what it takes? None before you have passed my trial."

"You just said no Builder has ever tried." I shrugged. "Maybe I will surprise you."

"I doubt that very much." With those words, I stepped forth from the shadows.

"What the fuck?" I cried, taking in the being before me. It looked exactly like me, right down to the scar on my neck I'd gotten from trying to shave with an old-fashioned razor.

"If you wish to complete the trial, Builder, you must do one thing," the Dark Arthur said before touching his T-shirt with one hand. "You must defeat me." He smiled. "It will not be easy to do because I am you."

"Only I am me," I replied, and as I hefted Caliburn, the other me did the same. Only unlike Caliburn, his sword seemed to pulse with pure, unrelenting Darkness.

"That remained to be seen, Arthur Curie. For I have looked into your soul, and I have found you to be quite normal indeed." Dark Arthur raised his free hand and gestured for me to bring it. "Now come."

Something about this felt off to me, and as I

stood there gripping Caliburn, the wrongness of the situation was damned near overwhelming. It was weird because while I knew Michelle had told me the trial was always different, I couldn't help but think if the trial was really by combat, one of them would have succeeded. They were all amazing warriors, and while I'd gotten better, I was still, well, me.

That meant I had to fight this challenge like me.

"Are you scared or do you wish me to attack first?" Dark Arthur asked, cocking his head to look at me. "The first would not surprise me, and I do not think you want the second."

"What do people normally do?" I asked, raising an eyebrow and considering its words. They felt off. Hell, this whole thing felt off.

"They attack me," Dark Arthur said after a time.

"Then I want you to attack me." I gripped my sword and waited.

"Are you sure?" Dark Arthur asked, the vaguest tinge of interest filling his voice. Then he tightened his grip on his weapon. "Very well."

He charged, sprinting across the sandy beach toward me. I'd like to say it was fast, but it wasn't.

Not really anyway. I don't mean to say it was slow either because it wasn't.

It was just, well, my speed. That was certainly interesting.

As Dark Arthur slashed at me, clearly trying to decapitate me with his first strike, I ducked. The blade passed over my head, missing me by a hair's breadth. Only before I could counter-attack, the sword whipped around, coming back at me, and I instantly recognized the maneuver as one I'd learned when I'd spent the year in Mammon's domain. It was *Slash That Separates Rain Droplets*.

Again I dodged. It was hard since it was quick and precise, but I knew the maneuver and knew what it was supposed to do. Stepping sideways with *The Wind That Flings The Sand*, I brought my sword up, catching the blade before flinging it backward.

"Are you just going to copy my attacks?" I asked as Dark Arthur recovered his footing and looked at me.

"They are not copies." He shook his head, his grin widening. "I am you, and they are mine."

"That's just silly talk." I shrugged. "Why don't you try again?"

"With pleasure." Dark Arthur raised his hand, and I saw it begin to fill with Hellfire. Only it was

Caliburn's Hellfire, not that from the earring. I wasn't sure how I was able to tell, but I just could. What's more, I also knew I could stop it.

As he threw the fireball at me, I lashed out with *Lightning That Arcs Across The Sky*, catching the fireball and deflecting it away. As it spiraled off into the ground behind me, I peered at the guy before me. He had to know I could easily deflect such an attack, so why would he do it?

"That's not going to work." I shook my head, and as I did, something in my brain sort of clicked.

He may have looked like me, and had similar moves, but he was just a guy in a shirt and jeans.

"Why is that?" he asked, and he was genuinely curious. "I know all your tricks, Builder."

"Thing is, they aren't tricks." As I spoke, he seemed confused. "They are just me for better or worse."

"I don't understand. A man is only the sum of his parts and nothing more." He touched his ear, and I realized he had The Cold Embrace of Death in his ear. That was odd.

As ethereal armor appeared around him in a flash, I stopped and stared at him. He did have what looked like Caliburn, and he did have Sam's Armament, but he didn't have the others.

He lacked the Ruthless Crown of Pride I'd received from Lucifer as well as the Relentless Grips of Greed, the Uncontrollable Binding of Lust, the Remorseless Chain of Envy, and even the Merciless Greaves of Wrath. It made me wonder what would happen if he hit me.

I blinked, concentrating on him as his sword began to glow with sapphire light, letting me know he was going to try to blast me.

The crown on my head glowed, and his stats popped into view.

Name: Apparition of Reflection
Health: 84/84*
Mana: 162/162*
Strength: 38/100*
Agility: 46/100*
Charisma: 22/100*
Intelligence: 84/100*
Special: 78/100*
Unique Ability: Mimic

As I sidestepped the sapphire blast with *The Wind That Flings The Sand,* I read the note next to his stats.

*Note – These stats are subject to change based upon who is currently being mimicked.

My eyes widened. Were those my stats? I wasn't

sure, but it seemed likely given the circumstances. Not that it mattered. What mattered was that while he had managed to copy Caliburn and the Cold Embrace of Death, he hadn't managed to copy my other armaments.

A grin spread across my lips as he charged at me, and I instantly knew what he aimed to do. Skewer me with Caliburn. The thing was though, I had used the Remorseless Chain of Envy to steal Dred's healing ability…

I screamed in pain as he drove his sword through my chest. The blade punched out my back in a spray of blood, and as the Apparition of Reflection met my eyes, he laughed.

"All too easy," he said right before his chest practically blew apart as the Merciless Greaves of Wrath reflected the damage back to him sevenfold. It was a bit crazy to see because one moment he was standing there triumphant and smug, and the next his stupid douche face (yes, I get the irony) was filled with shock.

He staggered backward, hands slipping off the sword embedded in my chest as blood leaked from the open wound in his torso. Blood poured from the wound as I calmly pulled his sword free and tossed it to the sand beside my feet. It hit with an empty clang as I raised my hand.

"Dodge this," I whispered, summoning my own hellfire and unleashing it from only a couple feet away. The blast took him in the face, reducing his skull to fragments of ashen bone.

As the headless corpse fell to its knees, the horizon began to flicker, and a glowing golden seal fell rose from the ground in front of me.

24

As I moved toward the seal, I couldn't help but be in awe of it. It was pretty big, easily twelve feet in diameter and covered with twelve distinct runes. As I approached it, energy began to crackle along its surface, causing each rune to blaze with light every color of the rainbow.

Caliburn began to glow in my hand, and as I glanced at the weapon, I realized there was a spot in the middle of the seal that I could have sworn would fit my sword.

That was certainly interesting.

Wasting no time, I moved to the edge of the seal, and as I stared at it, I realized it sort of resembled a table with no chairs. Crazier still, the closer I got, the more Caliburn glowed. As I touched the disc with my hand, energy surged through me, and the hole in the center began to glow.

"Well, I guess I know what I need to do." Climbing up onto the massive disc, I made my way to the center until I was standing on the spot. "Time to put my sword into the hole."

As energy crackled around me, I drew a deep breath. Then I drove the sword into the golden table beneath my feet. Energy crackled overhead, and for a moment nothing else happened. Then the disc beneath my feet exploded into a flurry of scintillating sparks that threw me across the Plains of Desolation. As I struck the ground hard, I realized the horizon had shifted in color, losing the tinge of Darkness that had clung to it before.

"Arthur, what's going on," Michelle cried, and as I turned toward the sound of her voice, I saw the archangel racing toward me.

"What do you mean?" I asked confused, right before she tackled me to the ground. We hit with a thud, and as I lay there confused, she leapt to her feet, hands gripping her flaming whip-sword.

"Stay back!" she snarled, and as I tried to orient myself to what the fuck had just happened, I realized all the statues were moving toward us. Only that didn't make sense because they hadn't been moving a second ago. "If you come closer, I will cut you."

"You do not need to fear us, Archangel," the closest statue, the long-haired hippie with the claymore said. He had a deep, rumbling British voice. "For we have awoken to serve the True King."

"The true king?" Michelle asked, shooting me a confused look.

"What in the fuckety fuck are you talking about?" I added, scrambling to my feet. I knew they couldn't hurt me but there were twelve of these fucks, and I'd just fought a magical apparition. Only, that's when it dawned on me. The achievement.

Were these guys the lost warriors? Feeling dumb, I sighed.

"I think these are the guys I was supposed to find, Michelle," I said, gesturing at the statues. "I think they're going to help because I beat the challenge."

"You did?" she asked, and that's when she turned and gaped at me. "I didn't even…" she flushed. "I just saw them all coming toward you and thought you'd failed."

"No. Arthur has completed the trial and released us from our imprisonment," the statue said, and I realized the others had lined up behind him in ever increasing numbers, so it was like facing a triangle of heavily armed men. Only, they were still all the same gray stone color they had been before.

Odd.

"Who are you guys?" I asked, and then I said my next thought even though I felt dumb as fuck. "I mean, you're men."

"We are the Knights of the Round Table." The statue touched his chest. "Many years ago we were lifted to Heaven, and our souls were placed in these statues while we waited for the one who would defeat the Darkness to rise." The statue knelt before us. "I am Lancelot, please accept me and mine to your service, Arthur."

"The Knights of the Round Table?" I said, watching the others kneel as well. "Like King Arthur?"

"King who?" Michelle asked, giving me a quizzical look. "Are you a king? Is that why you won the challenge?" She flushed. "I did not realize you were royalty. You must have thought I was the biggest bitch…"

"No, stop, just wait." I sighed. "On Earth, there's a legend about an old king who had Knights of the Round Table." I waved my hand. "It's a really famous story."

"And you are named after this king?" Michelle said, looking me over. "Names have power, you know."

"I'm named after Aquaman, actually. He is also a king, but he's *way* less cool." That's when I got the "who the fuck is Aquaman" look and decided to press on because Lancelot and his merry men were still kneeling. "You may all rise. I accept you into your service."

As I spoke, golden, glowing script flashed in front of my eyes, but from the look of things, I was certain no one else could see it.

Achievement: Those who were Lost are Found has been completed.

You gain 10% Legitimacy with the Heaven faction.

"Thank you, my liege," Lancelot said before turning to the others. "May I introduce you to our battalion?"

"Yes, that would be great. The only one I remember is Galahad because he found the grail." I shrugged.

"You found the grail, my son?" Lancelot asked, turning to look at another knight who looked like a much younger version of himself. "Why did you not say so?"

"No." Galahad shook his head. "Sir Percival, Sir Bors, and I set out in search of it, but alas we never found it." He looked at the ground. "It is my eternal shame."

"I'm about to lose my shit," I said, swallowing hard. "I'm having a total fanboy moment. Did you know I was named after King Arthur?"

"I'm not following. What's the big deal?" Michelle asked, glancing at me as the knights began to explain how they had trekked across all of Britain in search of the Holy Grail but had not managed to find it.

"You'd understand if you were me, but you're not so just…" I took a deep breath. "You'd think I would be less excited, I mean I've met you."

Michelle blushed. Hard. "Arthur…"

"But these are the Knights of the Round Table."

"And just like that, you blew it," Michelle huffed, stepping away from me as she extinguished her whip-sword and sheathed it. "Maybe you can explain why they are so," she gestured at me, "this while we walk back to the city."

"Right, okay." I paused, trying to control myself.

"Can you guys please introduce yourself to Michelle, she's the Archangel of Justice."

"Isn't Michael the Archangel of Justice?" the one Galahad had called Percival responded. "And isn't he male?"

"No." Michelle shook her head. "Almost all angels are female. It's just that men wrote all the books."

"That sounds suspiciously like heresy," Percival replied, watching Michelle closely. "How do I know you're telling the truth?"

"Well, let's assume you're God," I said, gesturing at Michelle. "Would you want to be surrounded by hot chicks or hot dudes?"

"That… is an excellent point," Percival said, nodding his agreement. "I do enjoy the company of women more than men."

"We all do," Lancelot said.

"All except Lamorak, anyway." They all glanced at the biggest, strongest looking knight who just shrugged.

"I am what I am," he replied, his gaze flicking to me. "If that's a problem, we can arm wrestle over it."

"Nah, you do you." I shrugged, wondering how I was gonna deal with twelve giant statue men.

"Are you guys even equipped? You know, down there?"

"Alas no, we have shed our mortal bodies in favor of these stone ones so that we may serve the True King." He looked at me. "It is good to meet you, Arthur."

"So what was King Arthur like?" I looked to Lancelot. "You know, before the whole Guinevere thing?"

"I don't know what you're talking about," Lancelot replied, looking at me with confusion. "Who is Guinevere?"

"Arthur's wife. The one you um…" Yes, I totally did the finger going into the circle thing.

"I'm not following," Lancelot said, glancing at the other knights. "Do any of you know an Arthur or a Guinevere?"

"No," Percival replied with a shrug. "I didn't even know these blokes before I was plucked up to Heaven."

"And who, exactly, brought you to Heaven?" Michelle asked, looking somewhat annoyed. "Your whole presence here doesn't make a lot of sense."

"I was taken by the Archangel Jophiel," Sir Galahad replied. "Like my father before me."

Lancelot, and the others, nodded.

"Jophiel." Michelle made a fist. "I should have known."

"You should have?" I asked, not sure what confused me more, everything, or well, everything.

"She was always scheming, always trying to figure out ways to beat the Darkness, but none of them ever worked." Michelle glowered at me. "This has to be another one of her tricks."

"Either way, having a contingent of awesome knights seems fucking awesome." I gestured to them. "They're all huge and made of stone."

"I will reserve my judgment until I see them on the field of battle," Michelle said. "Until then, they're just walking hunks of rock."

"We can hear you, you know?" Lancelot said, coming up beside me and glancing at Michelle. "And if you would like a demonstration of skill, I would be happy to show you. Just point me in the direction of a foe, and I will vanquish it post haste."

"You'll get your chance," Michelle said, gesturing at the horizon. "For Darkness never waits long before it tests our mettle."

"You hear that lads," Lancelot called, turning back to the other knights. "We will have foes aplenty!"

As a cheer burst from their lips, I couldn't help

but wonder about something else. Galahad had said they had never found the Grail, but in the myths, he had definitely found it. I'd have to look at the myth a bit more, but it seemed like a lot of those stories might not be true. After all, Lancelot didn't seem to know about King Arthur. What if that was supposed to be me?

If it was, maybe the reason Raphael hadn't been able to figure out more about the *Restore the Hallowed Host* achievement was because I needed Galahad and the others to complete it, like, I dunno, a chain quest? It seemed a bit reasonable, especially since that achievement had referenced the Holy Grail, but as I thought about it, another thought struck me, and I found myself annoyed with Lancelot.

If I was Arthur, who was Guinevere?

25

A claxon was sounding in the distance by the time we reached Heaven city? Capital Heaven?

"Dang!" Michelle said which didn't seem quite strong enough of a word to me because the entire fucking horizon was alive with dragons. Just a cursory glance netted me almost a dozen, and what's more, the ground was literally alive with lizard men and beholders. Ravagers stomped through the distance, so numerous I almost wanted to cry.

"How is that possible?" I asked, sprinting toward the far gates, my heart pounding, even though everything in me told me that maybe, just maybe, I ought to run the other way. "Has there ever been a force that size before?"

"No!" Michelle cried right before she took to the air in a massive flurry of beating wings, her flaming sword in hand.

Well, that wasn't good at all. I had no idea how we could take so many... unless... The waves were supposed to be comparable to our strength, had something happened? No... surely it couldn't be?

As Michelle flew straight at the closest dragon, sword-whipping around her, I glanced over my shoulder at the Knights of the Round Table who were easily keeping pace with me. "Can you guys do something?"

"Yes, my liege!" Lancelot replied, and before I could blink, the twelve knights were just gone. I stopped and stood there blinking for a three count before turning back to the fight as death cries filled my ears. The knights had charged into battle, but I wouldn't call it that.

No. It was a fucking slaughter.

In the time it took me to reach the gate, the knights had decimated the forces coming toward us. Dragon, beholder, ravager? It mattered not before their might.

Like a scythe cutting through chaff, they cut down the armies of Darkness, laying waste in a way I hadn't thought possible.

"Holy fuck," I mumbled, finally stepping onto the battlefield. Only there was only a handful of enemies left.

"Where the fuck did you find those guys?" Uriel asked, glancing at me. She was covered in blood, but if it bothered her, it didn't show. Only when she caught me looking, she smirked. "It's not mine."

"Those are the Knights of the Round Table. I freed them, and now they fight for truth, justice, and the Arthurian way." I nodded to them as the last of the enemies fell, and we found ourselves standing on an empty battlefield.

"Well, I hope the boss shows up soon. Otherwise, this fight just got kind of boring." Uriel glanced at her wrist. "Fortunately, I've got a big old knight to seduce." She pointed at Lamorak and licked her lips. "Yummy."

"He's gay." I shrugged. "And doesn't have a penis."

"Well, that's a bummer." Uriel sighed. "So, you busy?" She waggled her eyebrows. "Seems I've got a few minutes—"

A shriek erupted from the horizon, and I turned in time to see what looked like a giant scorpion cross the breach. It had claws the color of blood and a stinger the size of Uriel. In fact, as it moved, I was wondering how big it actually was because I could only see the front half and it blocked out most of the horizon.

"To arms!" Lancelot cried before leaping into the air, Claymore a blur of steel. As his blade slammed into the man-sized claw, an earsplitting crack resounded across the horizon.

The claw tore from the scorpion's arm in a spray of black ichor, and as it crashed to the ground, Percival hurled his sword right into the creature's eye stalk. The scorpion shrieked again, eye exploding like a pus-filled balloon as it tried to backtrack into the Darkness.

Only, before it could take even a few steps, Galahad and Lamorak rushed forward, taking out its legs with swings of their axes. The scorpion tottered, trying to regain its balance before slamming headfirst into the earth, throwing up a wave of sand as the rest of the knights charged in, tearing the creature to pieces in the time it took me to exhale.

Then it was over, and we were all standing there with nothing to do.

"That was insane!" Uriel shrieked, grabbing me by the arms and shaking me. "Your bros are awesome!"

"My liege," Lancelot called, coming toward me with the massive chunk of dark blood that had been taken from the corpse of the scorpion. "What would you like us to do with this shiny rock?"

"That's Dark Blood." I pointed to it. "Can you collect them from all the corpses and bring them to…" I stopped.

Normally, I'd have Sally process them before sending them to Sam for use or to Buffy for sale. Only Sally was still running the infirmary. There wasn't anywhere to take them.

"This is where I'm going to ask you a question, and you're going to tell me an answer that I hope isn't 'we crush them and sprinkle them on salads,'" I said, turning to Uriel. "What do you do with them?"

"The rocks?" Uriel shrugged. "Nothing really. We used to store them in a big building on the North side of town, but once it was filled, well, we just leave them on the field now. They dissolve after a few days which is good because, as I said, we have a building full of them."

"Can you direct Lancelot to the building so he can bring them all in," I said, trying not to get mad. I mean, it wasn't their fault they didn't know how to utilize them. We could change that though. Giving the angels Dark Blood infused weapons and armor would make them considerably stronger, you know, for the time when the knights didn't run roughshod over the entire field of battle.

"I guess." Uriel shrugged. "Do they really taste good on salads?"

"You know, I've never tried it." I shrugged. "I was making a joke."

"I kinda wanna try it now," Uriel mused, scratching her cheek as Lancelot approached.

Leaving the two of them to hash it out, I went to find Sally. As I went, I sighed. While I'd managed to get the *Rebuild Heaven* achievement to twenty-five percent, and the *Outfit the Troops* achievement had climbed to fifteen percent on account of the repairs Sam had already done to their weaponry, the *Heal the Rift* achievement was only at seventy-five percent. I'd figured it would be nearly done what with the alliance between Heaven and Hell, but all that work had barely gained me five percent.

I wasn't quite sure why. I'd have to make a point of asking Raphael about it when I got the chance and also ask her about the Grail. Now that I'd found the knights, maybe new information would reveal itself. After all, in the story, Galahad had found it. Maybe I just needed to send him on an epic quest and wait a while?

Either way, now wasn't the time to deal with that either. Now was the time to address the Dark Blood issue. To do that, we had to get processing. The walk to the infirmary didn't take long, and when I arrived, I quickly found Sally leading a group of both demons and angels. There were more of the battle clerics, especially since it seemed many of the angels had an affinity toward it, which made sense, but there were also healers from the Guild below. That was good because they were a lot better, at least on the infirmary side.

"Hey, Sally. How are you?" I asked, walking over to her. She looked a bit worn around the edges, and when she saw me, she tried to smile and run a hand through her blonde hair.

"I'm okay." She took a sip from her steaming porcelain cup. "Now that we actually have staff, things are running smoother." She let out a long breath. "Bit of a learning curve though. I never thought I'd be running an entire infirmary." She shrugged. "Maybe you wanna think about getting some admin staff from Hell…"

"Nope." I shook my head. While I knew a good administrator was worth its weight in gold, I didn't even want to try to use Hell's entrenched bureaucracy for the task. No, that'd just lead to Michelle smiting someone.

"Was worth a shot." Sally leaned against the counter. "So, is this a social call?"

"Unfortunately, no." I gestured at the infirmary. "You've done a great job with this, but there's a problem."

"With the infirmary?" She looked around the room, eyes fixing on one of the battle clerics for a moment. A girl with long red hair and freckles. "How so?" Was it me, or did she seem annoyed?

"Not with the infirmary." I shook my head.

"Arthur, I'm getting confused, and maybe it's because I haven't slept in two days, but can you just tell me what you're going on about?" Sally turned her gaze back to me and sipped from her cup again.

"We have a warehouse full of raw Dark Blood." I wanted to gesture at it but realized I didn't know where it was. "On the north side," I added sheepishly. "Some from Dragons and beholders, and every other kind."

"And you need someone to process it?" Sally asked, sighing. "Do you know how long that would take?" She shook her head. "Even if we had an

Alchemists' lab, which we don't, I can't do that job and this one."

I wanted to say something like "Not with that attitude" which was what my old boss would have said after laying down an impossible task, but I didn't because I was a kind and considerate person. Sort of.

"If I have an alchemist's lab set up, will you be able to do it? Do you want to do it?"

"Hmm," Sally mused, thinking. "I suppose I would. I always enjoyed the alchemy a bit more because it's quiet. If you got me a couple apprentices, I could probably knock out the easy stuff quickly enough, and Shara can basically run this place." Sally gestured at the redhead. "Get the lab, and we'll talk."

"Awesome, Sally. You're the best." I gave her a hug. "I'll go talk to Maribelle and Buffy."

"Right." She nodded, right before she got really serious. "And, Arthur, don't even consider coming back to me with this alchemy business until Crystal is in Heaven."

I flushed. I'd completely forgotten about her friend. Well, not forgotten about her, but had forgotten she'd stayed back in Hell. I'd just naturally assumed she'd come up with the merger, but evidently, that hadn't been the case.

"I'll take care of that too, Sally. I honestly feel bad about it." I sighed. "Really."

"I don't want you to feel bad about it. You're busy, but if you want me to do as you ask, I'd appreciate it." She gave me a wry smile. "And you will *really* appreciate *our* appreciation."

26

"How's my favorite carpenter?" I asked, sidling up to Maribelle.

"I'm your only carpenter," Maribelle snorted, turning and giving me a quick hug.

"That doesn't matter." I touched my heart. "You wound me."

"Is that so?" Maribelle asked, raising an eyebrow at me. "Because, truthfully, I find that hard to believe."

"Either way, you're still my favorite carpenter." I grinned and surveyed the building she was working on. It was mostly just a frame, so I couldn't even tell what it was without looking for a tooltip.

"What do you want, Arthur?" Maribelle gave me a sidelong look. "Sex is out of the question. I'm all sweaty." She looked down at herself. "I'd have to take a shower, and I *really* don't have time for that."

"Wait, sorry, give me a second." I looked her up and down. "I'm picturing you in the shower right now."

She flushed. "Please tell me that's not why you came here."

"No, of course not. You are a valued member of this team." I finally stopped picturing her naked, but it was hard because well, she'd brought it up, and now that I thought about it, the two of us hadn't had near enough sex since we'd got to Heaven. In fact, we'd had no sex, and that was very upsetting to me.

"That is not at all what the look on your face says." She glanced back at her apprentice from Hell who was starting to scream at a carpenter angel. "The kids are starting to get rowdy."

"I was just thinking I needed to take you out for a nice dinner, maybe crack open some wine—"

"I'll be done around seven." Maribelle glanced at her non-existent watch. "And instead of all that, how about you grab a couple bottles of beer and meet me in the shower?"

"That sounds like a plan." I nodded, wondering where the showers were. So far, I'd only seen baths here, and they'd been communal. I'd been sneaking off in the middle of the night to bathe when no one was looking, which, yes, was odd, but after I'd accidentally walked in on a pair of indisposed angels, I'd decided discretion was the better part of valor.

"So, why did you really come here?" Maribelle asked once again. "Because I have things to do. I know it may not seem like it because I stop and give you attention when you come around, but really you're just absorbing time from this whole city." She gestured at her apprentice who was now bludgeoning the poor angel's board with a hammer like it owed her money. "It's going well, as you can see."

"We need an Alchemy shop." I twisted like I could point to Sally who wasn't anywhere near us, realized I was an idiot, and just smiled dumbly.

"That's not in the plan," she said, and when I looked at her dumbly, she reached into her back pocket and pulled out a rolled up piece of parchment. "Here." She offered it to me.

I took it and unfurled it. I couldn't read it, of course, but the tooltip accompanying it gave me the gist of the idea.

"Why is the alchemy shop not even on the plan?" I asked, looking back at her. "You have a menagerie on here."

"The menagerie is a joke." Maribelle rolled her eyes. "It's to make sure people are reading."

"It's made of glass." I tapped the paper. "Is that so you can see the animals better?"

Maribelle looked at me for a long time, and I was getting the strong impression she was rethinking our earlier deal.

"Do you want me to build an alchemist's lab?" She raised an eyebrow. "Because if you do, we're going to have to kick something else off." She gestured at the frame. "This is for the fletcher."

A quick glance at the paper let me know fletcher was eighth on the list, after armory, blacksmith, infirmary, and a few other important seeming buildings. Oddly, showers was seven. So, they hadn't existed. Well, that made me feel better. Let no one say that Arthur Curie wasn't one perceptive individual. That's for damned sure.

"We can kick off the glass menagerie," I said, cracking a smile.

"Done. We will put it in place of the imaginary building." She wiped her hands. "That was easy." She turned to go back to work.

"Can you turn this into the alchemist's station?" I gestured at the not-yet-a-fletcher.

"We would have to retrofit some stuff. It'll cost

another…" She tapped her chin a couple times. "Twenty percent? Maybe thirty? Depends on a few things." She kicked at the frame. "Framing is the same, but there's a lot more ventilation in an Alchemy Lab, and that requires some ducting and other things. Needs a stronger floor too. Maybe bomb proofing."

"Do we have the extra materials?" I asked

"Probably." She pointed at the list. "I'll have to reorganize that a bit, I think because it's sort of based on materials. We probably won't be able to do the apothecary because the ducting was earmarked for that." She bit her lip. "You can tell Uriel you stole her ducting, by the way. She was really into the whole herb thing."

I laughed, and when Maribelle continued looking at me, I wiped my eyes. "Wait, you're serious?"

"Yeah?" She gave me an odd look. "She said she grew lots of different herbs, had all sorts of strains, and asked if we could work in an apothecary." She shrugged.

"Right, you can tell Uriel I shut down her pot farm." I rolled my eyes. "Do the Alchemist's next. Evidently, there's a ton of Dark Blood just waiting to be harvested."

"On that note, I have a request." Maribelle pulled out her hammer and showed it to me. "Look."

"It's a hammer?" I replied, confused.

"With your Builderness." She waved a hand at me.

"Oh, okay."

Journeyman's Hammer
Type: Tool
Class: Carpentry
Grade: B
Durability: 475/1,700
Enchantments: None
Ability: None

"I'm not understanding." I shook my head. "It seems like a normal hammer?"

"Exactly." Maribelle crossed her arms over her chest.

"I'm not following you at all." I shook my head.

"I want a better hammer, you fuck." She shook it at me. "Everyone else gets better swords and armor and whatever. I have a normal hammer and a normal saw and a normal everything." She glared at me. "And I'm *really* good in bed." The last part sounded suspiciously like a threat, like she wouldn't have sex with me anymore unless I got her some upgrades. I knew she didn't mean it, of course, but either way, I still felt bad about it.

"Oh. Well, we can get better tools for you." I tried to shake off my confusion. "That shouldn't be a problem."

"It is a problem." She sighed. "It's not just the tools. It's my standing in the Guilds. I'm really not feeling like I'm progressing at all. I'd have earned a better hammer, maybe Journeyman three, if I could go back and take the test, but I doubt you have the weeks I need to do that." Maribelle sighed. "Buffy even got me a Master's kit, but I can't use it for some reason. Everything gets all fucked up when I do, so I've been stuck with this hammer."

"Oh." I think I was starting to understand. Maribelle wanted better gear, but she wasn't high enough level to actually equip it.

"Yeah. 'Oh.'" She sighed. "Can you figure something out?"

"Give me your hammer," I said, and without a word, she gave it to me.

Do you want to upgrade Journeyman's Hammer to Grade A? Base cost 3 steel ingot (Grade A).

"Do we have steel ingots somewhere?" I asked, looking over at her.

"You'd have to ask Sam." She shrugged. "I work with wood."

"I'll be right back." I nodded at her.

"I need my hammer, Arthur." She watched me for a moment. "I earned it."

"Use one of theirs, okay?" Then before she could protest more, I made my way to Sam's new shop.

It was a lot bigger than the old one had been and had been attached to the armory, which was cool. As I stepped inside the armory, I found her apprentice busy polishing a set of swords that looked way higher quality than what the angels normally used.

"Hello," her apprentice said, and as she caught sight of me, her face turned red, and she swallowed. "Oh, sorry, Mr. Arthur, sir. I'll go get Sam." She vanished so quickly, I could have sworn she'd left a dust cloud in her stead.

Still, a moment later, Sam came out, wiping her face with a rag. "You scared Mixy."

"I have no idea how," I said, shaking my head. "I literally said no words to her." I frowned. "I probably should have said hi, but she ran off too quickly."

"It's because you're a big deal." Sam walked over to me and leaned over the counter.

"I am not. At least I don't feel like it. I'm just me."

"Be that as it may," Sam said, shrugging. "You make her shy."

"Um… sorry?" I shrugged. "Anyway, I have a question. Do we have any steel ingots? Grade A preferably."

"Yeah, I think so. Why?" She looked from me to the hammer and back. "You do know it only takes one ingot to make a hammer right?"

"Yes, but Maribelle can't equip the better ones." I waved off the line of thought before Sam could ask me what I meant. "And she *really* likes this hammer."

"Right…" Sam shrugged. "I'll go get some." She cocked her head to the side. "Mixy bring me three grade A steel ingots."

"By get some, you mean order your shy apprentice to get it for me?" I asked as the girl emerged, looking so flustered, I actually felt bad.

"Pretty much." Sam turned and looked at the girl. "Help Arthur with anything he needs, okay?"

"Anything?" she squeaked going wide-eyed.

"Yeah." Sam stepped through the curtain, leaving me alone with the girl.

"I won't need much, okay?" I said, nodding to her. "If I could get the ingots?"

"Right. Sorry. Okay." She came toward me in a flurry of motion before dropping the ingots onto the counter. "What else do you need?"

"A moment." I put the hammer down and stared at it. I'd never actually done this before. What if it exploded or something? "And maybe stand back."

She did as she was told, moving against the far wall, and seeming relieved by it. "Is this far enough?"

"Yeah, sure." I turned my attention back to the hammer and initiated the upgrade.

Sapphire light wrapped around the hammer and the ore both. Then the ore seemed to sublimate into gas before coalescing around the hammer. There was a loud pop, and another flash of light, and then the hammer sat there, looking cleaner, but not a lot different.

Only it was different.

Journeyman's Hammer
Type: Tool
Class: Carpentry

Grade: A
Durability: 2,000/2,000
Enchantments: None
Ability: None

Do you want to upgrade Journeyman's Hammer to Grade S? Base cost 16 steel ingot (Grade S).

27

An hour later, I set out in search of Maribelle and found her sitting on a tuffet eating curds and whey, which seemed strange because she was talking to a spider that had sat down beside her. I know, right?

"I've got something for you," I said, marching over and proudly displaying the hammer. "Bask in the Glory of an S double plus hammer." I waggled it.

"Oh wow," Maribelle said, eyes going wide as she caught sight of the tool. "It's so big." She bit her lip. "Can I touch it?"

"Of course," I smiled. "This tool is all for you, baby."

"Really?" She flushed, looking from the

hammer to me and back again. "You mean I don't have to share it?"

"Who would you possibly share it with?" I asked, raising an eyebrow at her.

"Other girls?" She shrugged, taking it from me. "Wow, it's so light, but I can feel the power throbbing inside it." She ran her hand up the handle a few times, stroking its length. "I can't believe you did this for me." She beamed.

"Well, you were right. I hadn't been very fair to you. The others all have Dark Blood enhanced weapons, so…"

"You mean?" Her eyes got huge. "This is a Dark Blood infused hammer. Those cost a fortune."

"Well, I made it, so it just cost us some materials." I kicked at the sand, suddenly embarrassed. After I'd upgraded the hammer to S double plus and used a total of one hundred S Grade ingots, I'd gotten Sally to take a break long enough to refine some Dark Blood. Then I'd gotten Sam to do her infusion thing. In retrospect, it seemed like overkill for a hammer, but I was willing to bet the hammer would pound the fuck out of a nail.

"It's not nothing," Maribelle said, getting to her feet and wrapping her arms around my neck. "It's really thoughtful." She nodded. "I can tell you put a lot of work into it."

"Well, you mean a lot to me, Maribelle. I know I'm busy and don't have as much time to spend, but even still, I do want you to be happy."

I was going to say more, honest, but she kissed me then, and I sort of forgot about it for the rest of her lunch break.

"I don't even know what I'm doing anymore," I said as Maribelle finished buttoning up her shirt, which was, quite literally, one of my least favorite things to watch.

"What do you mean?" she asked, picking up her new hammer and putting it into her tool belt. "You have lots of stuff to do." She nodded. "As do I. Need to build you an Alchemist's lab." She fingered the hammer for a second. "Thank you."

"You're welcome." I nodded to her, and as I did, I pulled open her stats menu.

Name: Maribelle
Experience: 217,376
Health: 78/78
Mana: 121/121
Primary Power: Carpentry
Secondary Power: None selected
Strength: 35/100

Agility: 43/100
Charisma: 27/100
Intelligence: 53/100
Special: 66/100
Perk: Rank 10 Carpenter

I blinked a couple times. "Whoa."

"What's wrong?" Maribelle asked, looking up from her hammer.

"I haven't upgraded your stats?" I asked, unable to believe it.

"You did a little bit with my skills, but never with my stats, no." She shook her head. "Why?"

"I just feel dumb. Give me a second." I quickly spent the thirteen thousand or so experience to bring her Strength, Agility, Intelligence, and Special to ninety-five.

It was a touch strange since for most classes, it requires either strength or agility, but carpentry seemed to require both. Still, she had so much accumulated experience, it was a moot point. Even after that spend, she still had over two-hundred thousand experience left. The thing was, I didn't really have anything to spend it on since most of her trees were maxed. No. Her problem was the same as before. She needed a higher rank to unlock better gear and more skill trees.

That needed to be fixed, but at the same time, I couldn't spare her for the time to fix it. Man, I was becoming my old boss.

"What did you do to me?" Maribelle asked, shaking her head in disbelief as newfound intelligence filled her eyes.

"I basically doubled all your stats. You are literally two to three times stronger, faster, and smarter." I smiled. "I could do more too, if there's something else in particular, you would like."

"This is like what you did to Sally and the others, huh?" She looked at her hammer, and some of her excitement had faded.

"Yeah." I clapped her on the shoulder. "I'm sorry I didn't do it before."

"I'm almost glad you hadn't." She shut her eyes and took a breath. "I'm sort of thinking about things I never had before. Nothing seems so simple." She sighed.

"Annabeth complained about the same thing, but you'll find you get used to it." I gave her a hug. "Besides, you were always smart. Like, really smart."

"I know that." She shrugged. "It's just strange." She shook her head. "Anyway, I better get back to work. Sorry about getting so bent about the hammer. It's really great, and I like it a lot, and you totally can't have it back, but we probably could have used the resources elsewhere."

"Pfft, resources." I rolled my eyes even though I could still hear Sam screaming at me after she'd found out how much ore I'd used. It turned out I could combine three ore to make one of a higher quality…

"The look on your face tells me I'm right." She bounced. "I'll make good use of that." With that, she turned on her heel and strode off, leaving me to stand there beside her tuffet and her stupid spider.

"I'm a girl spider," it said, even though I didn't ask.

"Of course you are," I said, right before I sat down beside it.

"I make really nice webs, but alas I have no one to share my webs with." It moved a bit closer. "Would you like to come into my web?"

"I'm good." I picked up Maribelle's half-finished bowl and looked at it. The contents looked unappealing in a way I couldn't explain, but I was intrigued nonetheless. I carefully put my index finger into the goop before sucking on it.

"Ugh!" I exclaimed, putting the bowl down. "How can she eat that?"

"Are you actually asking me?" the spider asked. "Because I don't know either." She gestured at the tuffet. "All I know is people like to come to my tuffet to eat it." Have you ever seen a spider shrug? It's kinda weird.

Not sure how to take that, I nodded to the spider before making my way to Raphael. Now that I'd settled the whole alchemist thing, I needed to get a move on with the next achievement *Restore the Hallowed Host*.

If I didn't, then it wouldn't matter if I finished the others because I'd still be down thirty-five percent Legitimacy with the angelic armaments, and that wouldn't be enough to free the angels or save Gabriella.

28

The claxon sounded as I reached Raphael's archives, and as I turned toward the horizon and saw even more creatures coming through the breach, a trumpet blast filled my ears.

"Ow!" I cried, reaching up and clasping my ears as the knights hit the battlefield like a tidal wave of force, wrecking everything in their path, including a new crab monster that seemed like it'd be fun to fight. Only before I even had that thought, the crabs and everything else was dead.

The claxon stopped, and I sighed. Goddamned OP motherfuckers. Ah well, I didn't really wanna fight monsters, anyway. I had achievements to get so I could become the mother-fuckin' hero of Heaven, fight another dude and take all his women. Or something. I wasn't even sure anymore.

I turned back to the door and knocked. There was no response, so I knocked again. Then I waited an appropriate amount of time before knocking again. This time the door opened to reveal Raphael, only she had bags the size of Texas under her eyes.

"Hey there pretty lady," I said, smiling at her. "How *you* doin'?"

"Fine," she said, looking me up and down. "Do you need something? I'm busy." She heaved out a breath. "It's why I didn't open the door. You were supposed to just go away."

"I was wondering if you have any more information about the *Restore the Hallowed Host* achievement." She frowned as I finished speaking.

"No." She shook her head. "I got really excited because new text appeared in one of the pages after your statue buddies showed up, but it doesn't make any sense. I've been trying to figure it out, but alas, all my research has turned up nothing."

"Can I see it?" I asked, wondering what it could say. "Maybe I'll have a different perspective?"

Raphael looked at me for a long time. "When was the last time you slept?"

"I don't know." I scratched my head. "I vaguely recall sleeping a few days ago, I think?"

"And you don't think that's a problem?" she sighed. "You're acting weird."

"How am I acting weird? I just wanna know about the achievement." I narrowed my eyes. "That's literally the main thing I've been doing. Trying to complete these achievements. I created an entire industry to do that."

"You used almost all our steel to make a hammer." She looked at me. "Yes. I heard about it. Michelle is livid and don't get me started on Uriel."

"The herb garden?" I asked, rolling my eyes.

"They're medicinal." Raphael waved off the comment. "I'll show you the book, but after you have to promise you'll go take a nap, okay?"

"I will promise to think about a nap." I flexed. "I feel great."

"Did you just flex at me?" the Archangel of Providence asked, one eyebrow snaking up over the top of her glasses.

"Yes?" I rubbed my face with my hand. Maybe I did need a nap.

"I'm really more of a brains than brawn girl." She shrugged. "Anyway, let's get this over with. Most of what I found is just the myth of King

Arthur. You know, Sir Bors, Galahad, and Percival set out and looked for it. Galahad eventually found it. You know that stuff." She yawned.

"We could nap together, you know." I followed her inside as I thought about what she had said. So Galahad had found the grail in the stories but not in real life, and he'd had Percival and Bors with him. Interesting. "You seem tired too."

"I'm not going to sleep with you, Arthur." Raphael glanced at me over her shoulder, and she didn't seem slightly amused. "Ever."

"I didn't mean it like that." I waved off the comment because I hadn't, but I didn't want to defend myself. "I think the whole damned city could use a nap."

"Right." She rolled her eyes as she opened the door to her study and stepped inside. "There's the book." She pointed to a green, leather-bound tome.

I obviously could not read the book, but I could read the tooltip next to it.

The way to the grail has been lost but is now found.

"Well, that's helpful," I sighed and rubbed my eyes. Maybe I did need a nap.

"Let me guess, you expected to come in here and just figure it out?" Raphael scoffed, and I suddenly realized why she had been icy toward me. I was stepping all over her shit. I'd have never done that with Sam, Sally, or any of the others, so why had I thought I could out scholar the scholar? Because I was tired and an ass, probably.

"I need to apologize." I sat down on the plush crimson couch along the far wall. Man, was it comfy. I could just lay down and…

"For what." Raphael looked at me, more curious than anything else.

"For not taking your skills and such seriously. I wasn't trying to imply I was better. I am way not better." I gestured at the room. "I've read lots of books, but most are about elves. None of them are academic. That you have read all this and know it so well? That's amazing."

"What kind of elves?" Raphael moved across the room toward a shelf on the bottom left. "Tolkien or…?"

"I lied. I don't know about elves at all. I was making a joke. In fact, I think I've read exactly one series with elves, and no one else has." I sighed. "I was just trying to sound cool. Mostly I read books about vampires and stuff, but not any of the girly stuff."

"Pity, I quite like elves." Raphael frowned at me

as she pulled out a book with a dragon on the cover. "This is my favorite one."

"That is literally the only book about elves I have read... how did you?" I shook my head. "Are you fucking with me?"

"Yes, a bit." She moved and sat down next to me on the couch. "I've read every book you've read Arthur. *Every book.*" She thumped the cover. "I've read your school records, your tax returns. Everything." She smiled crazily. "I know everything about you."

"That's kind of an invasion of privacy." I swallowed, wondering all what she knew about me since she had said everything. Hell, even I didn't know what my school records said since they wouldn't give them to me because I still owed them money.

"It is, isn't it?" She put her arm around me. "Now then, care to take a nap." She gave me a really creepy smile. "I could read you a bedtime story."

"Actually, I have to go..."

"Good." She glared at me and got up. "I was hoping you would leave. Not trying to be rude, but I'm busy." With that, she moved back to her desk and sat down. Had she just made all that up to freak me out? I wasn't sure, but it'd worked.

"I'll just show myself out." I got up.

My response was met with only laughter, but I didn't care. I was too tired to argue. A nap was sounding pretty good.

There was just one problem. I had a lot to do, and Gabriella didn't feel any closer to being rescued. Rubbing my eyes with my hands again, I wondered if they had coffee in Heaven, and if I could pour a five-hour energy drink in it.

Only as I stepped outside, the only thing I could think about was the line about the grail from the book.

The way to the grail has been lost but is now found.

As I turned the phrase over in my mind, another claxon sounded, and the horizon came alive. Once again, the knights charged into battle, and as I watched them tear apart a wave that dwarfed the one from a few minutes ago, an idea hit me.

29

"I want to take Bors, Galahad, and Percival back to the Plains of Desolation to search for the Holy Grail," I said, and yes, I could hardly believe I had said those words, so take that for what you will.

"You can't take thirty percent of our defenses," Michelle replied, looking at me like I was crazy. "And not on some hunch."

"It's not thirty percent, it's twenty-five percent." Yes, I winced as I said it, but she didn't bludgeon me.

"How will we defend ourselves?" Michelle asked, gesturing back at the field of dead Darkness warriors. "They did that in ten seconds."

"You've defended Heaven for millennia," I said,

crossing my arms over my chest. "I'm sure you'll be okay sparing them for a few hours."

"What if you get stuck in a time vortex for a year or something?" Michelle replied, and while I wanted to tell her she was being crazy, that'd already happened to me. Twice.

"Then you'll be fine." I sighed. "If I don't do this, we may not find the Grail, which means I won't complete the achievement, nor get enough legitimacy with Heaven to break the marks Dred placed on you." I took a step forward, putting my hands on my hips and stared down the Archangel of Justice. "And that means I can't save Gabriella."

"For all you know Gabriella has already given up her mark." Michelle glared right back at me. "There are people here who need your help, your protection."

"Michelle, I wasn't asking permission. I was telling you what is going to happen." I touched my chest with one hand. "They're my knights."

Michelle looked like she wanted to argue, but instead, she merely nodded. "If that's how you really feel Arthur, then go." She gave me a dismissive wave.

"Michelle," I said, and she turned her back on me.

"Go, Arthur." She walked away, leaving me standing there surrounded by hulking statues.

"Fine," I growled, but she didn't even respond. Sighing, I glanced at the knights. "Are you three ready?" I nodded to Galahad, Percival, and Bors.

"Yes, my liege," Galahad said, stepping forward. "I will fight with bravery and courage and help you to recover the grail."

"I'll do those things, but with style and panache," Bors said, stepping forward. Then he did a little flourish with his sword before sheathing it.

"I agree with Michelle," Percival said, glancing back at the archangel. "But if this is your request, Arthur, I shall help you find the grail." He stepped forward as well. "Let us make haste and find victory."

"To victory!" Galahad cried, pumping his fist in the air and causing the other nine knights to break out in cheer.

"Victory!"

"Well, I'm glad you guys are pumped. Let's go," I said, turning and heading back toward the Plains.

It took a lot longer to reach them than I'd expected, and I was surprised to find the landscape had changed. Where before it'd been pretty much unclaimed wildlands, now I saw different trade towns sprinkled throughout busily harvesting lumber, rock, and all sorts of other things. Man, Buffy had really been busy.

"Only as we passed by a mine, I remembered I'd never gotten the Heavenly Gold for Sam. While I wasn't sure where it was, and a cursory inspection of the mine with Mammon's gauntlets yielded little results, I resolved to find her some. I'd just, you know, probably have to ask where it was.

That was yet another thing I had to take care of. After all, what good was a wall with a giant hole in it? Sure, we'd managed to repel the Darkness's attacks thus far, but I was sure that would change, given enough time.

Now wasn't the time to think about the defense though. If I did, I might start to worry Michelle was right. Sure, I'd left nine of the knights behind, but what no one else knew was that the knights had a buff that increased their strength when they were together, and I had decreased their strength by twenty-five percent when I'd taken Percival, Galahad, and Bors.

It was a risk, but I had to do it. After all, if I didn't, I might not find the grail, and I *had* to find the grail. It was the only way I could save Gabriela, and I was damned sure going to do that if it was the last thing I did.

"The plains don't look any different," Percival said as we approached. "What should we be looking for, my liege?"

"I'm not sure..." I scratched my head as I looked around. He was right, it all looked the same. "There's got to be a clue though."

"Then we shall find it!" Galahad cried, charging forward to inspect one of the statue bases. The others glanced at him, shrugged, and then went to do the same.

As I watched them search, something about the line in the book kept bugging me.

The way to the grail has been lost but is now found.

It had to be a reference to the knights, since that achievement had been *Those who were Lost are Found*, but at the same time, nothing was really standing out to me.

I turned my eyes back to the knights and saw both Galahad and Bors were glowing. Not a lot or anything, but as my gaze flickered between them, I figured out why. They were standing near the pedestals they had stood on prior to being awoken. Those were glowing with the same color. Red for Galahad and blue for Bors. Interesting.

Percival, on the other hand, wasn't glowing, but he also wasn't near his pedestal.

"Percy," I called, and when the knight turned to me, I pointed toward where he'd once stood. "Can you go over there?"

"Back to my rest?" he asked, curious, and as he spoke, he glanced at his fellow knights. "Why in the blazes are you two glowing?"

"I'm glowing?" Bors said, looking down at himself. "By Scott! I am glowing."

"What sort of foul trickery is this?" Galahad cried, slapping at his chest. "Show yourself, foul cur! I shall fight you with bravery and honor!"

"Timeout. I think it's just the key to what we need to do next." I tried to calm them, but it didn't seem to work, so instead, I just nodded to Percival. "Can you please go stand over there?"

"As you wish, my liege." The knight moved to his pedestal, and as he did, he began to glow with emerald light.

"We're standing in a triangle," Bors said, glancing at his comrades before pointing to the disc that had once sat in the middle. "Do you see that?"

I followed his finger and found I did see that. Well, sort of. Sitting in the spot the disc used to occupy was what looked like a glowing ethereal keyhole. That had most definitely not been there before. It was a little weird, but then again, everything here was a little weird.

"I'm going to check it out," I said, pulling out Caliburn just in case the magic keyhole got any funny ideas. Only, the moment I unsheathed the blade, it began to glow. The symbols etched into the steel came to life with red, blue, and green energy.

With each step I took, the ground began to shake violently, so that by the time I reached the keyhole, I was having trouble standing. There was just one problem. Well, one other problem. I needed a key, and I didn't have one.

Still, the sword had worked to awaken the knights. Maybe it would work here?

I wasn't sure, but since I had no other ideas, I decided to go for it. After all, what was the worst that could happen?

Actually, I didn't want to think about that because I was *really* sure the Lady of the Lake wasn't going to give me another sword, and Dred seemed to be using his.

Taking a deep breath, I raised Caliburn, and then I did what I did best. I shoved my sword into a deep, dark hole.

At first, nothing really happened other than the

ground stopped shaking. Then an earsplitting shriek filled my ears. Light began to spill from the keyhole, right before it exploded in a flash of golden light that flung me onto my ass.

More shrieks filled the air, and as they did, the space in front of me began to crack like a car windshield.

"My liege, are you okay?" Galahad called, and I was sure he was about to run to me, but if he did that, I didn't know what would happen. Besides, I was okay. At least for now.

"I've got it," I said, getting to my feet. Then I took a deep breath and reached out toward the cracked split in reality. Touching that void sucked the heat right out of my hand even though I was wearing magic gauntlets and enshrouded in ethereal armor. That did not bode well.

"Who dares disturb my rest?" asked a voice from on high, and as I turned to look heavenward, something hit me in the balls.

Pain and the urge to vomit up my entire soul hit me as I collapsed to the dirt and found myself staring at a Scottish terrier wearing a green feathered hat.

"What the fuck did you do that for?" I croaked in the manliest way possible as my knights charged forward, ready to defend my honor. As I raised my hand to stop them, the glow left each of them.

I turned a worried eye back to the weird portal, but thankfully it was still there.

"I needed to make sure you were a dude," the terrier replied, sitting down in front of me. "You passed."

"You could have fucking asked," I cried while getting to my feet and signaling for my knights to let me handle this.

"That wouldn't be fun." The terrier tipped his hat to me. "Pleased to meet you."

"But, my liege, he has besmirched you," Galahad said, axe already in hand. "Let me carve honor out of his hide."

"It's cool." I turned back to the terrier. "Why did you need to know I was a guy?"

"Because if you were a chick, stepping into the Void of Desperation would rip your ovaries out through your nose." He gave me a horrified look. "It does not seem pleasant."

"Great." I took a deep breath, trying to ignore my sudden anxiety. "Why is it called the Void of Desperation?"

"Because only the truly desperate venture within." He gave me a wide grin. "And bro, I hate to say this, but you seem pretty fucking desperate." He shrugged. "It's cool though. I mean, why else would you be seeking the Holy Grail?"

"Is it hard to get or something?" I asked, looking at him. "I mean, lots of people seek the Holy Grail."

"Dude, are you being serious right now?" He looked at me like I was made of stupid. "It's in a place called the Void of Desperation which itself is in a place called the Plains of Desolation."

"Maybe it's like Iceland?" And when he stared blankly at me, I continued. "You know, made to seem worse than it is."

"Yeah, okay buddy." He pointed to the portal, and as he did, it opened into a yawning maw of a cave filled with screams. "That place is literally filled with suck." He shrugged. "Still, what you seek is in there. Mind the cave trolls."

"Cave trolls?" Percival said before spitting on the ground as we moved to enter the cave. "Man, I hate cave trolls."

"You and me both, brother." I nodded. "But I guess we'll deal with them, anyway."

"How many have you faced before, my liege?" Galahad asked moving beside me and peering into the cave. "I once slew fifty in a single blow."

"You always go on about that," Bors said, elbowing me in the side. "It's true, but just barely. He cut a rope that caused a bunch of lit dynamite to fall on a troll quinceanera."

"Trolls have quinceaneras?" I asked, sort of confused because that just seemed silly.

"The best quinceaneras," Percival added. "The only problem with them is the trolls."

"Anyway," I said, turning to the terrier. "Do we just go inside?"

"Yes." The terrier bobbed his head. "Well, you and one other only. Two will have to stay out here to keep the portal from closing." He shrugged as I opened my mouth to bitch. "Hey, I don't make the rules."

"Allow me to accompany you, my liege," Galahad said, thumping his chest.

"Agreed," Bors and Percival said in unison.

"Awesome," I said, glancing at Galahad. "Well, come on then. Let's kick some troll butt."

30

The first thing I noticed upon entering the cave was the smell of blood and despair. I shivered as it washed over me like a warm breath. Worse, I could barely see a damned thing.

Still, I was the Builder, and I had a bunch of awesome gear and a Knight of the Round Table. I could do this. Pushing my fears away, I called some of my power into Caliburn, causing it to glow bright enough for me to see. Only, it didn't reveal much. Just gray stone walls and a dirt floor.

"Smells like a bucket of awesome down here," I said sarcastically, glancing over my shoulder at Galahad.

"We should make haste my liege." The knight

inhaled sharply. "That is the smell of cave trolls, and many at that."

"Sounds good," I mumbled, sucking in a deep breath to calm myself as I gripped Caliburn and moved forward. The space was so small it bordered on making me claustrophobic.

We walked for only a few moments before coming to a sharp bend. While the smell of cave troll had grown with each step, I still hadn't seen any of the creatures, nor heard the sounds of a party, which was good I supposed. Still, the whole thing was making me anxious.

When I was fighting, I could ignore how scared I was. Sure, I was strong, and I was reasonably sure I could take a cave troll, but at the same time, I hadn't fought one. For all I knew, they'd be invulnerable or something.

"Their smell grows stronger, my liege," Galahad said, reaching out to stop me from turning the corner. "Perhaps it would be better if I led."

"Why is that?" I asked, glancing at him. "Do you know the way or something?"

"I do not, but I worry it may trapped. If one of us is to fall to the vile trolls' treachery, better it be me." He nodded. "You are much too important to the cause."

I wanted to argue with him, but at the same time, he was a walking statue inhabited by a Knight of the Round Table. If his happy ass wanted to go first, that was fine with me.

"Okay, you can go—"

A hand the size of a walrus grabbed Galahad and pulled him around the corner.

"Galahad!" I cried, racing after him, only to find him behind dragged across the ground. The giant hand was still wrapped around him, but it was attached to a tendril of serpentine flesh that snaked out into the darkness.

Without thinking, I called up a palm full of Hellfire and flung it into the darkness. As it flew through the air, shrieks filled my ears, and I saw huge, lumbering shapes cower away from the light of my fireball.

As the hellfire slammed into the far wall in a cascade of sparks, the shadows seemed to come alive with activity.

I lashed out with Caliburn, cutting through something I could barely see. My blade met with fleshy resistance an instant before hot blood splattered across my face, but I didn't let that stop me. I charged toward Galahad and unleashed a sapphire blast right into the tentacle.

It was strange because the tentacle turned to stone a second before impact and shattered into a billion pieces. The hand holding Galahad spasmed, and as it did, the knight tore free, leaping to his feet, axe already whipping about.

His weapon slammed into something with a wet thunk right before the knight got batted aside like a rag doll. As he rolled into the darkness, I realized the problem. These things needed dark, and the main reason they hadn't really attacked me was because my sword's glow was keeping them away.

"I'm okay!" Galahad called, but I could hear the strain in his voice. Still, his words gave me a target, and I lobbed more hellfire in his direction. As my attack exploded across the ceiling, Galahad severed another serpentine arm and backpedaled toward me, axe swinging like a helicopter blade.

"We need more light," I said as the knight approached. That will vanquish all of them.

"If it is light you need than light you shall have!" Galahad raised his left hand toward the ceiling. As he did, a pulsing ball of pure energy appeared within it. The spell wasn't enough to light the room, maybe just a few feet on either side, but that was because it was huge. "Quick, take them out, my liege. I will hold the spell as long as I can."

I glanced at him, and as I did, I realized that wouldn't be long.

Name: Galahad
Experience: 14,768
Health: 143/181
Mana: 32/43
Primary Power: None selected
Secondary Power: None selected
Strength: 93/100
Agility: 88/100
Charisma: 16/100
Intelligence: 16/100
Special: 27/100
Unique Ability: Knight of the Round Table

He just didn't have the mana to keep the light going long enough for me to kill a football stadium full of trolls. Then again, he had some experience…

As Galahad's mana ticked down, I quickly glanced through his skill trees, looking for his light spell.

Light
Skill: 2/10.

The user can summon a ball of light capable of lighting an area skill times 2 meters in diameter.

Right below the skill was an upgrade tab, but I

ignored it because even if I maxed the skill, it wouldn't light this room.

No, what I needed was something else, and I found it a moment later.

Solar Flare: This Ability allows the user to create a blinding flash of light, blinding all opponents within 20 meters of the user.

Requirements: Special: 50+, Intelligence: 40+

Cost: 4,000 Experience

"Perfect," I said, quickly upgrading his Special and Intelligence and then buying the Solar Flare skill. "Why don't you hit them with a Solar Flare?"

Galahad looked at me in confusion for a moment before understanding dawned across his stony face. He dropped his hand, causing the light spill to vanish before putting the back of his hands to his forehead. "You may want to close your eyes, my liege."

It was still bright behind my eyelids.

I didn't open my eyes until well after the smell of smoking corpses filled my nose. As I looked around, using Caliburn to light my way, I saw all the trolls had been turned into charred husks.

"I think I beat my record," Galahad said, moving closer to me. "How did you teach me that attack?"

"I just used your experience to buy it." I waved my hand dismissively as I looked around. Part of it felt too easy, but then again, I wasn't the one that was supposed to be in here. No, the Destroyer was supposed to be here, and he couldn't give skills to the knights.

What should have happened was that I'd have fought the trolls while Galahad's light slowly faded away. Only, like with the shade I'd fought outside, the trial didn't quite be set up for my abilities.

"I do not know what that means, my liege," Galahad said as the door along the far wall opened to reveal a corridor that twisted off into the darkness. "But I am glad you have such a power. This would have been nigh impossible without it."

"I just had a similar thought." I pointed to the door. "What do you suppose is in there?"

Galahad inhaled. "I can't smell anything but burned bodies." He shrugged. "Perhaps it is the grail?"

"Perhaps," I muttered, moving closer. I mean, he was probably right, but if I had learned anything, no treasure would be left unguarded, and while this room might have been tough, I had stolen Dred's healing ability. He would have been able to fight through it no matter how badly they'd hurt him. The fact that I'd cheesed the room didn't mean that the next room wouldn't have a boss. No. It'd have something designed to stop someone who could fight his way through a stadium full of trolls, and that concerned me.

A lot.

Worse, Galahad only had around nine thousand experience left. If I needed more than that to upgrade his abilities to beat the next room, we were screwed.

31

"Fee Fi Fo Fum, I smell the blood of an Englishman," warbled a voice from deep within the new room. As we stepped inside, the room came alive with torches that spiraled outward along the walls, casting the entire place in ethereal blue light.

The ground beyond the platform where we stood reminded me of grating, and through the slats, I could see creatures moving below. As I tore my gaze from whatever lurked below, the rest of the room finally lit up, revealing a grotesque humanoid creature lounging upon a pile of skulls while picking its yellowed-crooked teeth with what looked like a rib bone.

"How has this creature acquired so many bones?" Galahad asked me, glanced from the massive stringy-haired giant to me and back again. "Is there another way in here?"

"Be he alive, or be he dead, I'll grind his bones to make my bread," the giant cried before I could respond to Galahad's excellent point. Then it moved, climbing to its feet, and as I watched it, I realized I barely reached the top of its ankle.

"And how will you cook this bread, you vile cur?" Galahad called back, glaring at the creature who just blinked at him with sunken, yellow eyes.

"I don't think you're going to reason with the giant," I said, gripping Caliburn tightly. I wasn't even sure how to go about attacking something this size. Its ankles were like redwoods, and even if I had a chainsaw, I didn't think I could get through them. Worse, I was fairly certain it could just step on me, and while I might heal, it wouldn't be much of a fair fight, especially since I couldn't reach any vital organs from where I stood.

"That's no giant," Galahad said as his axe began to glow with red light. He pointed the weapon at the creature as it stood there, waiting for us to make a move. "That's a titan."

"A titan?" I replied, confused. "Like the Greek gods?"

"No." Galahad shook his head. "This is a black

knight titan." He smacked the back of his neck. "The weak spot is here."

"Seriously?" I asked, looking at the creature who was licking his lips. "How the fuck am I going to get up there? Shoot it?"

"Their skin is too hard for ranged attacks to penetrate. Usually, we use grappling hooks." Galahad shrugged. "It's not so bad. You shoot them high into the walls and zip up there and slash them apart. Pretty easy unless their smart, and this one doesn't seem smart." He sighed. "I don't have a grappling hook though."

"Me either." I could tell the creature wanted to rush us, only it hadn't. That was curious. "It's also not attacking."

"Indeed, my liege. Usually the moment they smell a mortal man, they charge." He swallowed. "They're much faster than they look. I've seen them easily outrun a horse." He frowned, and I realized the bravest knight was a bit scared.

"Well, if it isn't going to attack us yet, we can think of a strategy." I pointed to the grates. "There's clearly something down there." I stamped my foot. "And this is grating, so something must happen." It was a little weird because so far, the encounter reminded me of something straight out a video game. The ones where the boss didn't do anything until you attacked, at which point all sorts of crazy shit would happen.

It was weird because if I knew Dred, the guy would have just charged in and beaten the fuck out of the titan. Well, probably. After all, this fight was designed for someone like him, not me. I had no idea what most of his powers did, but they seemed like they were all meant to make him an unkillable killing machine, whereas mine weren't.

This probably was meant for someone to go in and try to melee the thing down in some way, but with what Galahad told me, that seemed impossible. After all, how were we to get to its neck? Climb my way up it like a beanstalk?

I took another look around the room for something like that, but there wasn't a lot there, just torches and the bone pile, and whatever lurked below the grating.

"My guess is that if we don't defeat the titan in a certain amount of time, the grating opens up." Galahad pointed to the edges of the room. "See those hinges? They'll allow the floor to drop out."

He looked to be right, but that was curious too. Galahad had told me that usually they used grappling hooks to get to the walls, and if that were the case, one would just need to wait until the floor fell out, and the boss fell into the pit. Of course, that might not kill him, but since we lacked grappling hooks, well, that was out of the question.

Or was it?

As I looked around the room, I recalled when I'd moved through the dwarven dungeon. I'd used Mammon's gauntlets to carve handholds into the walls. Would that work here?

I wasn't sure, but either way, I was going to find out. Only as I stepping off the platform and onto the grating so I could get a closer look, the creature charged.

Its huge, lumbering steps caused the ground to shake violently beneath my feet. As it ate up the distance, I whirled, bringing my sword up just in time to try to block a me-sized fist. The blow slammed into me with so much force, my armor shattered.

My body hit the far wall with a wet squelch, and as pain shot through my body, I saw it turn toward Galahad.

"For the King!" he cried, rushing forward in a blur of speed. His axe smashed into the creature's shin with a resounding clang that shot sparks into the air but didn't do a lot else.

"You are not flesh." The titan regarded him for a moment before kicking him away. The knight flew across the room, slamming into the pile of bones. Debris went everywhere as Galahad struggled to stand and failed. I could see why. His health had dropped by over half from that single blow.

Not good.

I knew part of it was that he wasn't receiving his cumulative Knight of the Round Table buff, but part of it was that this thing just seemed unstoppable. Especially since I knew my damage had been reflected back to it sevenfold. Only if it had actually gotten hurt, I couldn't tell.

Still, his attack had bought me time to heal. I pulled myself to my feet as the creature came loping toward me, massive knuckles dragging along the steel grating like some kind of gorilla.

I threw a sapphire blast at the creature who didn't even bother to block or dodge. My attack splashed across its skin before disappearing into the ether. Damn.

Quickly pulling up its stats, I swallowed.

Creature: The Black Knight Titan
Type: Titan
Class: Boss
Health: 2173/2181

Mana: 402/403

The guardian's palm came flying toward me like he intended to squash me like a bug. Dodging, I tried to leap onto its arm as its hand crashed into the grating where I'd stood. Only my feet slipped off its skin like it was made of oil and I was wearing butter shoes. I fell flat on my back as the titan raised its hand like it expected me to be smashed beneath.

"Die, cur!" Galahad cried, charging the titan once more, and once again his attack bounced off the back of the titan's leg.

This time, he didn't even draw the creature's attention. Instead, its gaze fixed on me as I scrambled to my feet. It drew in a large breath, its nostrils flaring.

"I will swallow you whole, and when I shit out your bones, I will boil them into stew."

"That's kind of disgusting," I said, backpedaling as it reared back to try to crush me with an overhead swing. "And I thought you were going to make me into bread?"

"I will do that third."

As I threw myself forward, rolling between its tree trunk legs, its fists slammed down on the metal. I came to my feet, whirling around, and as I did, I wished I had Sathanus's teleport ability. If I did, I could just pop up there.

I blinked.

Wrath.

The archangel could not only fly, but she could teleport.

I slammed my hand against the mark on my shoulder and called upon the power of the Archangel of Wrath. I felt her out in the distance, but she was there.

"Sathanus, can you come to me? Please?" I asked aloud as crimson light flared from the mark and the titan whirled to face me. "Like, right now." It felt like I was shouting down a large tunnel.

The titan tried to grab me this time, and I lashed out with Caliburn. My blade clanged off its hand with enough force to rattle down my arms. Worse, it didn't stop the creature's attack. Hell, it didn't even slow it.

The titan's hand closed around me, and it squeezed. Pain exploded through me as it raised me toward its gaping mouth.

"Take me instead!" Galahad cried, and before I could quite understand what had happened, I was back on the ground, and Galahad was in the monster's grip. Had he done some sort of switch places technique? I wasn't sure but either way, I was free. Galahad on the other hand…

The titan stopped, hand halfway to his lips and peered at the knight. "You are not blood and flesh," he snarled, glaring at Galahad. "You will upset my stomach!" He flung Galahad away. This time the knight seemed ready for it, and he managed to roll through the fall, but I suddenly didn't care because the creature was coming toward me.

Since counterattacking hadn't worked, I opted to try to dodge. I threw myself to the side as the creature's foot came down where I'd been only a second before. Then I reached up toward the ceiling, trying to call the stone above us with my gauntlet so I could drop it on the big bastard.

Only as I did, the titan kicked me. My ribs shattered right before I crashed into the wall. My head smacked into the stone with a sickening thud. As darkness encroached upon my vision and I slid to the ground, the titan started coming toward me once more.

32

"Please, Sathanus," I mumbled even though my mouth tasted like blood. I knew I'd heal the damage given time, but since the creature wasn't far away, I knew I didn't have much. "Come!"

The mark on my shoulder flared as the titan approached and peered down at me. Its hand reached out, and as it plucked me from the ground and moved me toward its open maw, a flash of blinding crimson light filled my eyes, and the dwarven archangel appeared in front of me.

"What is so damned important?" she cried, glaring at me.

Before I could explain, a trumpet blast filled the air, so loud that the titan covered its ears. I fell the ten or so stories to the ground and smashed into the grating. Agony exploded across my body as the dwarf landed beside me.

"What is all that racket?" she asked, scooping me up and carrying me backward before the titan could recover.

"My liege, the floor as started to open!" Galahad pointed at the hinges, and I realized he was right. "I think your friend has triggered the mechanism since it was meant to be the two of us."

"Fuck," I mumbled as Sathanus looked over at him.

"What's the statue on about?" she asked, confused.

"This is a two-person quest, and you're three. I think it triggered the floor, and now it's going to drop us into the pit." I was gonna say more, but the titan was coming toward us, and what's more, its skin had turned from sickly yellow to bright red. That definitely wasn't good, and with the way it was moving, I knew we were in trouble.

Wrath tossed me toward Galahad before leaping into the air, nimbly avoiding the creature's attack. Then with a flash, she teleported behind the titan and slammed her blazing axe into the back of its neck in exactly the place Galahad had indicated was its weak spot. Only, instead of doing anything at all, her attack bounced off. That didn't make sense.

"What manner of creature is this?" Galahad asked, inhaling sharply. "'Tis no ordinary titan."

Wrath teleported again as the titan swung at her, and I could have sworn it had gotten way faster.

"I think we triggered a berserk timer." I swallowed, thinking about how games often required you to beat a boss within a certain timeframe before the boss got impossibly stronger. "I don't think we can kill it now."

"I do not know what that means, my liege, but I fear you are right." He pointed toward the titan as Wrath once again slammed her axe into the back of its neck. Just like last time, her attack bounced off. The thing was, she was the Archangel of Wrath, and as her body was glowing with crimson light in a way I'd never seen it before, I was fairly certain she was using a lot more than one percent of her power.

Worse, even with the ability to teleport, she was barely dodging the creature's attacks.

"There's got to be a way to beat it." I looked around hurriedly, trying to ignore how the grate beneath my feet was opening. Tentacles were already starting to reach up from below, and I knew that before long they'd grab us and pull us into its depths. Sure, if we lasted long enough the grate would spill us down there, but I was betting that the more the gap in the grate widened, the more tentacles would come through.

It sort of made sense because Galahad knew you needed to attack from the air. That was why he'd suggested grappling hooks. If I'd gone with my original plan, or had those handy grappling hooks, the tentacles would just pull me down off the wall. Worse, I was starting to think that maybe the creature's weak spot hadn't been its neck.

I turned back to the bone pile, and as I did, I had a really bad idea.

"Galahad, whatever happens, just take care of Sathanus, okay?"

"As you wish, my liege," the knight replied.

"Hey, you fuck! Come at me!" I snarled, sprinting toward it right before it batted Wrath from the sky like an annoying gnat. The archangel hit the far wall with enough force to crack the stone, and as she slid down leaving a bloody snail trail in her wake, the titan turned toward me once more.

It was practically frothing with energy as its eyes sighted on me.

"Get in my belly!" it cried, and this time when it reached out, I didn't try to dodge.

Its fingers once against wrapped around me, and as its mouth opened wide, I saw Galahad start to move.

"Stay back!" I cried, right before the titan swallowed me whole. The smell was unlike anything I could comprehend, and as its throat muscles convulsed around me with bone-crushing force, I lashed out with Caliburn.

This time, my blade cut deep into the pink flesh of its throat, before clanging off the backside of its skin. Still, as I slid down, slicing my way through the flesh, I came to a stop as it narrowed, the throat muscles too damaged from my attack to push me down further.

I smiled. I might not be able to cut through the skin from either side, but I could definitely cut through his insides. I reached out, driving my free hand into the soft flesh, and as I hung on, acidic globules of saliva splattered all over me. I tried to ignore the pain as I hung there in its throat and the damage was reflected into the glistening flesh all around me. As the smell of burning meat, both mine and the titan's, hit my nose, the creature began to shake violently.

Something slammed into the other side of the throat, and as it did, I realized it was choking on me. Good. Biting down the pain flooding through me, I hung on with all I could. I knew I didn't have much time though, what with the grate opening. While I was reasonably sure it hadn't sent us tumbling down to meet the tentacle monster, I also knew if I waited that long, I'd go down with the beast, even if Wrath and Galahad somehow managed to avoid becoming octopus food.

Pushing the pain down, I planted my boots against the sides of the things throat, bracing myself as best as I could, I conjured Hellfire with my free hand and sent it flying upward. The blast of flame charred the flesh of the monster's throat before slamming up into its brain pan. The entire creature spasmed and a gust of air from below ripped by me as it screamed. The sound blew out my eardrums, but I didn't care.

Calling upon my power once again, I hurled gob after gob of Hellfire upward. As my fourth blast exploded, and I readied my fifth, the creature collapsed. We struck the ground with enough force that I'd have probably been knocked unconscious if

I wasn't so tightly packed inside its throat. And, you know, wasn't surrounded by cushy muscle to break my fall.

Even still, as we hit the ground, I wasn't sure it was dead. No. I had to be sure. Jerking Caliburn from the confines of the monster's throat, I crawled forward. Steam curled off my gauntlets as I went, the cooked meat smell of the inside of the creature filling my nose as I moved. It was probably dead but probably wouldn't save my friends.

Reaching the roof of its mouth, I whipped out Caliburn and drove it upward through the roof of the creature's mouth with all the force I could muster. The glowing steel plunged through its soft palate right before I drew my blade sideways, slicing open the flesh and dousing myself with blood.

Gripping Caliburn, I unleashed a sapphire blast that blew open the creature's mouth. Foul smelling ichor cascaded around me as I stared at the bloody bone of its skull. That's when I felt the thing start to move, though I wasn't sure how.

Its jaws opened, and as I saw its fingers, I knew it meant to reach in and pluck me out. I smashed into its skull with my sword. Only, like with the creature's skin, my blow just bounced off. That made sense. After all, I'd blasted it at point-blank range, and it wasn't so much as smudged.

As its fingers came in, I slid backward, trying to escape it, and as I did, I thought of something. The creature's weak spot was supposed to be at the base of its neck.

I whirled around, sliding down its gullet once more as its fingers pressed back into the darkness. The whole of its body rumbled as it triggered its gag reflex.

"Fuck!" I muttered as its throat seemed to split below me into twin tubes. Did one lead to the stomach and the other to the lungs? I wasn't sure, both because I barely knew anatomy, and I had no idea how the inside of a titan worked.

Either way, I didn't care because in front of me was a glowing bit of flesh the color of day-old sludge. I wasn't sure what it was, or if this was the weak spot, but either way, I was instituting a new rule of thumb. When in doubt, hack at the glowing thing.

I lashed out with Caliburn, driving the blade to the hilt into the glowing bit of flesh. Blood exploded out of the wound, coating me from head to toe, in hot, sticky gunk as the entire creature spasmed. Then I was falling.

As the creature disintegrated all around me, I slammed into the grating with bone-shuddering force. It was open, and as I saw tentacles writing from the two-meter-wide opening, I instinctively curled back. Only they too were dissolving into mist.

33

"Well, this has been fun," Sathanus said, sidling over to me as I picked myself up and dusted myself off. "Next time you need something, call someone else."

"Thanks for your help, Sathanus," I said, nodding to the archangel. "You really saved us."

"Yes, thank you, dwarf. Your skills are most impressive," Galahad agreed.

"I barely did anything more than provide a distraction." The Archangel of Wrath stroked her beard. "Now, if you'll excuse me, I've got things to do." She stood there looking confused.

"Okay," I said, waving to her. "Thanks for coming."

"It's not working," she said, concern filling her

voice. "I just tried to teleport back, but something is keeping me here." She glared at me. "If I'm trapped here forever, I will rip out your spleen through your dick."

"You don't even know where my spleen is," I said, hoping we weren't trapped here because I didn't see any obvious exit in the room. If there was nowhere to go and she couldn't teleport... well.

"It's in the upper left quadrant of your abdomen." She poked me hard in the tummy. "Right there."

"Man, I felt that all the way up my arm," I said, taking a step backward and raising my hands defensively. "I'm sure there's a way out of here."

"There better be." Sathanus glared at me.

"My liege, come hither. The monster has dropped something." Galahad stood a few feet away pointing at what looked like a broken piece of sword.

There was a stat icon over it, so I did my thing.

Blade of Strange Girdles

Type: Longsword

Durability: 0/11,000*

Enchantments: Godly Focus*

"Hmm," I said, staring at the menu. "It's got

some kind of ability, but its durability has been worn down…"

"Wow," Sathanus said, rolling her eyes at me. "The entire hilt of the thing is missing, and you could tell it was broken? Impressive."

"Well, it's a bit more complicated than that," I said, scanning the note next to the durability. "It's actually in three separate pieces. So it's not just broken, it needs all three to be fixed. There's nothing intrinsically wrong with that blade I guess."

"Other than it's broken?" Sathanus snorted. "As I said. Really helpful."

"What does the ability do, my liege?" Galahad hefted the piece of blade. "It feels very powerful. If we were to forge it once more, I believe it could be quite formidable."

"Right, sorry." I opened the enchantment Godly Focus.

Godly Focus – For those worthy enough to draw the Sword of Strange Girdles from its sheath, they will gain the ability to accomplish any task, no matter difficult. However, those deemed unworthy will be instantly destroyed by drawing it.

Note – This ability will not take effect unless drawn from set piece **Memory of Blood.*

"Well, that sucks," I mumbled, before telling them what it'd said.

"So, it would seem we must quest for the remaining pieces as well as the scabbard." Galahad nodded. "Perhaps it is here? Mayhap the weapon was broken by the titan?"

"It's worth a look," I said, looking around hopelessly. Pretty much the only thing in the room was the bone pile, and the odds of finding something within it seemed, well… a needle might have been easier.

Then again, I was the builder, right?

I walked over to the pile, and opened the tooltip. I soon found, much to my chagrin, that every single item in it was categorized. I glanced through the list for a second before finding what I was looking for. Pulling the bone free of the pile, I examined it.

Papagustes
Type: Bone
Durability: 0/11,000*
Enchantments: Flesh of the Serpent

"You're in luck," I said, holding the piece of bone up. It sort of like the cross braces of a sword. "I guess this bone is part of it. The thing even has an ability."

Flesh of the Serpent — This ability allows the holder to resist excessive heat.

"It would seem so," Galahad replied, taking it from me, only as he tried to fit it to the sword, I could tell it wouldn't work. "It seems we are missing the other cross brace."

I nodded at turned back toward the bone pile. After all, it didn't help to look. Still, it took me scanning through nearly each and every bone before I found it.

Ertanax
Type: Bone
Durability: 0/11,000*
Enchantments: Endless Struggle

"Here you go, Galahad." I gave him the next piece. "It also has an ability."

Endless Struggle — This ability allows the holder to never grow tired.

As Galahad took the piece, he laid it on the ground next two the blade and Papagustes. Then, he slowly tried to fit them together. As he did, the sword began to glow with all the colors I'd ever seen, and as I watched, it solidified into a blade with a handle of bone.

Sword of Strange Girdles
Type: Longsword

Durability: 33,000/33,000

Damage: 2D20

Enchantments: Flesh of the Serpent, Endless Struggle, Godly Focus*

"Tis quite amazing, my liege," Galahad said, picking up the sword, and as he did, it glowed even brighter. He brought it over and offered it to me.

"Why don't you keep it? I already have a magic sword." I gestured at him with Caliburn. "I don't need two."

"Are you sure, my liege? This sword feels much too powerful for me to rightly keep it." Galahad swung the weapon tentatively through the air, and as he did, the far wall opened, sliding up into the ceiling to reveal a passageway.

"I'm sure." I nodded toward the opening. "Seems like you've got the magic touch."

Galahad looked down at his shoes. "Thank you, my liege. Your words make me joyous." Only he didn't look joyous. He looked embarrassed.

"Well, let's go then," Sathanus said, moving toward the passage. "As much as I like you both, which I don't really, I would like to get back. I had things to do." She sighed. "Lucifer is going to be pissed when she finds out I wasn't busy quelling the dwarven rebellion."

"There's a dwarven rebellion?" I asked, following her toward the new passageway.

"Yeah, but it's like ninety percent crushed." Sathanus shrugged. "I wouldn't worry about it."

"Do I want to know why there is a dwarven rebellion?" I said as the passage opened up to reveal a massive room that was more or less identical to the one we'd come with, except it didn't have grating. It did, however, have a pedestal in the middle, but from where I stood, I couldn't make out what was on it.

"No." She shook her head. "Better if you don't. Just know that when Lucifer asks, I'm throwing you under the bus."

"All right," I said as Galahad joined us in the room. The sword in his hand began to glow, and as it did, a matching glow came from the pedestal. Then, before I realized what was happening, the sword tore from Galahad's grip and spiraled across the room.

My eyes opened in shock as a wooden scabbard wrapped in crimson serpent skin rose into the air to catch the blade. Then the now sheathed weapon settled back onto the pedestal like it was daring us to take it.

"What should we do about that?" Sathanus

asked, and before I could tell her that I had no fucking idea, Galahad strode into the room.

"Tis my sword, my liege. I will check it." He swallowed hard, and I realized that while he was scared, he was trying to put on a brave face.

"We can all check it together," I said, moving to follow him, but before I could Sathanus stopped me.

"No. If that thing explodes, I don't want you anywhere near it." The dwarf spoke so quietly that only I could hear her, but as she said it, I remembered what Galahad had told me earlier about him being expendable. Was that why he'd decided to go get the sword?

"Maybe we should check and see if there's another way?" I asked, recalling the tooltip I'd read for the ability Godly Focus. While I wasn't able to tell from where I stood, if that was the set piece *Memory of Blood*, drawing the sword might kill Galahad.

"There is no other way," Sathanus said, gesturing about the room, and I had to admit she was correct. While large, it was just four empty walls. No doubt, pulling the sword free of the pedestal would open a passageway like it had in the previous rooms.

"Fine," I grumbled displeased. After all, I was the leader, I ought to be doing this.

"All is well, my liege," Galahad said when he picked up the sheathed weapon a moment later. "Nothing appears to have happened."

I waited for a few heartbeats because it seemed like something should have definitely happened, especially since he'd basically tempted fate, but when nothing did, I let out a sigh of relief.

"There's still no way out." Sathanus swallowed anxiously. "I think he needs to draw the sword."

"That could kill him," I said as Galahad approached. "Under no circumstances are you to draw that weapon."

"Are you sure, my liege?" He looked around. "I think the dwarf may be correct."

"It's too risky. Not when we haven't searched for another clue." Even as I said it, I knew it was likely hopeless, and they were both probably right. Still, we had to try. I'd feel a lot worse if we didn't and then drawing the weapon didn't do anything besides kill Galahad.

"Very well," Galahad nodded, and tried to strap the weapon to his thigh, but it was way too heavy for his belt. "Alas, this weapon requires a girdle."

"A girdle?" I asked, confused. "What do you mean?"

"A girdle attaches to the belt to help balance the weight of a sword so it doesn't flop everywhere." Sathanus shrugged. "We don't have any way of making one."

"Well, great." I sighed. "Let's just look around."

We did, but after almost an hour of searching, we turned up nothing.

"I think we need to draw the sword," Sathanus said once more as she pressed on the same brick for the fifth time. "We all know what has to happen here."

"It's up to Galahad." I looked at him. "You're the one who was able to retrieve it. If you want to try, go ahead, but if you don't, we will find another way."

"I fear the dwarf is correct. I must draw the sword." He took a deep breath. "I am not afeared."

"Great," Sathanus nodded. "Let's see what happens."

With that, Galahad tried to draw the weapon, only he couldn't. The moment it came more than an inch or two out of the sheath it snapped back. Only that didn't make any sense.

"What's going on?" Sathanus asked after he

tried a third time. "I thought it'd just kill him or something?"

I wasn't sure either, but as I looked at the tooltip flashing next to the sheathed weapon, I realized what the problem was. "Would you believe it needs a girdle?"

"Are you serious?" Sathanus asked, glancing from him to me. "How are we to make a girdle?"

"Percival's sister once made me a girdle with her hair. Perhaps we could do that?" Galahad asked, coming over and looking at the two of us. The thing was, I had short hair, and he was a statue. Hell, even Sathanus was bald. Wait a second…

"No." The dwarf said, taking a horrified step back. "Don't even think about it."

"It's the only thing that will work." I shrugged. "You do want to get out of here, right?"

"Not if it means cutting off my beard." She clutched her beard in horror.

"It will grow back," I said. "Otherwise that sword isn't getting drawn."

34

"By Lucifer's black hairy ass, if you tell anyone about this, I will murder you dead," Sathanus snarled, running one hand over her chin.

"You look really hot without the facial hair," I said, smiling at her.

She glared at me while Galahad fitted his beard girdle to the sword. "This had better work." She pointed her glowing axe at Galahad. "Because if it doesn't, even if drawing that sword doesn't kill you, I will."

"Wait, is Lucifer's ass really hairy?" I asked, confused because I'd seen her ass, and it was neither black nor hairy. In fact, it was pretty much the best ass I'd ever seen. And I'd seen a lot of spectacular ass lately. Hard to believe just a short while ago I was a Slurpee monkey, and now I'd literally seen the entire heavenly host naked.

"It's just an expression, you dumbass." Sathanus glared at me again. "Of course her ass isn't hairy. She cannot grow proper hair." Sathanus moved to stroke her beard but wound up clutching at empty air which was sort of sad. "Grrr."

"I think it will work. Thank you again, Lady Dwarf," Galahad said as he finished adjusting his new girdle. "Wish me luck." He gripped the hilt of his weapon and pulled. This time the blade slid free of the scabbard. Brilliant blue light exploded from it, and as it did, the pedestal in the middle of the room began to glow the same color.

There was another flash, and as I turned away, the entirety of the room shook. Whiteness exploded from every direction, moving outward in every direction for what felt like miles so that as I stood there trying to orient myself, I got hit with vertigo. It was like standing on nothing and not moving. Worse, every direction was an infinite abyss.

"Is that what I think it is?" Sathanus said, and I turned to find her staring mouth agape. I followed her gaze and saw what looked like a simple wooden cup in the center of what had once been the room. It was sort of hard to tell because, well, the room wasn't there anymore.

"I can feel it call to me, my liege," Galahad said, glancing at me. "What would you have me do?"

I wanted to tell him to go get it, but I had no idea what that would do. Would it summon God or Jesus or something? Hell, would it make someone melt like in that Indiana Jones movie? I wasn't sure, but either way, if anyone was going to touch that thing, it sure as fuck wasn't going to be me. I may have said I had Jesus in my heart, but a face to face with the guy? That, I did not want.

"Go get it," I said, swallowing hard. "You're the one with the magic sword."

"Very well." Galahad moved forward, his sword blazing in his hands, and as he stepped off the spot next to us and stumbled, the entire floor space between where we stood and the grail turned to fucking lava. Only, it didn't seem to bother Galahad.

In fact, he seemed just as surprised by it. As the lava flowed around him, he just stared down at it in confusion. That's when I realized the sword he had made him heat resistant. Was this why?

"I seem to be okay, my liege. I shall continue." When I nodded, he kept going. Taking another step, and then another. The lava pooled around his thighs but did not burn him.

"Magic bone or not, I'm glad that isn't me," I said, and as Sathanus nodded beside me, the distance between Galahad and the grail seemed to grow. In an instant, I could barely see the grail anymore.

"Fear not." Galahad looked to me. "I am not tired. I will return soon." With that he raced off, moving through the rising tide of lava with all the speed I knew he had. In only a few moments, both he and the grail had escaped from view.

"Well, at least he won't get tired," Sathanus said, glancing at me.

"Yeah, I just hope it won't take too long." I shrugged. "Once we get the grail, we still have to get it back to Heaven. Who knows what will happen then?"

"Why are you even looking for the Holy Grail?" Sathanus asked, looking at me, and as she did, I realized her beard had already grown back which was crazy.

"There's an achievement called *Restore the Hallowed Host* which requires me to get the Holy

Grail." I sighed. "That achievement will make it so I can use the Heavenly armaments in addition to the demonic ones. Then I'll kill Dred and save Gabriella."

"So all this is to save the dumb angel?" Sathanus sighed. "Would you do all this for me?"

The question struck me as odd, and as I thought about it, I realized I wasn't sure which made me feel bad.

"Most likely." I shrugged. "You're my friend."

"Then you're an idiot." Sathanus touched her chest with one hand. "I'm the Archangel of Wrath. I kill things for fun."

"Yeah, but you're my sociopath so it's fine." I smiled, and she frowned at me.

"For now." It was probably supposed to sound creepy or scary, like she was implying she'd kill me when she felt more like it, but I could tell she didn't want me dead, and even if I couldn't, she'd come to save me from the titan. She wouldn't have done that had she not wanted to save me.

"You say that, but you came to help me, and gave up your old beard." I gestured at her.

"That was different." She narrowed her eyes at me, giving me the impression I should drop it.

"Right, of course. My bad." I sighed, and

turned toward the horizon, and was surprised to see Galahad was on his way back with the grail. It was weird because the ending felt somewhat anticlimactic, but at the same time, I guess having the proper items for a quest tended to do that, and we'd already killed the boss.

I looked down at myself. Man, I really needed a shower. I was still covered in gunk, and now that I was standing next to the lava field, it was drying all over my clothes and body. Ugh.

"Well, this is exciting," Sathanus said, snapping me out of my reverie. Galahad stood before us, thigh deep in lava and holding a wooden cup I'd have ignored at the dollar store.

"I present to you the Holy Grail." He smiled. "I know tis the real thing because Joseph told me it belonged to his son when I finally reached it." He bowed his head and crossed himself. "Now we must return it to Heaven."

"Right, so, uh, how do we do that?" I asked, watching him climb out of the lava.

"We must merely drink from the cup." Galahad offered it to me. "That is what the spirit told me."

"You want me to drink from the Holy Grail?" I asked, taking it from him. It felt like a normal cup.

"Yes, my liege. I have already done so, and it is safe." He nodded to me.

"It's empty." I looked at it and shrugged. "Okay, whatever." I drank from the cup, and crazily, it sort of tasted like I was drinking water and then wine. As I swallowed, I realized I suddenly felt better than I ever had.

"Wow, that is amazing. I feel great." I held the cup in my hand and looked into it. The cup was still empty. "You try, Sathanus."

"I'm a fallen angel, Arthur. That might kill me." The dwarf shook her head.

"If you do not drink, we will be stuck here until time ends, and then we will sit here longer." Galahad looked at her totally serious. "That is what the spirit of Joseph told me."

"You heard the statue. He says the ghost said it was okay." Man, I felt really good. Better than good. "Drink up." I waggled the cup out at her.

"The thing with the spleen still applies," she said, snatching it from my hand, and for a second, I worried that she'd spill some of the precious nectar within. Only it was still empty.

Without another word, Sathanus tipped the cup to her lips. I watched her throat convulse as she swallowed and then a crimson glow surrounded her entire body and an exclamation appeared above her head indicating an urgent message.

Popping open the new tooltip, I gasped.

The user has drank from the Holy Grail within the Holy Host. All stats and abilities have been permanently increased by ten percent, including all those formerly at maximum.

"There's no way," I said, my gaze shifting to Sathanus so I could bring up her stats.

Name: Sathanus
Experience: 463,843
Health: 202/202*
Mana: 184/184*
Primary Power: None selected
Secondary Power: None selected
Strength: 105/100*
Agility: 97/100*
Charisma: 28/100*
Intelligence: 72/100*
Special: 103/100*
Unique Ability: Archangel of Wrath

My gaze shifted to Galahad, and I realized that his stats had increased as well.

Name: Galahad
Experience: 19,364
Health: 199/199

Mana: 99/99
Primary Power: None selected
Secondary Power: None selected
Strength: 102/100
Agility: 97/100
Charisma: 18/100
Intelligence: 44/100
Special: 55/100
Unique Ability: Knight of the Round Table

"This is crazy, I feel way stronger than before," Sathanus said, stroking her beard. "And my beard has regained its luster." She was right, it looked more vibrant than it had even before she'd cut it off to make Galahad's girdle.

"Yeah," I said, nodding. "But, um, how do we get out?"

"I presume through the door, my liege." Galahad pointed behind me, and I turned to find there was now a door there made of polished mirror, which was weird because there was nothing behind me but endless white.

"Okay, so through the looking glass we go," I said, glancing at Sathanus. "Can you keep the grail safe?"

"Keep it safe. You'll be lucky if I even give it back to you." She stroked it lovingly. "I don't even like wine, but I love this stuff." She took another sip.

"I'm going to take that as a yes," I said, turning back to the mirror, and as I reached out to open it, the surface rippled into a swirling void that sucked me and my companions inside.

35

As the scenery changed, I found myself in the middle of a forest with the trees made of polished mirror. There was a lake off to my lest, and as I watched silvery mist waft off of it, Sathanus and Galahad appeared next to me looking just as disoriented.

"By the great bearded black ass of Lucifer," Sathanus said, gripping the grail tightly as she spun in a slow circle. "We're hosed."

"Um… why is that?" I asked, trying to keep the sudden fear swirling in my belly from overwhelming me because Sathanus looked absolutely terrified. It was a little weird because aside from lake silver mist, the scenery seemed pretty normal.

Okay, yeah, the trees were all polished mirror, and the sky was just a reflection of the ground, but given that we'd just been in a room full of unending white, that wasn't really as vertigo-inducing.

"This is the forest of mirrors." Sathanus gestured at the closest tree with her axe.

"And what's so bad about the forest of mirrors?" I asked, raising an eyebrow as I stared at the only thing on the horizon that seemed at all different. The lake. Its bank was rocky and the water within seemed to churn violently. If that was where we needed to go, it was definitely not going to be fun, but it didn't seem impossible especially since the archangel could cry, I couldn't really get hurt, and Galahad was, well, him.

"It's the gateway to all realms. Even ones completely unlike ours." She gestured at a tree. "Each of these leads to a new place, a new realm." She took a deep breath like she was trying to calm herself.

"So we need to find the right portal. Got it." I took a deep breath and tried to call on my Builder powers. Only nothing happened. Like, I felt my power come as I called, but no tooltips, menu bubbles, or anything at all appeared. There was absolutely no way to discern which portal went where, and that seemed very bad.

"Joseph did not speak about this." Galahad

looked at me. "The portal was supposed to return us to the Plains of Desolation."

"So what went wrong?" I looked around once again before approaching the closest tree. That's when I realized two things. One, it wasn't a true reflection. I could see a whole other world through the tree, and two, I had no idea which of the billion trees we needed to get back to our realm, let alone back to Heaven.

"That's not the problem, Arthur." Sathanus pointed toward a tree several hundred meters away. "That's the right portal. I can feel the call of our realm. That whole grove leads to our home."

"Okay?" I started toward it. "So what's the problem?"

As I took a step, I heard the roar of a motorcycle followed by horrible sleepy hollow laughter. I spun, just in time to see a girl with skin like chocolate riding a bright red Harley.

She was clad in stilettos, fishnet stockings, a short black vinyl skirt, and a fire engine red crop top, and as she came at us like a bat out of hell, her dark red hair fluttered behind her in a way that made me think of wind blowing bloody entrails through the air.

"She's the problem," Sathanus said, and instead

of moving to attack, she just tucked the grail into a pouch.

"I shall defend you," Galahad said, pointing his new sword at the woman as she approached. "Escape while you can."

"That's not necessary." Sathanus took a deep breath. "We're here because she wants us here. If not, the portal would have worked."

"That's bad?" I asked, looking to Sathanus. "If she wants us, maybe it will be okay."

"Yeah, the tax man often wants to see you too. Is that ever good?" Sathanus raised an eyebrow at me as the vixen unslung a fucking morning star and started whirling it over her head. "Or, you know, did that."

"I'm kind of okay with Galahad's plan," I said, especially since none of my Builder powers seemed to work. That might mean my armaments didn't work. If they didn't work, would I heal if she hit me? I wasn't sure, but I really didn't want to find out.

"No. If you run, she'll chase us." She unfurled her wings and made herself bigger. "Act like a predator, not prey." Sathanus hefted her axe even though it wasn't glowing anymore.

It seemed like great advice, except, well, I felt

like prey. Still, maybe the dwarf was right. Better to stand our ground than run away.

Following Sathanus's lead, I gripped Caliburn and tried to make myself seem awesome, while Galahad unslung his axe, hefting it in one hand and the Sword of Strange Girdles in the other.

Oddly, it seemed to work. As the vixen approached, she dropped her morning star and ceased her laughter before skidding to a stop a few feet from us.

"Do you not fear me, Sathanus?" The woman raised an eyebrow. "That is… unwise. Your powers will not work here." She threw her head up and laughed. "For I am the Princess of Mirrors, and all is as I wish it to be!" Her lips curled into a smile. "I am a god here."

"What do you want?" Sathanus asked, and her voice held way more confidence than it had a moment ago. Only, I couldn't see why. The archangel was strong, but if she was as powerless as I was…

"What makes you think I want something, Archangel?" The princess sat there for a moment, drumming her fingers on the metal of the cherry-red Harley.

"We both know we're not supposed to be here,"

Sathanus said, gesturing to our trio. "That means you came and got us. Why?"

"You're taking all the fun out of this." She sighed. "Very well. I shall tell you what I want, and you can do it in exchange for me letting you leave."

"I really don't have time to do a quest for you." I sighed. "I already have a lot on my plate."

"You'll want to do me this favor." She smirked. "Trust me."

"Let's just hear her out, okay, Arthur?" Sathanus gave me a warning look.

"Fine." I nodded to the Princess of Mirrors. "What would you have us do?"

"Two of your sisters have passed through here recently, and they have taken something that belongs to me." She pointed to Sathanus. "You must bring them to me so they can return what they have taken."

"Which two?" Sathanus asked instead of asking more important questions like why the fuck would we do that.

"Belial and Belphegor." She rubbed her hands together. "I had set this trap to capture them, but instead you have triggered it." She made a clucking noise. "Portal traffic is such a tricky business, you know. It'd be unfortunate if, I dunno, all your realms portals led to me for all time."

"What did Belial and Belphegor take?" I asked, somewhat confused. Those were the last two archangels I had needed to find, but they were also working with Dred. Or at least having naked fun time with him, anyway.

"A Mirror of Transference." The Princess pointed to one of the trees. "They grow on my trees and are capable of making a new realm when planted." She sighed. "I want it back."

"Why would they need to make a new realm?" I asked, and Sathanus shrugged.

"Don't know don't care." The Princess of Mirrors shrugged. "Just retrieve it, and in exchange, you will be rewarded handsomely."

"Okay." I nodded to her. "Send us home, and we'll get your Mirror of Transference back."

"Excellent." She held out her hand, and I shook it. "I look forward to doing Business with you."

With that, she tore off in a squeal of scorched rubber, leaving us standing there alone in the forest.

"Why do I feel like I just made a deal with the Devil?" I asked, sighing.

"Oh, this is way worse than that," Sathanus elbowed me in the side before heading toward the tree she'd pointed out earlier. "And you've already done that."

"That's a fair point," I said, shrugging. I didn't know why it was a bad deal or anything, but I knew one thing. If Belial and Belphegor were in play, we had to find them. After all, I needed their Marks and Armaments. Getting them might give me enough power to stop Dred even without completing the rest of the achievements.

36

After we reappeared in the Plains of Desolation, gathered up Percival and Bors, and bid Sathanus farewell, we headed back to Heaven with the Holy Grail. Part of me still couldn't believe we'd found it, and only after about a day or so.

I could practically taste the achievement. Once I got it, I'd be at forty-five percent legitimacy with Heaven, and my Armament of Death would be that much stronger. While not necessarily game-changing, especially since Dred had six legitimate armaments (I was assuming Sam's still worked for him) he also had two demonic ones.

Assuming his were also at twenty-five percent legitimacy, and I had no reason to think they weren't, that only gave him a one armament advantage. If I could then get either Belial's or Belphegor's, I'd be strong enough to challenge him without having to complete the armaments, and if I got both? Well, I'd be more than able to save Gabriella.

"We must hurry, my liege!" Galahad said, drawing my attention toward the horizon as we approached the main city. My eyes widened in shock.

I wasn't sure if it was because we'd found the grail, or if Dred had finally had enough, but the sky was quite literally alive with dragons. The ground seethed with so many ravagers, I could scarcely even see any other creatures save for one. A giant tarrasque, Godzilla-looking mother fucker that was busily slamming its bulk against the barrier spell protecting Heaven. With each blow, I could see concentric sparks of color radiate outward, and if this barrier was anything like the one we'd had in Hell, I knew it wouldn't be long before it got through.

Once that happened, well, I'd seen enough Godzilla movies to know what'd happen.

"Go!" I cried, pointing at the army besieging Heaven. The three Knights of the Round Table nodded before charging forward in a blur. The moment they touched the hallowed ground of the city, the buff affecting the knights went back to full strength. Even still, I wondered if it would be enough.

Part of me wanted to rush in and help, but as I stared at the massive kaiju, the Grail pulsed in my hands. What would happen if I completed the achievement now? I wasn't sure, but from the way drinking from it had boosted the strength of my party, I was willing to bet it wouldn't be a small thing, and right now, well, we needed all the help we could get.

Charging into town, I pulled out the grail and found it glowing with golden light. As I moved through the streets, the glow brightened or darkened depending on which turns I took. Deciding the grail knew what was best, I moved my way through the city while trying to maximize the glow.

An explosion rocked the city, nearly throwing me from my feet as I approached the center of town. Only, it didn't look like I remembered it. There was now a sculpture of Michelle. She stood blindfolded, one hand outstretched toward the horizon while her other clasped her blazing sword. Part of me wanted to smile as I saw it.

Annabeth was smart, no doubt, she'd used this statue to ingratiate herself to the archangel who wasn't keen on things like art, despite their many benefits.

Still, I had a problem. The statue occupied the spot where the grail needed to go. Approaching it carefully, I held out the grail, trying to find another spot. As I did, I realized I could place the item in her empty hand. At least, that seemed the best spot.

"Well, here goes nothing…" I mumbled before setting the Holy Grail in the outstretched palm of the statue.

Light exploded from the grail as it began to glow with every color of the rainbow. Energy leapt through the air as sparks crackled all along the surface of the statue before ripping outward in a concentric ring of blue light.

I threw my arms, desperate to block, but as the light swept through me, I suddenly felt at peace with the whole of the world. Then the light was passed me, and as I turned to watch it flow outward, I saw the broken, battered buildings restored, the streets brighten. Hell, the sky above was clearer.

Then the ring struck the barrier, and the whole of it shone like a golden sphere of power. Sparks jumped from its surface right before the giant creature assaulting it screamed. Its entire body evaporated as the light passed through it, enveloping the battlefield and obliterating everything in its path.

In an eye blink, there was nothing left of the massive force, but that didn't seem to stop the light. It slammed into the Darkness, and the sound was like a sonic boom. The whole of the horizon crackled and popped as the Darkness itself was pushed backward until I couldn't even see it on the horizon anymore.

I blinked, stunned by the sight of lush fields that suddenly appeared in the wake of the Darkness's retreat, and for a second, I wondered if all of Heaven had been cleansed. I'd have to find out, and as I thought about seeing how far out the cleansing wave had actually pushed the Darkness, a notification appeared in front of my eyes in shimmering golden text.

Achievement: Restore the Hallowed Host has been completed.

You gain 10% Legitimacy with the Heaven faction.

37

"I'm not sure why Belial and Belphegor would want a Mirror of Transference," Michelle said rubbing her chin as she stared at the grail clutched in the statue's hand. "Could Dred be trying to gain an achievement as well?" She looked to me. "It stands to reason that if there is a Heaven based one, there would be a Hell based one as well."

"Why now?" I asked, hoping that wasn't true. If Dred was completing achievements, that might make my gains moot. "Why wouldn't he have done them over the last thousand years?"

"He did not have demonic armaments before," Michelle said, and the coldness in her voice surprised me. "Dred is nothing if not methodical. He spent a lot of time trying to get my mark and armament, but now that he has it, and presumably Gabriella's, well, that just leaves Hell's armaments." She took a deep breath. "Think about it. Why else would he let your friends live? He could have killed the archangels when he attacked, but he didn't. That must mean he needs them alive for some reason."

"Maybe he didn't have time. Gwen did shove him back into the portal." Even as I said it, I wondered if it was true. Dred was strong, and if he wanted me dead, I'd have been dead. It hadn't been like with Nadine where I was pretty sure she'd done everything in her power to let me win. No, this was different, and the sad thing was, I believed Michelle.

"Could be, but we also do not know what Dred has been up to this entire time, nor why Belial and Belphegor have stolen the Mirror from the Princess of Mirrors." Michelle turned her gaze back to the grail. "It could be something else entirely, but if anyone does know, it will be Lucifer."

"Lucifer?" I asked, raising an eyebrow. "Why would she know?"

"Lucifer has been in Hell while you have been here. I know she has been actively rebuilding it, so if something happened down there, she might know something Sathanus does not. In fact, it's likely.

Sathanus is, well, kind of dumb when it comes to big picture things. Lucifer isn't." Michelle took a deep breath and exhaled slowly. "Furthermore, she'll have better insight into what Belial and Belphegor are doing. She might even know why they want the Mirror of Transference."

"You're starting to sound like you want to go talk to her." I watched Michelle very carefully as I said the words, but she gave no discernible reaction to having heard them.

"I have already spoken with Raphael," Michelle said after letting the silence hang in the air for a moment. "She does not know why they would want the Mirror, nor much about it." She took a deep breath, giving me the impression she was keeping something close to the chest.

"But?" I asked, trying to prompt her on. "None of that would make me think we should go talk to Lucifer. I mean, I will, but for you to suggest it seems off. Is there something you're not telling me?"

"What I do know is this. During the war that sundered Heaven, Lucifer sought a mirror, but there were none available at the time." Michelle met my eyes. "I never found out why she wanted it, but I suspect it's time to find out."

"Ah." That made a lot more sense. If Lucifer

had wanted one, she likely knew what the two archangels would use it for. Or at least would have a good idea. "Let's go speak to her." I glanced at the city. "Otherwise our options are to stand around and wonder while other people rebuild the city, and even with the bonus granted by the grail, we've got at least another month before Heaven will be rebuilt. Who knows what they'll have done if we wait that long."

"You are correct." She bit her lip. "Let us go see my sister." With that, she began walking toward the rift at the far side of the city. Part of me had expected it to have been healed when I'd restored the Grail to Heaven, but it still looked the same as ever.

This time when Michelle offered me her hand, it was trembling. Was she scared? It seemed unlikely because she was the least scared person I'd ever met.

"Is everything okay?" I asked right before she leapt from Heaven.

"Yes," she replied as we landed. "Everything is fine."

"See, when girls say things are fine, that usually means they are not." I smiled at her, and she frowned.

"You are very perceptive, Arthur." She didn't elaborate further as we headed toward the Graveyard of Statues. While I wasn't sure if Lucifer was there, I was willing to at least check before I tried to call her with my mark. That might piss her off, especially if she reappeared and saw Michelle. While the elder archangel had definitely been protective of her sister, Michelle had been pretty hammered at the time. Who knew how their reunion would go with Michelle acting more, well, like herself.

"Something feels off," I said as we entered the gates. "For one, the gates are opened, and I don't see any guards."

"Indeed." Michelle inhaled sharply causing her nostrils to flare. "I smell magic in the air." She licked her lips like she was tasting the air. "Belphegor. This is her doing."

"Is she here?" I asked, looking around but seeing nothing out of the ordinary. Even still, worry crept down my spine. If Michelle thought Belphegor was here, and she was aligned with Dred, well, what if Dred was here too?

"Yes, I think so." Michelle nodded. "Can you call my sisters?"

I shut my eyes and tried to open my marks, but

as I tried, I found it incredibly difficult to do. If trying to call Sathanus while I'd been in the Void of Desperation had been like screaming down a long hallway, this was akin to screaming from across a continent.

"Something is interfering," I said, shaking my head. "I can use my powers and the like, but I cannot reach any of them. At least not easily." I met her eyes. "What do you want to do?"

"I think that is Belial's magic. She has a way of making true communication impossible. They must both be here. We must find them." Michelle nodded fiercely. "Let's go." She pulled out her whip-sword, and as it blazed to life, she began moving through the town like she knew exactly where to go.

"Do you know where they are?" I asked as I drew Caliburn and followed behind her. "Because you seem to be heading toward the other side of town awfully purposefully."

"The scent of Belphegor's magic is stronger that way." Michelle looked at me. "What is in that direction?"

"The barracks, mostly. Some other stuff, but mostly just barracks." As I spoke, Michelle nodded once.

"That makes sense, Arthur. As Archangel of

Sloth, Belphegor can make entire cities fall asleep. No doubt she has done that." Michelle sighed. "No doubt your townsfolk are all tucked in their beds fast asleep."

The idea that the archangel was strong enough to make our entire city fall asleep was maddening, and it made me wonder why they had come. After all, it was obvious none of the other Archangels were here, but then again, I had no idea why they wanted the mirror either.

"That's probably for the best," I said, glancing at the barracks and finding Michelle was right. I could see soldiers, merchants, and everyone in between all fast asleep in their beds through the still open doors and windows. "It means none of them have died."

"True." Michelle let out a slow breath, and for a second all I could hear was the snap-crackle of her weapon. "Then again, neither of them ever really liked getting their hands dirty. So it somewhat surprises me their running around like this."

A loud crash to my left stopped me from replying, and I turned to see two women burst out of one of the barracks.

One had long auburn hair and was so tanned I thought she might have fallen asleep in a tanning booth. She was pretty, but only in that, "I'm kind of curious what you look like naked" way.

The other one had short black hair and was, quite frankly, large, but not in a bad way though. No, while she was chubby, it was definitely all in the right places.

Both of them were dressed in armor that made me think of what the lizard men commonly wore, which seemed a touch strange since I could see wisps of Darkness coming off them like it was burning away.

"Belial, Belphegor stop!" Michelle cried, surging toward them.

The two women turned, and as they did, the thin one held out her hand. "Michelle, it is you who will stop." Green light burst from her fingertips, and as it struck Michelle, it wrapped around her like several sets of chains before shattering into etheric shards.

For a second, I thought Michelle had broken the spell, but then I realized she was only moving as fast as she had been a moment before.

"This is perfect," the bigger one said, turning her sparkling blue eyes on me. "Builder, where is the room that Gabriella occupied?"

"Why would I tell you that," I said, letting loose

a blast of sapphire light at her. I don't know if it was because she was surprised, or what, but by the time she seemed to comprehend my attack, the blast hit her in the chest, knocking her off her feet. She flew backward, crashing through the wall of the barracks and hitting the ground.

I surged forward as her sister turned to look at me. As she raised her hand, presumably to slow me like she had with Michelle, I flung a gob of Hellfire at her. It smashed into her outstretched hand, and she screamed as fire engulfed her flesh like it was made of tissue paper.

As her arm disintegrated into a pile of ash, my knee smashed into her stomach. The blow sent her flying backward across the ground. She bounced like a broken mannequin as the spell surrounding Michelle shattered, and the Archangel of Justice sped up to real-time.

"I'll get Belial," she said, turning on her heel and heading into the barracks after the larger girl. "You get Belphegor."

"Okay!" I said because I'd been going to do that, anyway. I mean, I wasn't sure what Belial's powers were exactly, but Belphegor's slow could get us all killed. That definitely needed to be neutralized.

The Archangel of Sloth was starting to get to her feet as I came up beside her and drove Caliburn through her back, pinning her to the ground like a macabre butterfly. Part of me wanted to try to stop her without killing her, but at the same time, I'd been fighting Wrath for a while now. While I had no way of knowing how strong Belphegor was in comparison to Sathanus, I didn't want to take any chances. No. I was going to use maximum strength and hope I could keep them off-guard.

Belphegor screamed as my sword tore through her body, and as she tried to twist, I wrenched the blade sideways. Her eyes went wide with pain right before I kicked her under the chin as hard as I could. The blow snapped her head backward with a crack, and she slumped to the ground, eyes rolling up in the back of her head.

"Wait, are you unconscious?" I asked, somewhat surprised that had worked. It would never have against Wrath, but then again, Belphegor didn't really seem as formidable. Maybe what Michelle had said was true. Maybe she just wasn't as good?

A loud crash tore my attention from Belphegor, and as I turned, I saw Belial explode through the wall in a cloud of debris. The Archangel of Gluttony bounced once before coming to her feet. The left side of her face was battered and bloody, and as Michelle strode confidently from the broken building, the Belial glanced at me.

"Belphegor," she murmured, and as she stepped toward me, I reached back toward Caliburn. It was still buried in Belphegor's back, and while it held her in place, I'd definitely pull it free and use it if Belial came at me.

"You can't win, Belial," Michelle said, and her voice held that same edge of command I'd often heard on the battlefield. "Concede, and I'll let you live." Her whip-sword crackled as she raised it. "You couldn't beat me on your best day, and I doubt you could beat the two of us. Surrender is the only way you'll live."

"No." She bit her lip. "It is not." Then before I could blink, she spun on her heel, tearing a hole in the space beside her and disappearing inside it.

"Dammit!" I cursed, taking a step forward because I needed the both of them. "Did you know she could do that?"

"No." Michelle shook her head. "But the power smells like Dred's. No doubt the Darkness has augmented her ability to flee." The words made a slight frown curl Michelle's lips downward. "We will have to be more careful with that one." Michelle gestured toward the unconscious Belphegor. "Good job taking her down."

"It was a lot easier than I thought it would be, honestly." I looked back at the archangel.

"That is because you avoided her spell. If it had hit you, your speed would have been greatly reduced, and she would have crushed you with ease. Beyond that power, she is not much. I remember telling her she relied on her magic too often." Michelle smiled. "I suppose her arrogance worked in our favor." She knelt down beside the archangel. "Now remove your sword so I may bind her."

"You will do no such thing!" Lucifer boomed, and as her voice filled my ears, I realized I could feel all the archangels again. Was that because Belial had retreated? I wasn't sure, but I was willing to do so.

I turned and saw the Devil marching toward us in full battle regalia.

"Wait, what's going on?" I asked, suddenly confused. Lucifer had never had a problem with Michelle being in Hell before, why did she want to stop Michelle from subduing Belphegor.

"She means to take Belphegor's powers for Heaven." Lucifer gestured at the fallen archangel.

"That is not acceptable." Lucifer's power began to fill the air as sparks of purple energy leapt from her skin. "You think you can take what's mine after I have given you so much?" Lucifer narrowed her eyes. "You would dare?"

"I don't, and I wouldn't," Michelle replied, standing and gripping her whip-sword like she was ready to throw down. "You always think people are trying to steal from you sister, but it's just not true." Michelle glared at her sister. "You would do well to remember we're supposed to fight side by side." She pointed one finger at me. "I was just trying to help Arthur."

Lucifer's gaze flicked to me, and while I got the impression she wanted to argue, as I nodded to her, she relaxed a smidge. "I want to believe you, Michelle."

"Then do." Michelle crossed her arms over her chest. "Stop making everything into an issue of me versus you, and think of the cause. For once. Just once. Think of the cause."

Lucifer bristled and her eyes narrowed. Her entire body pounded like a cat about to spring, and as she opened her mouth to no doubt scream at her sister, I spoke up.

"Actually, Michelle suggested we come down to

talk to you about them. She thought you would be the most knowledgeable." Lucifer's gaze flicked to me as I spoke. "We just happened to find them looking for Gabriella's room."

"Why were they looking for Gabriella's room?" Lucifer asked, features softening as concern filled her voice. "What are they after?"

"I'm not sure," I said, glancing at the fallen archangel. "But I, for one, aim to find out."

38

"Okay, here's how this is going to go," I said, pacing back and forth in front of Belphegor who was too busy being tied to a chair with enchanted ropes to do much more than nod at me. I was angry at her, and angry at Dred, and angry at myself, but this was different. If I couldn't get her to tell me what I needed to know, who knew what would happen to Gabriella?

"I'm going to ask you questions, and if you don't respond the way I like, I'm going to stab you. Considering you're still bleeding from the Mortal Wound given to you by Caliburn, that should concern you." I paused. "Be a good girl, and I'll heal you?"

"You're going to stab me more?" she asked, looking at me. "That doesn't seem very creative."

"I work with what I have," I said, unsheathing Caliburn and pointing it at her. "And I have a sword."

"Geez, maybe you need to take a fucking chill pill." Belphegor rolled her eyes. "You know, catch more flies with honey, and OMG, did you just stab me?"

"Yes," I said, tearing Caliburn out of her leg and holding it up, so her blood spattered across the ground. "You're right. I should chill, but you know what, fuck it. I will stab you until you take me seriously, cool? Cool." I stabbed her again just to make sure she was taking me seriously.

"Why do you keep stabbing me?" she cried, bucking against the magic ropes to no avail. "Ask me a fucking question."

"Oh, I will," I said, right before I stabbed her again. "But I have to get all my stabbing out."

"Arthur, are you fucking mental?" Lucifer asked, interrupting me while I was interrogating Belphegor.

"No?" I said, looking at the Devil as she stepped inside the room. "Why?"

"You're just stabbing her for no reason," Lucifer

replied, grabbing me by the shoulder and pulling me away from Belphegor. "Have you even asked her why she was here or why they want the Mirror of Transference?"

"Is the Devil really the good cop?" Belphegor asked, eyes flicking between us.

"See what I'm dealing with?" I said, pointing at the archangel in frustration. "She's been totally unhelpful."

"Yes." Lucifer snapped her fingers and flame shot from the floor, burning the archangel to a near cinder. As her screams filled the air, Lucifer snapped her fingers again, and the flames extinguished, leaving a flash-fried archangel sitting there screaming because her flesh had been melted off.

"I changed my mind," I said, glancing from Belphegor's charred husk of a body to Lucifer and back again. "I am nowhere near that much of a psychopath."

"Which is why you need to let me do this." She patted my cheek. "Preserve your innocence. Being the evil torturer doesn't quite suit you. Me on the other hand." She grinned. "It's my jam."

As she spoke, I realized she was probably right. After all, she was the Devil. She was supposed to be the master of torture.

"Okay." As I spoke, Lucifer flicked her wrist, causing Belphegor to miraculously heal, which was something I'd not thought possible.

"So, Belle, here's how this is going to go," Lucifer said moving toward the Archangel of Sloth and straddling her. "I'm going to keep lighting you on fire and healing you until you tell me why you're here, why you joined Dred, and why you want the mirror. Do you understand?"

"Yes," Belphegor said before shuddering. I had to admit, Lucifer had the bad ass bitch thing down.

"Good." Lucifer nodded before leaning in so her lips were close to the woman's ear. "Because I'd hate for something bad to happen to you." She smiled. "You know, like getting buried in an anthill while covered in honey."

"I would prefer for that to not happen as well," the archangel replied, eyes fixed on Lucifer.

"Then we are in agreement." Lucifer grinned, leaning back slightly. "Why are you're here, Belle?"

"Dred sent us to find Gabriella's armament." Belphegor's eyes flicked to me. "He hasn't been able to break her yet because she is holding out hope he will come find her."

"Why do you think it's here?" and as I spoke

because if it was here, wouldn't Gabriella have given it to me?

"She said it was," Belphegor replied, swallowing hard. "But we couldn't find it."

The words hit me hard. It had been here, and I hadn't even thought to ask Gabriella about it this whole time? Man, I was an idiot.

"Why are you helping the Destroyer?" Lucifer stood then.

"He offered us a chance to win, to serve at the right hand of the Darkness itself." Lucifer lit her on fire, and her screams filled the air for a full minute.

"The Darkness will not win," Lucifer replied, once again healing the Archangel of Sloth.

"You haven't seen what I have, Luci." Belphegor looked at the ceiling. "Everything you've faced… it's nothing."

"That isn't a reason to concede, you sniveling worm. That is a reason to fight harder, to rail against your cage." Lucifer shook her head. "Have you become such a coward?"

"I'm not a coward, just a realist." She took a deep breath. "Have you seen an old one, Luci?"

"Those aren't real," the Devil shook her head. "That's myth."

"It isn't myth." The way Belphegor said it made

me think she was telling the truth, but that didn't seem possible because Lucifer really didn't believe her. "You think Dred is strong?" She shook her head. "He's a fucking amoeba beneath the Empress's toenails. Only worth note because he has Excalibur."

"What's so great about Excalibur?" I asked, holding up Caliburn. "This sword came from the Lady in the Lake."

"Excalibur is the blade destined to *destroy* the Darkness," Belphegor said, shaking her head. "Your sword is nice, but it is not Excalibur."

"You're awfully forthcoming, sister," Lucifer interrupted. "Why?"

"You lit me on fire." She took a deep breath. "I know you. Worse will come so I may as well tell you." She sighed. "Dred won't come for me either. He has my mark and armament. I'm useless now." She sighed. "Imagine being me and serving that toad. He's the most powerful man in the universe, and he's basically nothing before the Generals of the Dark."

"The Generals of the Dark?" I asked, totally confused. "What is that?"

"You've seen the heavenly host, right? It's the same thing but within the Darkness. It's why Dred wants power so much. He doesn't really care about me or you or Heaven or Hell. He just wants to kill those sons of bitches." She sighed. "At least that's what he says." She met my eyes. "It's why I joined him."

"Is she really saying Dred is a good guy?" I looked at Lucifer. "Is that what you heard?"

"I heard it, but I do not believe it. I have felt his soul, and it is corrupt beyond measure." She shook her head. "When you concede to the Darkness as he has, you cannot easily walk away from it." Lucifer looked at Belphegor. "Why does he wants the Mirror of Transference?"

"To make a new realm to seal away all the generals. Once he does that, the Empress will be weakened." The way Belphegor said those words made me think she was hiding something, and not just because she wouldn't look at us.

"He means to make a prison world with it?" Lucifer asked, rubbing her chin. "It's pretty smart, actually."

"No. Something is off." I shook my head. "Even if that was true, why does Dred want to fight the Darkness and us?"

Understanding dawned in Lucifer's eyes. "He is using the power of the Darkness to become strong enough to crush our world. The Empress allows it because even if he had all your strength, he is nothing."

"Yeah, I got that part. That's why he is the bad guy." I nodded. "He's helping the Darkness."

"Dred could have killed you, Arthur, but he didn't. Surely you wonder why?" Belphegor said, and I had to admit it was true. I had wondered.

"It crossed my mind." I met her eyes. "Do you know why?"

"Because you make things easier for him. With the Darkness focused on you, on what you've done, he can move freely. Lay his trap and spring it. Then when they are all locked away, he will kill you and claim this world for himself." Belphegor shrugged. "It's simple, really."

"So, he's still a douchebag." I sighed. If I understood this correctly, Dred wasn't really working with the Darkness. He was merely using it to gain power before he double-crossed it. The thing was, I'd faced him, and I didn't believe that for a second. I just wasn't sure why.

"It's a good plan," Lucifer said, looking at me. "Makes a lot of sense."

"No. It doesn't." I let out a slow breath, trying to order my thoughts. "The Empress bargained for

Dred. She wouldn't do that for someone that doesn't matter." I shook my head. "That means he has to matter a lot."

"Of course he matters," Belphegor said. "He's Dred."

"He can't matter and not matter," I snarled, and as I glared at the archangel, I realized something. Everything about this was all wrong. I took a deep breath and pointed at Belphegor. "She spilled the beans after three seconds of torture, Lucifer. Does that seem like what would happen?"

"Well, yes. Belphegor is notorious for—"

"That's exactly my point." I rubbed my face. "I think he wanted her to tell us all these things. She talked too easily for Dred to have taken her into his confidence. We know Dred has been working with the Empress of Darkness for Millennia. Does he really seem the type to lay out his schemes to *her*?"

"No. He doesn't." Lucifer looked at me. "What do you think? I can see your mind whirring."

"I think he did want the mirror to set a trap, only I don't think it's for the generals or anything." I met Lucifer's eyes. "I think it's for us."

"For us?" Lucifer asked, confusion filling her face as she flicked her gaze to Belphegor. "Why would he do that? He could have killed us many times over."

"No. He can't. Not really." I shook my head. "He can't kill you guys because ultimately he wants your Marks and Armaments. We know that."

"Even if I believe he could kill you," Lucifer said with a shrug. "Why would he trap you?"

"What happens if I get trapped in some crazy time void like your training ground with all my armaments and everything? There's essentially no more Builder, no more armaments, no more marks. In short, he is a lot more likely to win if I'm locked away and not dead." I sighed loudly. "It's why she's here to find the armament, I bet."

"What do you mean?" Lucifer asked, coming toward me.

"She's bait." I looked right at Belphegor. "Do you know where Gabriella is and how to get to her?"

"Of course," the Archangel of Sloth replied. "Why would I not?"

"That's why," I said, gritting my teeth. "Because once she tells us where Gabriella is, we'll have to go after her, and then we'll get trapped."

39

"Arthur, wait," Lucifer said, coming after me as I stormed out of the room. I was so angry I could barely think.

"No," I snarled, whirling on her. "I will not wait. Everything I did was to save Gabriella, and that asshole played us. I bet this was his plan from the beginning. The whole reason he came here. He didn't care about Gabriella's armament. Not really anyway. He just wanted me to go after her." I shook my head. "The whole thing is a trap."

"It was always a trap, Arthur," Lucifer said, reaching out and grabbing my chin, forcing me to meet her eyes. "You were always going to go after her. That was never in question."

"This isn't that." I took a deep breath. "What if he only captured Gabriella because he wanted to trap me?"

"I don't think that's true." The Devil shook her head. "He wants the Armament. He wants them all. I could feel it in him. Capturing you will be a bonus, after all, then he will get all your Armaments." She stroked my cheek. "Do not feel as though you are responsible."

"I suppose you're right," I said, taking a deep breath and trying to calm myself. "If he'd originally wanted to capture me, he would have already had the Mirror."

"Exactly." Lucifer smiled at me then. "I think you've scared him, and that's why he's changed plans. Think about it."

"What do you mean?" I asked, confused. "He has millennia of skill and training and almost all the armaments."

"Sure. He's got six Heavenly Armaments and two Hellion ones." Lucifer shrugged. "But you have five Hellion Armaments, and with the Achievements you've gained, your single Heavenly one is worth as much as both of his."

"That's still one less, which is a lot less." I shook

my head. "It's not enough to save Gabriella. Especially if I'm walking into a trap."

"That would be true except for one thing." She pulled me back toward the room and pointed inside. "If you take Belphegor's that gives you six and a half."

I stopped. She was right. In my anger, I'd completely forgotten. While she had given the Mark and Armament to Dred, if I could break her bond with Dred, I could still get her Mark. Maybe the boost in power would be enough?

"Six and a half marks anyway, but I guess beggars can't be choosers." I nodded to Lucifer. "I'm going to go back in there, while I do, can you do me a solid?"

"Um… okay?" Lucifer's eyes filled with confusion. "What do you need me to do?"

I told her, and she stared at me for a long moment. "I will do my best, but I do not know if Michelle will agree."

"Just try." I shrugged. "I think you might be surprised."

"And if she says no?" Lucifer asked, looking down at her shoes.

"She won't." I smiled. "Trust me."

"You're a man, you can't be trusted." Lucifer rolled her eyes at me. "But I shall try, anyway. It is time Heaven and Hell became united in this fight."

"Good."

With that, I made my way back inside and stared at Belphegor who was still tied to the same chair. Only instead of threatening her or anything, I pulled up my own chair and sat down in front of her.

"You've returned." The Archangel of Sloth looked at me. "Why?"

"We both know Dred is going to leave you to rot." I waited until she nodded. "Give me your Mark."

"It won't do you much good without my Armament, and Dred has it." Anger laced her words. "The bastard doesn't even use it because my Armament is a pair of boots and he likes Raphael's better because it has a healing ability."

"I would like to use it, and I will use it if you help me get it." I shrugged. "Or you can stay tied to that chair for pretty much ever."

"If I give you my Mark, you must free me." She looked at me. "Otherwise, you can go fuck yourself."

"After I return safely with Gabriella, I will

release you." I touched the spot over my heart with my index finger. "Promise."

"And should you perish or become trapped during the attempt?" She watched me carefully.

"Then you'll still be released." I shrugged. "But hopefully, with your help that won't happen."

"You do know I cannot give you my Mark while I am still bonded to Dred." She sighed. "This conversation is pointless."

"I can break the bond with him," I said, standing. "Tell me where it is, and I will break it."

"How can you do that?" she asked, looking at me like I was a very strange bug.

"Raphael showed me how to do it in Heaven. Granted, that was for the Heavenly ones, but something tells me that this will be even easier, since I'm the one you should have marked in the first place." I smiled. "Not that I'm annoyed or anything."

"It is on the small of my back," she said, leaning forward as much as she could. "He will know when you break it. He knew when you broke Samael's mark."

"I've been wondering about that?" I circled around and knelt down behind her. "What happened because of that?"

"He can still use the Armament, and is still

empowered, but he can no longer draw from her in times of need." Belphegor smiled. "It made me wish you had gained Uriel's Mark because then he would be forced to use mine."

"He would need more Legitimacy to use it." I reached out and touched the small of her back, and as I did, I felt a spark of cold wrongness emanate from her flesh just as I had with Sam. Only this was way worse. With Sam, the Mark itself hadn't felt wrong, just tainted. Everything about this one felt wrong.

"That is also true." Belphegor shrugged. "He has not yet completed the demonic achievements, and I do not think he will bother."

"Why is that?" I asked, surprised.

"Do you really think he will rebuild Hell or outfit it to face the Darkness?" she asked, laughing. "He is the Destroyer, not the Builder."

"That's a fair point," I said, wondering what the other achievements for Hell might be. For all I knew, they would be easier to get.

Still, I didn't care about that now. I had to focus on breaking Dred's bond with Belphegor. Then I could gain her power and go after Gabriella. Shutting my eyes, I reached out toward the Mark she shared with Dred. As my fingers touched her skin, I felt a surge of energy flow from my fingertips into Belphegor. Unlike with Sam, I actually knew what I was doing though, so instead of trying to tear it free, I merely unraveled the edges.

It was easier than I expected because as my power touched the spot on her soul where the bond had formed, the mark seemed to dissolve. I took a deep breath. No wonder Raphael had insisted I gain full legitimacy before I remove any of their marks. The way this was going, I had more than enough power to rip this free.

Then again, that was because I had one hundred percent legitimacy versus Dred's twenty-five percent. When I wanted to remove the angels' marks, I'd be battling against an equal force, and they wouldn't be acclimated to Hell as Sam had been.

As I continued to draw Dred's energy away, I replaced it with mine, slipping my own bond in its place so by the time it was done, it was like rubbing away the flaky skin after a sunburn had healed. That isn't to say it was quick.

"All done," I said four hours later.

"It's strange," Belphegor said, looking over her shoulder at me. "I expected it to hurt a lot more."

"I told you I knew how to do it," I said, shrugging. "And you have to remember something. You're supposed to be bonded to me." I touched the small of my back. "There's something to be said for legitimacy."

"Yes." She nodded. "I have to say, I feel better than I have in a long time." She smiled. "If I'd known bonding to you would feel this good, well…" she sighed. "What's done is done."

"I do want to know something though," I said, moving back to the chair and sitting down. I was tired, but not as tired as I thought I'd be. "Why did you go to Dred instead of to me?"

"What do you mean?" she asked quizzically. "When Belial and I awoke a few months ago, Dred was already there waiting. We didn't even know you existed. He offered us power, strength, and the chance to have revenge upon Heaven. After so long asleep, it seemed like a good deal in exchange for having to do very little." She frowned. "Only it wasn't as he made it out to be. After he used our power to defeat Michelle, we became less than nothing to him. Had we known he had joined forces with the Darkness, we never would have helped him, but by the time we found out, it was too late."

"I believe you," I said, standing. "And thank you."

"I hope you succeed," she replied as I moved to the exit. "But you're much nicer than he is. You'll need to work on that."

40

"Arthur, is this really your plan?" Michelle asked the moment I walked out of the room. She stood there with one hand on her hip while she pointed at Lucifer with her other. "Because this sounds a lot more like her plan."

"No. It's my plan." I looked over at Lucifer. "Unless she's told you a different plan."

"I have not." Lucifer shrugged. "She just called me a liar and said I was insane and then marched over to talk to you."

"You expect me to work with her?" Michelle raised an eyebrow. "Are you mad? I threw her out of Heaven."

"I do expect you to work with Lucifer. It is the only way this ends well." I took a deep breath, hoping she'd agree. "Think about it. No one else will succeed but the combined forces of Heaven and Hell."

"Arthur, your plan involves storming Dred's stronghold. It's insane." Michelle came closer. "You could die, or worse, be trapped for all eternity."

"Which is why I'm trusting you, both of you really." I glanced from her to Lucifer. "I don't know if you care about me or not, or even Gabriella, really, but I know you care about Heaven. This is the only way to save it because if we don't stop Dred, he will win." I met Michelle's eyes. "Do you want him to win, Michelle?"

"No." She looked at her feet for a long time before turning and looking at the Devil. "I will allow you into Heaven."

"You will?" Lucifer seemed shocked. "I don't know what to say."

"Say you're sorry for breaking up our family because you're too damned stubborn to do what you should do." Michelle sighed. "That's all I want. Apologize, and I'll consider the matter closed. We can ally Heaven and Hell and set Arthur's plan in motion." She smiled slightly. "The ball is in your court sister."

"You would really forgive me?" Lucifer swallowed hard and took a step back.

"Yes." Michelle sighed. "Truthfully, I always would have. We're sisters. I'll probably always forgive you."

"I'm sorry." Lucifer looked at the floor. "I'm sorry for everything I put you through, everything I did. It was—"

"Just stop right there," Michelle waved her hand. "I don't want to hear your explanation or any justifications." She touched her chest. "I'm the Archangel of Justice. Your motives are plain to me." She smiled. "It is enough to hear you apologize, sister." Michelle took a step forward and wrapped her arms around Lucifer. "You are forgiven."

As she spoke, glowing golden text appeared in front of me, and I nearly leaped for joy.

Achievement: Heal the Rift has been completed.

You gain 10% Legitimacy with the Heaven faction.

"What?" Lucifer asked as Michelle released her. She wiped her eyes because she must have gotten something in them.

"I got another achievement." I smirked. "Apparently, getting you two to kiss and make up, scored the Heal the Rift Achievement, which brings my legitimacy to fifty-five percent."

"That means you only need to finish rebuilding Heaven and outfitting the troops to gain full faction recognition," Lucifer said, nodding. "Then you'll be strong enough to break the bonds Dred has placed on my sister." Her gaze flitted to Michelle who was looking at me like she was pondering something.

"Indeed," Michelle said, but it was clear she was barely paying attention. "We will not be able to speed either of those along. Buildings and weapon-making both take time." She lapsed into silence for a moment before turning to Lucifer. "Sister, would you make preparations? I wish to speak with Arthur alone."

A sly grin spread across the Devil's face. "Sure, don't do anything I wouldn't do." Then she unfurled her wings and sprang into the air, her body a glowing red beacon of light as she made her way toward Heaven.

"There is much she would do that I would not," Michelle said idly before turning her attention to me. "I never thought this day would come."

"That you'd let the Devil back into Heaven?" I asked, slightly shocked myself. Never had I expected it to happen.

"No." Michelle waved off my comment. "That she would ask for forgiveness." Michelle bit her lip.

"Anyway, that is not what I wished to speak to you about."

"Oh?" I asked, raising an eyebrow at her. "What did you want?"

"You are greater than fifty percent legitimate now." She looked right at me, and I got the impression she could see into my soul. Only instead of finding me wanting, she merely took scope and nodded.

"Yeah." I touched the earring Sam had given me, *The Cold Embrace of Death*. "I can feel how much stronger my bond is with Samael."

"I wish you to break my bond with Dred." Michelle met my eyes. "Before you go."

"I probably can't." I turned and gestured toward the room where Belphegor was still tied up. "I could easily take hers because I was the legitimate, I dunno, markee, I guess. And we're in Hell where my powers are strongest." I shook my head. "I don't think I can break yours in the same way."

"Are we not in Hell?" she asked, moving closer to me. "Are we not in the very seat of your power?"

I looked at her for a long while. Part of me wanted to try, to take the mark, but honestly, I thought it might not work, and what's more, it would hurt a lot. What if all it wound up doing was weakening her to the point where we couldn't save Gabriella?

"No." I shook my head. "I need you to save Gabriella. Even if it works, you'll be weakened. I can't risk it."

"Have you even found Gabriella's Armament yet?" Michelle asked, and the question struck me as odd.

"Why do you ask?" I replied, worried I was stepping into a trap.

"Let us find it, and I will show you why you must take my mark at all costs." She looked around. "Where is her room?"

"Um… over there." I pointed toward the far building. It was the same one Sally and Crystal lived in and was one of the few that had proper rooms.

"Let us go then." Michelle nodded once before setting off toward it.

"I still don't see what this has to do with anything," I said, following along after her. "At all. Heaven will be rebuilt soon enough, and then I can break the marks. I'm probably strong enough to fight Dred now."

"Perhaps." She shrugged. "But you are not certain." Michelle whirled on me in a flash. "Do you wish to fight me now, to see?"

"Now that you mention it..." I looked her up and down. I kind of did want to face her, to see if I could beat her. I felt much stronger now that I had Belphegor's mark, but at the same time, I could tell it wouldn't be enough. At least, not without the armament too.

"I can see in your eyes you think you would lose." Michelle nodded. "Let us find Gabriella's armament." With that, she stepped inside the Archangel of Love's room and snorted.

When I followed her inside, I saw why.

The room while not very big, was bright pink with a picture of a unicorn painted onto the wall above the tiny bed.

"There is a lot of pink in here," Michelle mused, gesturing to the bed which was covered with pink sheets and a pink comforter. "I did not know she had such an affinity for the color."

"Me either," I replied, wondering where she'd gotten all the pink linens, let alone found time to paint the room and draw a unicorn.

"It is sad." Michelle sighed. "I have known her for so long and yet, I know her so poorly. I ought to know her favorite color." Michelle bit her lip. "Ought to have helped her paint her old room."

"I'm guessing her old room is exactly the same

as everyone else's?" I glanced around, marveling at all the personal touches Gabriella had made. While there wasn't a lot of room, there was a small desk in the corner, and upon it sat a menagerie of sculpted horses in various stages of being painted. Had she done that?

"Yes, her room was similar to everyone else's. We did not have the resources to spare on such things." Michelle sighed. "Though now, part of me wishes I had let her decorate."

"It's okay." I smiled. "I'm going to get her back, and then you can help her paint her room in Heaven."

"I would like that." Michelle nodded, her eyes sweeping around the room. "Check there." She pointed to a potted plant in the corner.

"Check the plant?" I asked, raising an eyebrow.

"Yes." Michelle smirked. "Gabriella does not care for plants much. So she would have only brought it for it to be noticeable and out of place, but only to someone who knew her. It would be overlooked by others."

"How would anyone know that?" I asked, looking over at Michelle. "I didn't know that." I stared at her for a heartbeat. "Guess you know her better than you thought, eh?"

"Perhaps." Michelle's cheeks colored. "Check please."

I did as she asked, moving to the plant. It was just your garden variety shrub, where I would have expected flowers or the like, and now that I was looking at it, I could tell Michelle was correct. While I didn't know if Gabriella liked plants or not, she would have put flowers in her room, not a mangy shrub. This one wasn't even pretty, with sickly yellow leaves and little splotches of green spread out. Hell, it didn't even smell very good.

Kneeling down beside it, I pushed aside the bottom branches and looked into the pot. Sure enough, sitting right on top of the soil was a small red box.

"Is this it?" I asked, showing the tiny box to Michelle.

"Yes, I think so." Michelle smiled. "Gabriella always loved those puzzle boxes." The archangel held out her hand. "Can I see it?"

"Uh, sure." I handed the tiny box to Michelle who peered at it intently for a moment. Then her fingers became a blur of speed. A few minutes later, there was a loud click, and the box opened up, spraying glitter into the air that seemed to coalesce into Gabriella's face.

"Arthur, if you're hearing this message it means something has happened to me." Glitter Gabriella bit her lip. "I am sorry I could not give you this in person. I was too shy I suppose, but it doesn't matter now." She flushed, which was crazy because, you know, glitter. "Please, take my Armament, the *Endearing Gaze of Love*, as a token of my affection. Know that I do not blame you for anything. My time with you has been some of the best I have ever had."

Glitter Gabriella disappeared in a twinkle of light, revealing a bright pink gemstone in the center of the now opened puzzle cube.

"I don't know that I could have found that without you," I said because otherwise, I was going to get really upset and angry. I knew I'd need those emotions, but not now. Not yet.

"I do not believe that to be true," Michelle handed me the gem. "You will need me now though. Tell me, how does that feel?"

"Um… like a normal gemstone." I shook it a little before peering at it. I could see sparks of life inside, but it mostly just felt cold and dead in the same way Mammon's Gauntlets had felt cold and dead before I'd received her mark.

"Exactly." Michelle held out her hand. "May I see it?"

"Sure." I shrugged and gave her the *Endearing Gaze of Love*.

Michelle stared at it for a moment, and then it began to glow with soft blue light. She held it up, and I could see the spark of her power within it. "I can partially activate her armament, Arthur. I am the leader of Heaven." She met my eyes. "If you had my Mark, you could do the same." She shrugged. "It won't be as good as if Gabriella marked you, but it will be a lot better than nothing."

"Michelle, we talked about this—"

"Arthur, it is my decision, not yours." She held the gemstone out to me. "I wish you to save my sister. I will do anything to help you accomplish that, and if all I must do is endure some pain, I will do so gladly." She dropped the gemstone into my hand, and I could feel the warmth within it as love radiated out. Not Gabriella's per se, but Michelle's love of her sister, of her kingdom, of all those she swore to protect.

"Okay," I said, closing my fingers around the gemstone. "I'll do it."

41

It took three days, and the combined strength of all seven archangels bonded to me to break the bond between Michelle and Dred. Then another three days to recover. It was only now, on the seventh day that I was ready to face Dred.

"Do not worry about us, Arthur," Lucifer said, reaching out and adjusting my crown, as she did, she smiled. "I never expected Gabriella's gem to fit into my crown." Her eyes flicked to the pink gem now displayed prominently in the center like it'd always meant to be there. "It makes me think there may be more to the armaments than we previously thought."

"Yeah, I didn't even realize the crown was lacking a gem until Sam pointed it out." I smiled.

"I'm glad it worked though. Makes this a lot easier." I touched the gem. I still had no idea what it did, but having it did allow me to draw strength from Michelle. That was what I needed now.

"Hard to believe we wanted to put a gemstone of Love into the pommel of Caliburn." Lucifer nodded and gave me one last look before stepping back. We were standing at the rift that, according to Belphegor, would lead me to Dred's stronghold within the Darkness.

"Yeah." I met her eyes for a moment. "I'm counting on you and Michelle both. If this doesn't work..." I swallowed, hoping I wouldn't be trapped in a prison world for the rest of my life.

"It will work." Michelle clapped her hand on Lucifer's shoulder. "My sister can be quite... persuasive." She nodded to me then. "You should go. The moment we begin to help you, Dred will suspect us. You must distract him until we are finished."

"Yeah..." I turned to look back at the rift. This was it, my turn to step in and be the hero everyone thought I was. Just a little while before I'd been a scared orphan who dreamed of getting a cubicle job, and now I was going to go storm a castle in a void of Darkness, fight the strongest human on the planet, and save the Archangel of Love. Jesus, it was like the universe had no idea who I was.

"Good luck, Arthur," Lucifer said, waving to me as I turned to the rift and readied myself.

I could feel my heart pounding in my chest, my adrenaline surging through my veins, but mostly? Mostly I wanted to step through that rift and lay waste to everything Dred had built. It wasn't even really because the guy was an asshole, though that was part of it.

At the end of the day, he was a bully. He had used his power to do horrible things thinking no one could stop him. Now, it was time to stand up to him. He might be stronger, faster, and all around more skilled than me, but at the end of the day, I had to try. No. I had to win.

He didn't.

Hopefully, that would make the difference.

"Thank you for everything," I said, and before they could respond, I stepped into the brink.

After my body put itself back together, I found myself standing beneath a black matte sky sprayed with multihued starlight.

Before me was a massive castle made of sparkling obsidian. Its walls practically glimmered despite the lack of abundant light, and as my vision started to adjust, I could see shadows writing within the moat and along the walls. The drawbridge was up, but even if it wasn't, I knew better than to go that way. Belphegor had warned me of the wards clinging to it, and if I tried it, not only would I have to break through them, assuming I even could, I'd have to deal with an onslaught of Darkness warriors. Worse, Dred would know I was here.

I glanced at my wrist, wishing I had a watch. I had forty-five minutes to get in as far as I could before Michelle and Lucifer would make their move. If I wasn't to Dred by then, well, I'd have to become the distraction, and that'd make everything harder.

Sucking a deep breath, I wished I had Wrath's teleport ability once more. Hell, I wished I could have brought the archangel, but if I had, her mere presence could potentially alert Dred to our presence. That wasn't worth the risk. No. I had to do this on my own.

I moved forward, angling around the castle toward the front left corner. Up above I could see a guard tower, and while I couldn't make out if it was occupied since almost everything here was made of shadow, this was my best chance to enter.

Taking a page out of Galahad's book, I reached

down and activated the steam-powered grappling hooks attached to my thighs. It had been meant for titans, sure, but it would also scale walls just as well. And, after all, who warded guard towers. After all, who would be foolish enough to come in *that* way?

With a twitch of my thigh, the nearly silent grappling hooks burst from the canisters strapped to my legs with a hiss of steam. The projectiles slammed into the roof of the guard tower, and not waiting to see if anyone had heard or seen me, I initiated the recall feature. I wasn't as good with them as I'd have liked, though, and as the harness strapped to my upper body fought to keep me balanced, I was jerked into the air like a puppeteer's doll with too few strings. Fortunately, I didn't plan on going all the way up. As I shot toward the roof, I released the hooks, causing them to disengage from the stone walls and retract back into the canisters. The whir of the gears inside filled my ears as I flew through the window of the guard tower. I lashed out with Caliburn, removing the head of a lizard man who had moved to see what all the fuss was about.

As his head bounced across the stone at our feet, I crashed into him. The impact sent us slamming into the back wall. As his headless corpse crashed into the window facing into the courtyard, I gritted my teeth and spun. Caliburn flashed through the air, ending the other guard within in a spray of black ichor. I stood there, chest heaving and trying to ignore the pain from the impact of my landing. The lizard man had broken my fall with his body, but that didn't mean I hadn't suffered damage. Fortunately, I would heal.

A moment or two later, I was ready to go, and as I peered into the courtyard, I found it nearly deserted. There were only a few token lizard guards and a single beholder which didn't seem like nearly enough, but then again, Dred was a monster king. Who was going to attack him?

No. According to Belphegor, he had grown complacent. I hadn't believed it before, but now I did. Even Heaven, with the Knights of the Round Table to guard the city, had more defenses to guard grain houses than Dred seemed to have for his entire courtyard.

Watching the guards circle the courtyard, I inhaled and exhaled slowly. Then I took my leap of faith. Jumping from the platform, I careened downward, slamming into the top of the beholder below with my sword thrust downward. The blow,

The Builder's Wrath

combined with the momentum of my impact, reduced the beholder to jelly.

As the massive creature exploded outward, spraying pus, slime, and god knows what else out across the courtyard, my knees slammed into the cobblestone courtyard. Pain exploded up my legs as they shattered, but I clenched my teeth, trying not to cry out.

If I'd timed it right, I had ten seconds until the first guard would circle through here in the beholder's stead.

Healing only took five seconds.

I was on my feet and at the corner as the lizard man turned. His eyes went wide in shock as he spied the beholder, but before he could do much else, I drove my blade through his back while pulling him against the wall. Using the shadows for cover, I held him there until his struggles ceased and he collapsed to the ground.

After dragging his body to the side, I waited once more, repeating the procedure eight more times. As I threw the last corpse into the pile, I took a deep breath. I was sweating and breathing hard. Adrenaline pounded through my veins, and I'd barely begin.

Now came the hard part. Turning to the wall behind me, I sheathed Caliburn and raised my gauntlets. Using the same trick I had in the tunnels, I used the *Relentless Grips of Greed* to carve furrows into the sheer wall. Belphegor had told me that all the entrances were warded, but walls? Why ward those?

Part of me wanted to use the grappling hooks, but I was worried someone inside might hear me, or worse, that the impact of the hooks would trigger the wards within the rooms. And it'd waste what little steam I had left. Now that I was inside and had some time, I didn't want to waste the precious fuel. I might need it for later.

No. Climbing would be better, I could tuck myself against the wall and move unseen. I could conserve steam.

Moving up the wall, I took care to be as silent as possible. My muscles screamed with the effort as I pulled myself up, but with each foot I moved up the wall, I could feel Gabriella getting closer. I wasn't sure how exactly, only to say I could feel her through the gem mounted in my crown. Pausing long enough to pull my dark cloak tighter over my shoulders, I tried to harness my inner Spider-man.

Moving up the wall, with all the strength and quickness my armaments afforded me, I felt

Gabriella growing closer. It made things both harder and easier. Harder because it made me desperate to race to her, and easier because she felt like she was okay.

As I reached the parapet, the gem was practically glowing, and despite my best efforts to keep it shielded, I was worried the guards on the other side of the wall of the parapet would see it. I'd have to take them out.

Hanging there for a moment, I pressed the side of my head to the wall and listen. It took a few moments, but judging by the way they patrolled, there were probably only two or three inside. Granted there was a big difference between two or three, but it was what it was.

I shimmied to the right and waited until I heard a guard approached before I reached out, seizing the unfortunate lizard and jerking him backward over the edge. He flailed, clawing for purchase in the air, his hiss rasp of a voice sort giving a startled yelp.

The closer of the other two guards spun at the sound, and as his buddy exploded on the stones below like a bag of jam, the creature came closer, eyes narrowed in suspicion.

It said something in that weird Darkness

language I never understood, and when there was no response, he started to turn toward the third guard. Fortunately, that one was all the way across the castle.

Taking my chance, I leapt over the parapet and flung Caliburn. The pointy end hit the side of the lizard's head, skewering the creature. As it dropped to the ground, I darted forward, pulling Caliburn free. The third one saw me then. Well, sort of. As it spun back around at the commotion, I pulled myself against the wall.

The lizard man stared at the corpse of its comrade for a second before drawing its weapon and moving in to inspect the scene. The movement made a surge of relief rush through me. I'd been worried he'd sound an alarm, but fortunately, he'd decided to inspect the area himself.

As the creature approached, I sidled along the wall, so that as he passed me, I lashed out with Caliburn. The lizard man's life ended in a spray of ichor as the top part of his skull went in a decidedly different direction that the rest of his body. It was a little weird because he actually took a few more steps before the nerves in his body realized he was dead.

I spun toward the doorway to my left as it

The Builder's Wrath

collapsed to the ground and made my way toward it. As I'd moved to the right, the feel of Gabriella had lessened, but now as I returned to the left side of the parapet, I found it growing stronger again. She was definitely that way.

Smiling, I reached the door. She felt so close it was almost like being in her presence. Taking a deep breath, I reached out toward the door before stopping myself. What if it was warded?

I paused, trying to feel for traps with my magic, but alas, I wasn't a very good rogue. I felt nothing more than the same heady feel of Darkness all around me. Still, I was worried. Belphegor had been pretty adamant about not using any normal entrances, and this was a pretty normal entrance. Granted it was three or four stories in the air, but still. Nearly everything I'd encountered could fly. Dred would have warded this door if he was smart.

Moving to the side, I tried to find another way that seemed less obvious, but the rest of the wall was more sheer stone. That left me with a problem. I could go through the door and risk triggering whatever wards were inside, or I could try breaking through the wall. Part of me wanted to try using one of the guards to unlock it, but Belphegor had told me that wouldn't work, though she hadn't explained why. Now that I was here, I wished I'd pressed for more details.

"What would someone smarter than me do?" I wondered, putting my head against the wall and listening for sounds. Unfortunately, I couldn't hear anything within, and I had no idea if that was a good thing or a bad thing.

Placing my hand on the stone, I reached out with Mammon's gauntlet, and as her power pulsed through the mark on my neck, I realized I could feel how thick the wall was. Only a foot or so. That seemed like a lot, but was it really?

Shutting my eyes, I concentrated, drawing upon the power of my marks. My breath came out as mist while the stone in front of me began to pull free. My heart began to hammer, and I started to sweat as I used my power to remove a small section of the wall so I could see inside.

As the stone came free, I leaned against the wall and took a deep breath. That had taken a lot more out of me than I'd expected it would, but even still, I had my hole. Peering inside, I quickly realized the room was a sort of hallway with stairs that headed both to the upper and lower levels within.

More doors branched off inside, leading to what presumably was the rest of this floor. Still, there were no guards to be seen inside, which made sense. After all, there were supposed to be guards out here.

Wiping the sweat from my brow with the back of one hand, I gripped Clarent. As the power of the marks rushed through me, I slashed at the wall. My magic-fueled blade cut through the obsidian like butter, and in only a moment I had a big enough hole to climb through. It had been louder than I'd wanted, but so far, it didn't seem to attract anyone which was good.

Making my way inside, I felt the press of the magic within. All across the doorway to my left, sigils flared, making me think that going through the wall at the end of the hallway had been smart. Even from here I could feel the strain of their power, desperate to incinerate me or worse. Had I gone through that door, I'd have been dead.

Putting that thought out of my mind, I looked around, trying to ascertain where to go. Moving to the stairs, I first tried up, and when the glow of the gem faded and the connection to Gabriella lessened, I knew it wasn't that way. Nor was it down.

My eyes fixed on the door that led deeper into the castle. Gabriella was that way. I knew it.

Moving forward, I pressed my hand to the door

and felt for traps. Again, I felt nothing in particular, which wasn't very helpful. Worse, there wasn't enough room to try the wall here.

"It would be my luck that I'd trigger an inner alarm," I muttered, gripping the door handle and pressing it in. When I wasn't immediately incinerated or turned into a toad, I let out a breath.

Belphegor had been pretty sure none of the inner doors were warded, but pretty sure wasn't one hundred percent. Still, in this case, wishes had been horses.

The room beyond was another hallway, only it branched off into what looked like rooms on one side while the other looked out over a large ballroom. Not seeing anyone inside, I crept forward, careful to keep myself to the shadows, but there were no guards at all.

Still, with each step I took, the feel of Gabriella grew stronger. She wasn't far now. In fact, as I passed by the third of six doors, I stopped. That was where she was.

I swallowed, turning to look at the door before me. It wasn't any different from the others and appeared to be made from some kind of dark wood. There was just one problem. I could feel the magic coming off of it. Someone had sealed it with magic, and I knew that if I opened it, something crazy would happen.

That's when I had an idea.

Hurrying back outside, I grabbed the closest of the dead guards and dragged him inside. By the time I reached the door again, I was breathing hard from the effort, but sure enough, as I raised his hand to the door, I felt the lock disengage.

Dropping the corpse, I pushed on the door, and as it swung open, I found myself staring at Gabriella. The archangel sat on a plush, four poster bed covered in bright pink sheets working on a quilt made of brightly-colored squares.

"Gabriella!" I cried, stepping inside and looking around. Buckets of paint, a few paintbrushes, and an easel sat against the far wall, which had itself been painted with a rainbow. That was odd. Shouldn't it have been more, well, dungeony?

Gabriella's gaze flicked toward me, and her eyebrows furrowed. "Who are you?"

42

"I'm Arthur," I said, confusion filling me. "What do you mean who am I?"

"Arthur?" she shook her head as I approached. "I don't know anyone named Arthur."

"Gabriella, you know me." I took a deep breath. "I'm the Builder."

"The Builder!" she gasped, one hand going to her mouth in shock. "The one who stole my Armament and means to aid the forces of Hell against Heaven?"

Her words threw me for a loop because it sounded like she believed them. Only how could she possibly believe them after everything we'd been through, after everything I'd done to come save her?

"No," I said, but before I could do more, she leapt to her feet.

"Guards!" she cried, hands curling into fists. "Come quick!"

Her words seemed to resound through the air, and as they did, the shrill cry of a claxon nearly blew out my hearing. I staggered forward, my hands going to my ears, which was made further complicated because I was holding Caliburn.

"Stop," I cried, trying to shout over the noise. Only it didn't seem like Gabriella heard anything, or at least, if she did, it didn't bother her.

"I won't let you kidnap me." She narrowed her eyes, bringing up her fists. "I won't."

"Gabriella," I said right before she decked me.

Her fist caught me on the underside of my chin, snapping my head backward and throwing me across the room. I hit the doorframe hard and felt something pop inside my back. As I slumped to the ground, she rushed forward.

I dodged. Barely. Her knee slammed into the stone where my head had just been with so much force the wall cracked.

"Stop attacking me," I said, scurrying away from her as she whirled on her foot and tried to kick me. I caught her leg, and before I realized what I was doing, I flung her across the room. She smashed into the bed, shattering the wood before slamming into the wall. The stone broke, cracking in concentric circles as she slid to the ground, clearly hurt.

"That's enough, Builder." Dred's voice filled me with, well, dread, and as I spun in a slow circle, I saw him standing there.

"What did you do to her?" I cried, one hand snaking out to point at Gabriella.

"Nothing." He shrugged. "Belial did all the heavy lifting on that one." His eyes flicked to the gemstone in my crown. "Thank you for bringing me that by the way." He held out his hand. "Give it to me, and I'll kill you." He grinned, causing the scar across his cheek to stretch grotesquely. "Trust me when I say it is a good deal, Builder."

"Fix her," I snarled, gripping Caliburn tightly.

"I cannot." His smile widened. "Not in my job description."

I charged him, sword arching through the air, and as I did, he shook his head. "You should have just let me kill you." As I reached him, the entire world exploded into scintillating light. My entire body felt ripped apart, and I realized I'd triggered some kind of trap. No. Not some kind. *The trap.*

In an instant, I found myself locked away in a room the size of a jail cell with no doors and only a single small window. Through the murky glass, I could see Dred standing there and smiling.

"I had wished to get the armament first, but alas, with you trapped there until time itself ends, I doubt I'll be needing it." With that, he moved toward Gabriella.

I wasn't sure what he was going to do to her, and even though everything in me wanted to rail against my cage, I knew that it wouldn't do any good. Instead, I took a deep breath and tried to reach out with the power of my marks, but like I'd expected, nothing worked. I couldn't feel anything at all beyond these four walls.

As Dred knelt beside Gabriella, I shut my eyes and tried not to get pissed off.

"You're awfully calm for a rat in a cage," the Princess of Mirrors said, and my eyes opened to see her standing just beyond the wall with Michelle and Lucifer. "Where is all your rage?"

"I knew you would do it," I said, nodding to the two archangels.

"They can be quite convincing," the Princess of Mirrors said, shrugging. "It seems that the mirror can no longer be recovered and for that Dred must pay. Letting you do that for me, well, that's just so much easier." She rubbed her blood-red nails on her leather jacket. "Go."

As she said the word, the window behind me began to shimmer and shine before turning into a swirling vortex of force that sucked us back out into Dred's Castle.

The three of us hit the ground, causing Dred to spin on his heel.

"How?" he asked, right before his eyes fixed on the Princess of Mirrors, who was still visible through the shimmering mirror on the wall. "Clever." His eyes narrowed. "You always seemed clever, Arthur. Tis a pity I will kill you."

It was a bit strange because, for a second, I almost believed he would be sad to see me die.

"Gabriella!" Michelle cried, moving to rush forward, but Lucifer stopped her. "Are you okay?"

"Michelle?" Gabriella asked, confused. "I'm okay." She looked at her sister for a moment. "Why have you joined the Builder? Has he tricked you?"

"No." Michelle shook her head. "Dred has tricked you—"

"Don't listen, Gabriella," Dred said, cutting off the Archangel of Justice. "She has been fooled by the Builder."

"Oh." Gabriella's eyes narrowed at me. "Free my sister."

"Gabriella," Michelle pleaded, right before Dred rushed forward.

His fist lashed out, slamming into Michelle's gut and buckling the archangel over. Blood spurted from her mouth, and as Michelle sank to her knees, Lucifer glanced at me.

"Save Gabriella," Lucifer said, lashing out at Dred.

Only despite, the enhancements I'd made to her, Dred still dodged her blow. As Lucifer's fist knocked out a section of wall and sent it flying outward in a spray of debris, Dred pivoted and slammed his foot into her knee.

There was a sharp crack, and as Lucifer started to fall, Michelle attacked, throwing them all through the hole in the wall and into the ballroom below. They were buying me time, but it wouldn't be much. I had to make it count. I had to save Gabriella.

As I looked back toward Gabriella, an idea hit me. Dred had said it wasn't in his job description to fix her, but it might be in mine. Quickly bringing up her stats, I nearly shouted with joy because at the very bottom was a message I'd hoped to see.

Flaw: Influence of Belial

Influence of Belial– The user has been afflicted with a curse that has twisted her memories.

Would you like to remove this flaw? Cost 33,000 experience. Yes/no?

It wasn't even a question, and not just because Gabriella had almost a million experience. I spent the points, and as I did, the Archangel of Love blinked a few times.

"Arthur?" she asked, and as she took in the scene, confusion spread across her face. "What's going on?"

"Gabriella, we have to hurry." I moved across the room and grabbed her hand. "Lucifer and Michelle won't be able to hold Dred off for much longer."

"No, we have to help them." She looked me over and flushed as she laid her eyes on the gemstone within my crown. "You have to help them." She reached out, pressing her hand over my heart. A blaze of power filled me, and she grimaced.

"Did you just mark me?" I asked, swallowing hard as a surge of power unlike anything I'd ever felt before filled me. It was far beyond anything that had ever happened, and while part of it was coming from Gabriella herself and her mark, more of it was coming from the Armament itself.

"Yes." She nodded. "Now save my sisters." She pulled me into the hallway in time to see Lucifer go flying and slam into the far wall. Michelle followed her a moment later, and as the two archangels lay there confused, I realized I could feel their strength in a way totally different from before.

"Okay. I will draw his attention, you get them out of here." I looked at her, and as I did, I found her looking off across the hall with a weird look in her eyes. "Gabriella?"

"Sorry." She met my eyes. "I just need a moment, okay?" She touched my face as Dred stalked toward her sisters. "You'll be fine. I promise."

I wanted to argue, but there wasn't time. Dred had Excalibur out, and both Lucifer and Michelle were down.

"Fine!" I said, hoping she was right as I leapt down, swinging Caliburn through the air.

Dred spun as I careened downward and caught my blow on the flat of his blade, and I wasn't sure if it was my added weight and momentum or something else, but the blow actually knocked him backward.

The Destroyer himself stumbled backward, barely able to push Caliburn out of the way with his sword as he did so. I hit the ground a moment later, and even though I felt my bones crack from the impact, I shoved myself forward, ignoring the pain.

I whipped my blade out, and once again, Dred seemed to have trouble dodging. He feinted, and as I went to block, he reversed course lashing out at me. The thing was, the movement almost seemed slow. Not enough for me to block or anything, but enough for me to dodge.

The tip of Excalibur missed me by a hair's breadth as I executed *The Wind That Flings The Sand*. My elbow shot out, catching him on the side of the head, and the blow rocked him backward.

"You hit me?" he said, more shocked than anything. "How could you hit me?" His eyes narrowed as they raked over me. "You shouldn't even be able to see me."

"Power of Love, bitch," I said, darting forward, and for a few seconds, I actually had him on the run. As we fought and parried, I couldn't seem to land a blow on him, but then again, he couldn't get me either.

The problem quickly became apparent to me.

He was just way better than me, and while I was actually a touch faster than him, I couldn't hit him. Still, the difference wasn't enough to let him overpower me.

"It's been a long time since someone has pushed me this far, Builder," Dred said, and I could have sworn he sounded happy. "No wonder the Empress fears you so."

"The Empress fears me?" As I said the words, I hesitated.

Dred's boot caught me in the stomach, lifting me from the air and flinging me backward. I hit the far wall, slamming into it with bone-shuddering force. My teeth snapped together, and as I collapsed forward on my hands and knees, Dred rushed forward.

"No, but I thought it might shock you to hear." Excalibur came down to end my life.

43

The clang of metal resounding off Dred's skull as Gabriella slammed a pair of boots upside his head filled my ears an instant before the guy was flung across the room like a fucking ragdoll. He slammed into the far wall, shattering the stone and collapsing to the ground stunned.

"It's dangerous to fight Dred as you are," Gabriella said, offering me the boots. "Take these."

"What the fuck?" I mumbled, and as I touched them, I realized what they were. The *Uncaring Walk of Sloth*. Belphegor's armament.

Power exploded through me as the sigils emblazoned on them came to life in a flurry of emerald sparks. As Dred started to rise, I kicked off my own boots and pulled them on.

The Destroyer stood, eyes narrowed, and as he did, I threw my hand out at him. A scintillating net of sickly green light exploded from my fingertips, slamming into him as he charged at me. The magic wrapped around him, slowing him down enough for me to stand and brace myself for his attack.

I barely got my blade up in time. Excalibur slammed into my sword, throwing me back half a step, and as he tried to push me off balance, I dropped one of my hands and triggered the grappling hook on my thigh. The projectile exploded from the canister in a spray of steam, catching him in the underside of the throat before ripping out the back of his neck.

Blood sprayed over me as he looked at me wide-eyed. Choking bubbles of blood burst from his ruined throat, and as his hand fell from the hilt of his sword, and he stopped pressing down on me, I thought he was going to grip the wound.

Only, instead, he grabbed the hook, jerking it free of his flesh with one movement that drew me toward him. His knee lashed out, catching me in the gut and throwing me from my feet. I collapsed to the stone as he stood there, holding the bloody hook in his hand. As the wound closed on his throat, he jerked me toward him. I lashed out, and thanks to his decreased speed, I managed to slip Caliburn past his defenses and slam the weapon into his gut. His glowing armor turned away the blow, but it still staggered him.

Still, as I recalled the hook to the canister, he was already coming at me again. Worse, even with him slowed and with more power at my disposal than anything I'd had before, I knew I wasn't good enough to win. Powerful enough, maybe, but skilled? No.

Then again, I didn't have to beat him. I just had to escape. And I could hold him long enough to do that.

"Gabriella, get them to safety," I said, right before Dred countered, slipping by my next attack and slashing at me with Excalibur. The weapon ripped by me, gouging a flurry of sparks through my ethereal armor as it scraped across my torso. Pain leapt through me like every nerve in me had been lit on fire, and as my body struggled to heal the wound, I realized it was going to take a lot longer than normal.

Worse, he was already attacking again. His knee caught me under the chin, snapping my head backward.

"I don't know where to take them," Gabriella

said, moving toward her sisters while I stepped back, trying to ignore how my jaw felt broken while I parried his next blow. "Where is the portal?"

"The rift is just beyond the gate." I once again used *The Wind That Flings The Sand* to sidestep while conjuring a palm full of Hellfire. Unfortunately, Dred seemed to expect it. He pivoted and slammed his knee into my stomach as I tried to blast him, causing my fireball to slam harmlessly into the wall behind him.

Air whooshed from my mouth, and as I staggered backward, Gabriella picked up her two sisters, throwing both Michelle and Lucifer over her shoulders.

"You'd better hurry after us!" Gabriella cried, her wings extending from her back. "Because once we leave, you're going to lose thirty percent of your strength and speed."

"What?" I asked as Dred came at me again, trying to capitalize on my sudden hesitation. He was slower, but almost not enough for it to matter because he was still so much better than me.

"My armament, it boosts all your abilities by ten percent for every ally within fifty or so meters." Gabriella was lifting into the air, heading out the way I had come in.

Her words made my blood grow cold because while I'd succeeded in sidestepping his thrust, it'd been close. Too close.

Worse, Dred smiled at me. "How long do you really have, Builder?" he nodded toward Gabriella's fleeing form. "How long?"

He renewed his attacks, coming at me even harder than before. As I fought, dodged, and parried, I knew why her Armament had made me feel so powerful. I was getting a five and a half percent boost (my legitimacy times the buff it gave me) for each of them.

Once that was gone, I'd be almost twenty percent slower. And I was barely keeping up now. Dred seemed to know that, which made sense because he wasn't deaf. Now, he was just focused on keeping me off balance until she left.

"What's it going to be, Arthur?" Dred asked, Excalibur flashing through the air and driving me back. "Will you turn and run, giving me your back, or will you make your allies stay and watch you die?"

"How about option B?" I asked as I realized something. I didn't give a goddamn about Dred finding out I was here now. It was time to play my trump card.

I flung a blast of Hellfire at Dred, and instead of dodging, he tanked it, allowing it to slam into his chest and dissipate as he came at me. I didn't try to dodge his swing as Excalibur jerked outward because I'd heal. Hopefully.

Instead, I put my hand on my shoulder and called upon Sathanus. The moment our power sparked, Dred drove his blade into my gut. As he ripped it out of me, spilling blood and thicker bits across the floor, I collapsed to my knees struggling to remember how to breathe.

"You might think you'll heal, but how well will you do that without this?" Dred grabbed my belt and pulled me to my feet.

"By my Grandmam's bearded beard!" Sathanus snarled, her axe lashing out in an arc that would have removed Dred's head from his shoulder's if she hadn't warned him with her battle cry.

Only, as he released me and sprang back barely avoiding her glowing axe, I realized that had been the point. Distance. Space. Time.

Sathanus grabbed me with one hand as her one-handed swing ineffectually cut through the air, and then we were gone.

We reappeared beside the rift just as Gabriella

stepped through it, and for a second, I thought we were home free.

That's when I saw the force coming toward us. Ravagers, dragons, everything was converging on the rift, sure, but that wasn't what scared me. Hell, even the battalion of kaiju I saw wasn't what scared me. No. It was the sight of what had to be the Empress. She stood in the back of it all, impossibly huge and menacing. Her grotesque body was covered in eyes and tentacles, and that was only what I could see of her because as I craned my head toward the sky, I realized I couldn't see past what I thought was her thigh.

"Is that who I think it is?" I asked, barely able to keep the tremor out of my voice. That thing felt impossibly strong. Like I was just a gnat buzzing around a flea on a rat clinging to a fucking planet. "How do we beat that?"

"I don't know, but now is not the time to figure it out." Sathanus met my eyes, and I could see the terror in them. "We should leave before she gets here. Before they all get here."

The thing was, as I followed Sathanus through, the only thing I could think about was how hopeless our situation had become. At the end of the day,

Dred was a man, and that thing? That had to be a god.

And we hadn't been able to beat Dred.

We reappeared back in Hell, just beyond the rift gate, and as we waited for something to come through, the other assembled Archangels bound the rift shut with their magic. All of Heaven and All of Hell save Belial. It would have been awesome if I wasn't so fucking scared.

"What do we do?" I asked, swallowing hard as I looked at everyone.

"What do you mean?" Gwen asked, coming forward to help Gabriella with the other two archangels. "You won? We have Gabriella back."

"For now." I swallowed, turning to look at the bound rift. The whole of the horizon at the edge of the Graveyard of Statues was Darkness, and within it lived a god who wanted nothing more than to crush us. "I mean what do we do about the Empress?" I swallowed, but I couldn't get any moisture in my mouth. "I saw her." I gestured at Sathanus. "She did too."

"Arthur, you'll figure out a way. You're smart like that, remember?" Gabriella said, and as she hugged me, I almost believed her. Almost.

THANK YOU FOR READING!

Curious about what happens to Arthur next?

Find out in The Builder's Throne, coming soon!

AUTHOR'S NOTE

Dear reader, if you REALLY want to read my next Builder novel- I've got a bit of bad news for you.

Unfortunately, **Amazon will not tell you when the next comes out.**

You'll probably never know about my next books, and you'll be left wondering what happened to Arthur, Gwen, and the gang. That's rather terrible.

There is good news though! There are three ways you can find out when the next book is published:

1) You join my mailing list by clicking here.

2) You follow me on my Facebook page or join my Facebook Group. I always announce my new

books in both those places as well as interact with fans.

3) You follow me on Amazon. You can do this by going to the store page (or clicking this link) and clicking on the Follow button that is under the author picture on the left side.

If you follow me, Amazon will send you an email when I publish a book. You'll just have to make sure you check the emails they send.

Doing any of these, or all three for best results, will ensure you find out about my next book when it is published.

If you don't, Amazon will never tell you about my next release. Please take a few seconds to do one of these so that you'll be able to join Arthur, Gwen, and the gang on their next adventure.

Also, there are some Litrpg Facebook groups you could join if you are so inclined.

LitRPG Society

LITRPG

To learn more about LitRPG, talk to authors including myself, and just have an awesome time, please join the LitRPG Group.

Made in the USA
San Bernardino, CA
24 November 2017